INITIAL HERE	DESCRIBE THIS BOOK IN ONE WORD...
CH 1/30/15	COMPELLING!

THE
WINTER PEOPLE

Also by Jennifer McMahon

THE
WINTER PEOPLE

Jennifer McMahon

DOUBLEDAY

New York · London · Toronto · Sydney · Auckland

Copyright © 2014 by Jennifer McMahon

All rights reserved. Published in the United States by Doubleday, a division of Random House LLC, New York, and in Canada by Random House of Canada Limited, Toronto, Penguin Random House Companies.

www.doubleday.com

DOUBLEDAY and the portrayal of an anchor with a dolphin are registered trademarks of Random House LLC.

Library of Congress Cataloging-in-Publication Data
McMahon, Jennifer.
The winter people : a novel / Jennifer McMahon. —First edition.
pages   cm
1. Women—Fiction. I. Title.
PS3613.C584W56 2014
813'.6—dc23   2013026385

Book design by Maria Carella
Jacket design by Michael J. Windsor and John Fontana
Front-of-jacket photograph by Lawrence Perlman/Trevillion Images

ISBN 978-0-385-53849-7

MANUFACTURED IN THE UNITED STATES OF AMERICA

1 3 5 7 9 10 8 6 4 2

First Edition

3/14

For Zella

Because one day, you wanted to play a really creepy game
about two sisters whose parents had disappeared in the woods . . .
"Sometimes it just happens."

Q: Bury deep,
Pile on stones,
Yet I will
Dig up the bones.
What am I?

A: Memories

—A FOLK RIDDLE

THE
WINTER PEOPLE

Visitors from the Other Side

The Secret Diary of Sara Harrison Shea

From an introduction by the editor, Amelia Larkin

My beloved aunt, Sara Harrison Shea, was brutally murdered in the winter of 1908. She was thirty-one years old.

Shortly after her death, I gathered all of the diary pages and journals I was able to locate, pulling them out of dozens of clever hiding places throughout her house. She understood the danger these pages put her in.

It then became my task, over the next year, to organize the entries and shape them into a book. I embraced the opportunity, as I soon realized that the story these pages tell could change everything we think we understand about life and death.

I also contend that the most important entries, the ones with the most shocking secrets and revelations, were contained in the final pages of her diary, written only hours before her death.

Those pages have not yet been found.

I have taken no liberties when transcribing these entries; they are not embellished or changed in any way. I believe that, as fantastical as the story my aunt tells may be, it is indeed fact, not fiction. My aunt, contrary to popular belief, was of sound mind.

1908

Visitors from the Other Side
The Secret Diary of Sara Harrison Shea

January 29, 1908

The first time I saw a sleeper, I was nine years old.

It was the spring before Papa sent Auntie away—before we lost my brother, Jacob. My sister, Constance, had married the fall before and moved to Graniteville.

I was up exploring in the woods, near the Devil's Hand, where Papa had forbidden us to play. The trees were leafing out, making a lush green canopy overhead. The sun had warmed the soil, giving the damp woods a rich, loamy smell. Here and there beneath the beech, sugar maple, and birch trees were spring flowers: trilliums, trout lilies, and my favorite, jack-in-the-pulpit, a funny little flower with a secret: if you lift the striped hood, you'll find the preacher underneath. Auntie had shown me this, and taught me that you could dig up the tubers and cook them like turnips. I had just found one and was pulling back the hood, looking for the tiny figure underneath, when I heard footsteps, slow and steady, moving my way. Heavy feet dragging through the dry leaves, stumbling on roots. I wanted to run, but froze with panic, having squatted down low behind a rock just as a figure moved into the clearing.

I recognized her at once—Hester Jameson.

She'd died two weeks before from typhoid fever. I had attended her funeral with Papa and Jacob, seen her laid to rest in the cemetery behind the church up by Cranberry Meadow. Everyone from school was there, all in Sunday best.

Hester's father, Erwin, ran Jameson's Tack and Feed Shop. He wore a black coat with frayed sleeves, and his nose was red and running. Beside him stood his wife, Cora Jameson, a heavyset woman who had a seamstress shop in town. Mrs. Jameson sobbed into a lace handkerchief, her whole body heaving and trembling.

I had been to funerals before, but never for someone my own age. Usually it was the very old or the very young. I couldn't take my eyes off the casket, just the right size for a girl like me. I stared at the plain wooden box until I grew dizzy, wondering what it might feel like to be laid out inside. Papa must have noticed, because he took my hand and gave it a squeeze, pulled me a little closer to him.

Reverend Ayers, a young man then, said Hester was with the angels. Our old preacher, Reverend Phelps, was stooped over, half deaf, and none of what he said made any sense—it was all frightening metaphors about sin and salvation. But when Reverend Ayers with his sparkling blue eyes spoke, it felt as if he said each word right to me.

"I am he who will sustain you. I have made you and I will carry you; I will sustain you and I will rescue you."

For the first time, I understood the word of God, because Reverend Ayers spoke it. His voice, all the girls said, could soothe the Devil himself.

A red-winged blackbird cried out *conk-a-reee* from a nearby hazel bush. He puffed up his red shoulders and sang over and over, as loud as he could, his call almost hypnotic; even Reverend Ayers paused to look.

Mrs. Jameson dropped to her knees, keening. Mr. Jameson tried to pull her up, but did not have the strength.

I stood right beside Papa, clutching his hand, as dirt was shoveled down on the coffin of poor Hester Jameson. Hester had a crooked front tooth, but a beautifully delicate face. She had been the best in our class at arithmetic. Once, for my birthday, she gave me a note with a flower pressed inside. A violet it was, dried out and perfectly preserved. *May your day be as special as you are,* she'd written in perfect cursive. I tucked it into my Bible, where it stayed for years, until it either disintegrated or fell out, I cannot recall.

Now, two weeks after her very own funeral, Hester's sleeper

caught sight of me there in the woods, crouching behind the rock. I shall never forget the look in her eyes—the frightened half-recognition of someone waking from a horrible dream.

I had heard about sleepers; there was even a game we played in the schoolyard in which one child would be laid out dead in a circle of violets and forget-me-nots. Then someone would lean down and whisper magic words in the dead girl's ear, and she would rise and chase all the other children. The first one she caught would be the next to die.

I think I may have even played this game once with Hester Jameson.

I had heard whispers, rumors of sleepers called back from the land of the dead by grieving husbands and wives, but was certain they only existed in the stories old women liked to tell each other while they folded laundry or stitched stockings—something to pass the time, and to make any eavesdropping children hurry home before dark.

I had been sure, up until then, that God in his infinite wisdom would not have allowed such an abomination.

Hester and I were not ten feet apart. Her blue dress was filthy and torn, her corn-silk hair in tangles. She gave off the musty smell of damp earth, but there was something else behind it, an acrid, greasy, burnt odor, similar to what you smell when you blow out a tallow candle.

Our eyes met, and I yearned to speak, to say her name, but could only manage a strangled-sounding *Hss*.

Hester ran off into the woods like a startled rabbit. I stayed frozen, clinging pathetically to my rock like a bit of lichen.

From down the path leading to the Devil's Hand came another figure, running, calling Hester's name.

It was her mother, Cora Jameson.

She stopped when she saw me, face flushed and frantic. She was breathing hard and had scratches on her face and arms, pieces of dry leaves and twigs tangled in her hair.

"Tell no one," she said.

"But why?" I asked, stepping out from behind the rock.

She looked right at me—through me, almost, as if I were a pane of dirty window glass. "Someday, Sara," she said, "maybe you'll love someone enough to understand."

Then she ran off into the woods, following her daughter.

I told Auntie about it later.

"Is it really possible?" I asked. "To bring someone back like that?"

We were down by the river, picking fiddleheads, filling Auntie's basket with the curled fern tops, as we did each spring. Then we'd bring them home and make a creamy soup stuffed full of wild greens and herbs that Auntie had gathered along the way. We were also there to check the traps—Auntie had caught a beaver just two days before and was hoping for another. Beaver pelts were a rarity and brought a high price. They were once nearly as common as squirrels', Auntie said, but trappers had taken all except a handful.

Buckshot was with us, nosing the ground, ears attentive to every little sound. I never knew if he was all wolf, or only part. Auntie had found him as a pup, when he'd fallen into one of her pit traps after being all shot up by someone. She'd carried him home, pulled the buckshot pellets out of him, stitched him up, and nursed him back to health. He'd been by her side ever since.

"He was lucky you found him," I said after hearing the story.

"Luck had nothing to do with it," Auntie told me. "He and I were meant for one another."

I never saw such devotion in a dog—or any animal, for that matter. His wounds had healed, but the buckshot left him blind in his right eye, which was milky white. *His ghost eye,* Auntie called it.

"He came so close to death, he's got one eye back there still," she explained. I loved Buckshot, but I hated that milky-white moon that seemed to see everything and nothing all at once.

Auntie was not related to me by blood, but she cared for me, raised me after my own mother died giving birth to me. I had no memory of my mother—the only proofs of her existence were my parents' wedding photograph, the quilt she'd sewn that I slept under every night, and the stories my older brother and sister told.

My brother claimed I had my mother's laugh. My sister said that my mother had been the best dancer in the county, that she was the envy of all the other girls.

Auntie's people came from up north, in Quebec. Her father had been a trapper; her mother, an Indian woman. Auntie carried a hunting knife, and wore a long deerskin coat decorated with bright beads and porcupine quills. She spoke French, and sang songs in a language I never did recognize. She wore a ring carved from yellowed bone on her right pointer finger.

"What does it say?" I asked once, touching the strange letters and symbols on its surface.

"That life is a circle," she answered.

People in town were frightened of Auntie, but their fear did not keep them away from her door. They followed the well-worn path to her cabin in the woods out behind the Devil's Hand, carrying coins, honey, whiskey—whatever they had to trade for her remedies. Auntie had drops for colic, tea for fever, even a little blue bottle that she swore contained a potion so powerful that with one drop the object of your heart's desire would be yours. I knew better than to doubt her.

There were other things I knew about Auntie, too. I'd seen her sneak out of Papa's bedroom in the early morning, heard the sounds that came from behind his locked door when she visited him there.

I also knew better than to cross her. She had a fiery temper and little patience with people who did not see things her way. If people refused to pay her for her services, she'd call on them, sprinkle their homes with black powder pulled from one of her leather pouches, and speak a strange incantation. Terrible things would befall those families from then on: sicknesses, fires, crop losses, even death.

I tossed a handful of dark-green fiddleheads into the basket.

"Tell me, Auntie, please," I begged, "can the dead come back?"

Auntie looked at me a long time, head cocked to the side, her small, dark eyes fixed on mine.

"Yes," she told me at last. "There is a way. Few know of it, but those who do, pass it down to their children. Because you are the closest I will ever come to a child of my own, the secret will go to you. I will write it all down, everything I know about sleepers. I will fold up the papers, put them in an envelope, and seal it with wax. You will hide it away, and one day, when you are ready, you will open it up."

"How will I know I am ready?" I asked.

She smiled, showing her small teeth, pointed like a fox's and stained brown from tobacco. "You will know."

I am writing these words in secret, hidden under covers. Martin and Lucius believe I am sleeping. I hear them downstairs, drinking coffee and discussing my prognosis. (Not good, I'm afraid.)

I have been going back in my mind, thinking over how all of this began, piecing things together the way one might sew a quilt. But, oh, what a hideous and twisted quilt mine would be!

"Gertie," I hear Martin say above the clink of a spoon stirring coffee in his favorite tin mug. I imagine the furrow of his brow, the deep worry lines there; how sad his face must be after he spoke her name.

I hold my breath and listen hard.

"Sometimes a tragedy breaks a person," Lucius says. "Sometimes they will never be whole again."

If I close my eyes even now, I can still see my Gertie's face, feel her sugary breath on my cheek. I can so vividly recall our last morning together, hear her saying, "If snow melts down to water, does it still remember being snow?"

Martin

January 12, 1908

"Wake up, Martin." A soft whisper, a flutter against his cheek. "It's time."

Martin opened his eyes, leaving the dream of a woman with long dark hair. She'd been telling him something. Something important, something he was not supposed to forget.

He turned over in bed. He was alone, Sara's side of the bed cold. He sat up, listening carefully. Voices, soft giggles across the hall, from behind Gertie's bedroom door.

Had Sara spent the whole night in with Gertie again? Surely it couldn't be good for the girl, to smother her like that. Sometimes he worried that Sara's attachment to Gertie simply wasn't . . . healthy. Just last week, Sara had kept Gertie home from school for three straight days, and for those three days Sara doted on her—plaiting her hair, making her a new dress, baking her cookies, playing hide-and-seek. Sara's niece, Amelia, offered to take Gertie for the weekend, and Sara had made excuses—*she gets homesick so easily, she's so frail*—but Martin understood that it was Sara who could not bear to be without Gertie. Sara never seemed whole unless Gertie was by her side.

He pushed the worried thoughts away. Better to focus on the problems he understood and could do something about.

The house was cold, the fire out.

He peeled back the covers, threw his legs over the side of the bed, and pulled on his pants. His bad foot hung there like a hoof till he shoved it into the special boot fashioned for him by the cobbler in Montpelier. The soles were worn through, and he'd stuffed the bottoms of both boots with dry grass and cattail fluff, all layered over scraps of leather, in a futile attempt to keep the dampness out. There was no money for new custom-made boots now.

Blight had ruined most of last fall's potato crop, and they relied on the money they got from selling the potatoes to the starch factory to get through the winter. It was only January, and the root cellar was nearly bare: a few spongy potatoes and carrots, some Hubbard squash, half a dozen jars of string beans and tomatoes Sara had put up last summer, a little salt pork from the hog they'd butchered in November (they'd traded most of the meat for dry goods at the general store). Martin would have to get a deer soon if they were going to have enough to eat. Sara had a talent for stretching what little food they had, for making milk gravy and biscuits with a bit of salt pork into a meal, but she couldn't create something from nothing.

"Have some more, Martin," she would always say, smiling as she spooned more gravy onto biscuits. "There's plenty." And he would nod and have a second helping, going along with this myth of abundance Sara had created.

"I love biscuits and gravy," Gertie would say.

"That's why I make them so often, my darling," Sara told her.

Once a month, Sara and Gertie would hitch up the wagon and ride into town to pick up what they needed at the general store. They didn't get extravagant things, just the basics for getting by: sugar, molasses, flour, coffee, and tea. Abe Cushing let them buy on credit, but last week he'd pulled Martin aside to tell him the bill was getting up there—they'd need to pay it down some before buying anything more. Martin had felt the sour creep of failure work its way from his empty stomach up into his chest.

He jerked his bootlaces tight and tied them with careful knots. His bad foot ached already, and he wasn't even out of bed. It was the storm.

He reached into the right pocket of his patched and tattered work pants and felt for the ring, making sure it was there. He carried it everywhere he went, a good-luck charm. It warmed in his fingers, seemed to radiate a heat all its own. Sometimes, when he was out working in the fields or woods and he knew Sara wouldn't see, he slipped the ring onto his pinkie.

Every spring, Martin plowed up enough rocks to build a silo. But it wasn't only the rocks that came up—he'd found other things, strange things, out in the north field, just below the Devil's Hand.

Broken teacups and dinner plates. A child's rag doll. Scraps of cloth. Charred wood. Teeth.

"An old settlement? A dumping ground of some sort?" he'd guessed when he showed Sara the artifacts.

Her eyes darkened, and she shook her head. "Nothing's ever been out there, Martin." Then she urged him to bury everything back in the ground. "Don't plow so close to the Devil's Hand. Let that back field lie fallow."

And he did.

Until two months ago, when he found the ring out there, glowing like the halo he sometimes saw around the moon.

It was an odd ring, hand-carved from bone. And old, very old. There were designs scored into it, a strange writing Martin didn't recognize. But when he held it in his hand, it seemed to speak to him almost, to grow warm and pulsate. Martin took it as a sign that his luck was about to change.

He brought the ring home, cleaned it up, and put it in a little velvet bag. He left it on top of Sara's pillow on Christmas morning, nearly beside himself with anticipation. There had never been money for a proper gift, a gift she might truly deserve, and he couldn't wait for her to see the ring. He knew she was going to love it. It was so ornate, so delicate and somehow . . . magical—a perfect gift for his wife.

Sara's eyes lit up when she saw the bag, but when she opened it and looked inside, she dropped it instantly, horrified, hands trembling. It was as if he'd given her a severed finger.

"Where did you find it?" she asked.

"At the edge of the field, near the woods. For God's sake, Sara, what's the matter?"

"You must take it back and bury it again," she told him.

"But why?" he asked.

"Promise me you will," she demanded, placing her hand on his chest, gripping his shirt in her fingers. "Right away."

She looked so frightened. So strangely desperate.

"I promise," he said, taking the ring in its bag and slipping it into his trouser pocket.

But he hadn't buried it. He'd kept it hidden away, his own little good-luck charm.

He stood now, ring carefully tucked into his pocket, and walked over to the window. In the half-light of dawn, he saw it had snowed all night. That meant shoveling and hitching the roller up to the horses to make the driveway passable. If he got that done early enough, he'd get his rifle and go out into the woods to do some hunting—the fresh snow would make tracking easier, and with snow this deep, the deer would head where the woods were thickest. If he couldn't get a deer, maybe there would be a turkey or grouse. A snowshoe hare, even. He pictured Sara's face, lit up at the sight of him carrying in fresh meat. She'd give him a kiss, say, "Well done, my love," then sharpen her best knife and get to work, dancing around the kitchen, humming a tune Martin never could name—something that sounded sad and happy all at once; a song, she'd tell him, that she learned when she was a child.

He shuffled down the narrow stairs to the living room, cleaned out the fireplace, and lit a fire. Then he started one in the kitchen stove, careful not to bang the iron door closed. If Sara heard him, she'd come down. Let her rest, warm and laughing under the covers with little Gertie.

Martin's stomach clenched with hunger. Dinner last night had been a meager potato stew with a few chunks of rabbit in it. He'd ruined most of the meat with buckshot.

"Couldn't you have aimed for the head?" Sara had asked.

"Next time, I'll give you the gun," he'd told her with a wink. The truth was, she'd always been a better shot. And she had a talent for butchering any animal. With just a few deft strokes of the knife, she peeled the skin away as if slipping off a winter coat. He was clumsy and made a mess of a pelt.

Martin pulled on his wool overcoat and called for the dog, who was curled up on an old quilt in the corner of the kitchen. "Come on, Shep," he called. "Here, boy." Shep lifted his great blocky head, gave Martin a puzzled look, then laid it back down. He was getting older and was no longer eager to bound through fresh snow. These days, it seemed the dog only listened to Sara. Shep was just the latest in a line of Sheps, all descended from the original Shep, who had been chief farm dog here when Sara was a girl. The current Shep, like those before him, was a large, rangy dog. Sara said the original Shep's father had been a wolf, and, to look at him, Martin didn't doubt it.

Dogless, Martin opened the front door to head for the barn. He'd feed the few animals they had left—two old draft horses, a scrawny dairy cow, the chickens—and collect some eggs for breakfast if there were any to be had. The hens weren't laying much this time of year.

The sun was just coming up over the hill, and snow fell in great fluffy clumps. He sank into the fresh powder, which came up to his mid-shin, and knew he'd need snowshoes to go into the woods later. He plowed his way through, doing a clumsy shuffle-walk across the yard to the barn, then looped around back to the henhouse. Feeding the chickens was one of his favorite chores of the day—he enjoyed the way they greeted him with clucks and coos, the warmth of the eggs taken from the nest boxes. The chickens gave them so much and asked for so little in return. Gertie had given each bird a name: there was Wilhelmina, Florence the Great, Queen Reddington, and eight others, although Martin had a hard time keeping track of the odd little histories Gertie created for them. They'd had a full dozen before a fox got a hen last month. Back in November, Gertie made little paper hats for all the chickens and brought them their own cake of cornbread. "We're having a party," she'd told him and Sara, and they'd watched with delight, laughing as Gertie chased the chickens around trying to keep their hats on.

He came around the corner of the barn and felt the air leave his chest when he saw a splash of crimson on white. Scattered feathers.

The fox was back.

Martin hurried over, loping along, dragging his bad foot through the snow. It wasn't hard to see what had happened: tracks led up to the henhouse, and just outside was a mess of blood and feathers and a trail of red leading away.

Martin reached down, took off his heavy mitten—the blood was fresh, not yet frozen. He inspected the coop, saw the small gnawed hole the fox had gotten through. He hissed through clenched teeth, unlatched the door, and looked inside. Two more dead. No eggs left. The remaining hens were huddled in a nervous cluster against the back corner.

He hurried back to the house to collect his gun.

Gertie

January 12, 1908

"If snow melts down to water, does it still remember being snow?"

"I'm not sure snow has much of a memory," Mama tells me.

It snowed hard all night, and when I peeked out the window this morning, everything was covered in a thick fluffy blanket, all white and pure, erasing everything else—footprints and roads, any sign of people. It's like the world's been reborn, all fresh and new. There will be no school today, and though I love Miss Delilah, I love staying home with Mama more.

Mama and I are curled up, pressed against each other like twin commas. I know about commas and periods and question marks. Miss Delilah taught me. Some books I can read real good. Some, like the Bible, are a puzzle to me. Miss Delilah also told me about souls, how every person has one.

"God breathes them into us," she said.

I asked her about animals, and she said no, but I think she's wrong. I think everything must have a soul and a memory, even tigers and roses, even snow. And, of course, old Shep, who spends his days sleeping by the fire, eyes closed, paws moving, because he's still a young dog in his dreams. How can you dream if you don't have a soul?

The covers are tented up over me and Mama's heads, and it's all dark, like we're deep underground. Animals in a den. All warm and snuggly. Sometimes we play hide-and-seek, and I love to hide beneath the covers or under her bed. I'm small and can fit into tight places. Sometimes it takes Mama a long, long time to find me. My favorite place to hide is Mama and Papa's closet. I like the feeling of their clothing brushing my face and body, like I'm walking through a forest thick with soft trees that smell like home: like soap and woodsmoke and the rose-scented lotion Mama sometimes uses on her hands. There is a loose board in the back of the closet that I can swing out and crawl through; then I come out in the linen closet in the hall, under the shelves with extra sheets, towels, and quilts. Sometimes I sneak through the other way and go into their closet and watch Mama and Papa while they sleep. It makes me feel strange and lovely and more like a shadow than a real girl—awake when no one else is, me and the moon smiling down on Mama and Papa while they dream.

Now Mama reaches around, takes my hand, and spells into it with her pointer finger: "R-E-A-D-Y?"

"No, Mama," I say, wrapping my fingers around hers. "Just a little longer."

Mama sighs, pulls me tighter. Her nightgown is worn flannel. I work my fingers over its soft folds.

"What did you dream, my darling girl?" she asks. Mama's voice is as smooth as good linen.

I smile. Take her hand and spell into it "B-L-U-E D-O-G."

"Again? How lovely! Did you ride on his back?"

I nod my head. The back of it bumps against Mama's chinny-chin-chin.

"Where did he take you this time?" She kisses the back of my neck, her breath tickling the little hairs there. I told Miss Delilah once that we all must be part animal, because we have little bits of fur all over our skin. She laughed and said it was a foolish thought. Sometimes when Miss Delilah laughs at me I feel tiny, like a girl just learning her words.

"He took me to see a lady with tangled hair who lives inside an old hollow tree. She's been dead a long time. She's one of the winter people."

I feel Mama stiffen. "Winter people?"

"That's what I call them," I say, turning to face her. "The people who are stuck between here and there, waiting. It reminds me of winter, how everything is all pale and cold and full of nothing, and all you can do is wait for spring."

She looks at me real funny. Worried-like.

"It's all right, Mama. The lady I met isn't one of the bad ones."

"Bad ones?" Mama asks.

"Sometimes they're angry. They hate being stuck. They want to come back but they don't know how, and the more they try, the more angry they get. Sometimes they're just lonely. All they want is someone to talk to."

The covers fly off our heads, and the cold in the room hits my body and makes my skin prickle like it's being poked by a thousand tiny icicles.

"Time to get up," Mama says, her voice higher than it should be. "After chores and breakfast, maybe you and I can bake."

Mama's up now, smoothing the covers, fluttering around like a busy bird.

"Molasses cookies?" I ask, hopeful. They're my very favorite food on earth. Shep's, too, because now that he's so old he gets to lick out the bowl. Papa says we spoil that dog, but Mama tells him Shep has earned it.

"Yes. Now go find your papa and see if he needs help feeding the animals. Bring in the eggs, too. We'll need them for the cookies. And, Gertie?" she says, turning my face so that I'm looking right at her. Her eyes are bright and sparkly, like fish in a stream. "Don't mention your dream to him. Or anything about the winter people. He wouldn't understand."

I nod real big and leap to the floor. Today I'm a jungle animal. A lion or a tiger. Something with sharp teeth and claws that lives in a place far across the ocean where it's hot all the time. Miss Delilah showed us a picture book of all the animals Noah took with him on the ark: horses and oxen, giraffes and elephants. My favorites were the big cats. I bet they can walk real quiet, sneak around at night, just like me.

"Grrr," I snarl, pawing my way out of the room. "Look out, Papa. Here comes the biggest cat in the jungle. Big enough to eat you up, bones and all."

Martin

January 12, 1908

Martin had known Sara all his life. Her people came from the farm on the outskirts of town, out by the ridge. The Devil's Hand, people called it, the ledge of rock that stuck up out of the ground like a giant hand, fingers rising from the earth. *Haunted land,* people said. A place where monsters dwelled. The soil was no good, all clay and rocks, but the Harrisons eked out a living, trading the few things they could coax out of the ground—potatoes, turnips—for flour and sugar in town. The Harrisons were thin, almost skeletal, with dark eyes and hair, but Sara was different somehow—her hair auburn when the sun hit it; her coppery eyes danced with light rather than shadow. She seemed otherworldly to Martin, a siren or a selkie—a creature he'd read about in storybooks but never imagined might be real.

Sara's mother had died when she was born. It was just old Joseph Harrison caring for Sara and her older brother and sister, alone. But folks said he once had a woman who came around. She'd done the laundry, cooked the meals, nursed the children. People even said she'd bedded down with Joseph Harrison, lived with him for a time like a wife. She was an Indian woman who rarely spoke and wore clothes made from animal skins—that's what people said. Some said that she was half animal herself: that she had the power to transform into a bear or a deer. Martin remembered hearing about her from his own father; he said she used to live in a cabin up beyond the Devil's

Hand, and people from town would go to see her when someone took sick. "When the doctor couldn't help, you went to her."

Something had happened to her—an accident? a drowning? Something had happened around the time Sara's brother died. Martin couldn't recall the details, and when he asked Sara about it after they were married, she shook her head, told him he must be mistaken.

"The stories you heard, they're just stories. People in town love their stories, you know that as well as I do. It was just Father, Constance, Jacob, and I. There was no woman in the woods."

Back in grammar school, Martin had been shooting marbles with a group of boys in the schoolyard. His older brother, Lucius, was there, furious because Martin had just won his favorite marble after knocking it out of the ring: a beautiful orange aggie that Lucius had named Jupiter. Martin was holding up his prize, thinking about the orbits of planets, when Sara Harrison came sauntering over, her bright eyes glittering and catching the light much like his new marble. She looked so startlingly beautiful to him then that he did the only thing he could think of—he handed her the marble.

"No!" Lucius shrieked, but it was too late. Sara tightened her fingers around it and smiled.

"Martin Shea, you are the one I shall marry," she said.

Lucius snorted with laughter. "You're mad, Sara Harrison."

But Sara had said the words with such sureness, such conviction, that Martin never doubted the truth of them, even though he'd laughed at the time, surrounded by his friends and his brother, as if she'd told a joke. And it did feel like a joke, that a girl as pretty as she would choose Martin.

He'd been an odd boy—arms too long for his sleeves, face always stuck in a book like *The Swiss Family Robinson, Treasure Island, Twenty Thousand Leagues Under the Sea*. He longed for adventure and believed he had the heart of a hero. Unfortunately, there were no pirates to battle in West Hall, no shipwrecks to survive. Only the endless monotony of chores on the family farm: cows that needed milking, hay that needed to be cut. One day, he promised himself, he'd leave it all behind—he was destined for bigger things than being a farmer. Until then, he was just biding his time. He did poorly in school, daydreaming when he should have been studying, while his brother, Lucius, got top marks in the class. Lucius was stronger, faster, braver, even better-looking. Lucius was the one all the girls dreamed of marrying one day. So what, then, did Sara Harrison see in Martin?

He didn't know it at the time, but this was one of Sara's great gifts—the ability to see the future in these tiny pieces, like she had a special telescope.

"You won't leave West Hall, Martin," she announced at the Fourth of July picnic when Martin was twelve. Most of the town was gathered on the green, around the newly built bandstand. Some were dancing, others spread out on picnic blankets. Lucius was in the gazebo, playing the trumpet with a few men from town who made up the West Hall town band. Lucius, who would be going off to Burlington in the fall—his high marks had earned him a full scholarship at the University of Vermont.

"What makes you so sure?" Martin asked, turning to look at Sara, who had sat down beside him.

"Did you ever think that perhaps all the adventure you could ever want is right here?"

He laughed, and she smiled indulgently at him, then reached into the pocket of her jacket and pulled something out. The Jupiter marble.

She tucked the marble back into her pocket, leaned over, and kissed his cheek. "Happy Independence Day, Martin Shea."

He decided then and there that Sara had been right—she was the girl he would marry, and maybe, just maybe, *she* was the adventure he was meant for.

"Martin," she'd whispered on their wedding night, fingers curled in his hair, lips tickling his left ear, "one day, we'll have a little girl."

And, sure enough, they did.

Seven years ago, after losing three babies still in the womb and then their son, Charles, who'd died at two months, Sara gave birth to Gertie. The girl was tiny, so small; Lucius said she wouldn't live through the week.

He had passed his state boards and come back from Burlington to work with old Dr. Stewart, who soon retired, leaving Lucius the only M.D. in town. Lucius closed his leather medical bag and put his hand on Martin's arm.

"I'm sorry," he said.

But Lucius was wrong: Gertie attached herself to Sara and sucked and sucked, growing stronger each day. Their miracle child. And Sara glowed with happiness, the tiny baby asleep on her chest, Sara looking over at Martin with an all-is-right-in-the-world-now smile. Martin felt the same way and knew that no adventure he might ever have gone on could have had a happier outcome than this.

Though she no longer sucked at her mother's breast, Gertie had kept herself attached to Sara. They were inseparable, always intertwined, and they spelled secret words in each other's palms with fingertips. Sometimes Martin was sure they didn't need words to communicate at all—that they could read each other's minds. They seemed to have whole wordless conversations with their eyes, laughing and nodding at each other across the supper table. At times, Martin felt a little spark of envy. He would try to be in on their secrets and little jokes, laughing in the wrong places and getting a poor-Papa look from Gertie. He understood, and eventually came to accept that they had a closeness, a bond, that he would never be a part of. The truth was, he believed he was the luckiest man on earth to have these two for a wife and daughter—it was like getting to live with fairies or mermaids, some breathtakingly beautiful creatures he was not meant to understand fully.

He did worry though, that the losses of their previous children had made Sara cling to Gertie in a way that seemed almost desperate. There were days when Sara would not let the girl leave for school, saying she was worried that Gertie's nose was a little runny, or her eyes looked glassy.

In his darkest hours, Martin believed that, though she'd never say it, Sara blamed him for those dead babies that came before Gertie. Each miscarriage had nearly destroyed Sara—she spent weeks bedridden, weeping, eating only enough to keep a sparrow alive. And then Charles had been born healthy and strong, with a headful of dark curls and a face as wise as an old man. They'd found him breathless and cold in his cradle one morning. Sara wrapped her arms around him, held on to him all day and into the next. When Martin tried to take the baby, Sara insisted he was not gone.

"He's still breathing," she said. "I can feel his little heart beating."

Martin stepped away from her, frightened. "Please, Sara," he said.

"Leave us," she snarled, pulling the dead baby tighter, her eyes cold and frantic like those of a mad animal.

Finally, Lucius had to come and sedate her. Only when she was sleeping could they pry the child from her arms.

Martin believed the deaths were the fault of this place—the 120 acres that belonged to Sara by birthright. Other than her older sister, Constance, who'd married and moved out to Graniteville, she was the last remaining Harrison. He blamed the ledgy soil and barren fields, where almost nothing would grow; the water that tasted of sulfur. It was as if the land itself dared anything to stay alive.

Now, gun in hand, Martin moved east across the field as he pursued the fox, trudging along, his feet strapped into the bent-wood-and-rawhide snowshoes. His breath came out in cloudy puffs. His feet were wet and cold, soaked through already. The fox tracks continued in a straight line, out into the orchard Sara's grandfather had planted. The trees were unpruned; the few apples and pears they produced were woody, bug-filled, and spotted with blight.

Sara and Gertie would be out of bed now, wondering where he was. There would be a pot of coffee, biscuits in the oven. But he needed to do this, to kill the fox. He needed to show his wife and daughter that he could protect them—that if a creature threatened their livelihood in any way, he would destroy it. He'd kill the fox, skin it himself, and hand the pelt over to Sara, a surprise gift. She was clever, skilled with a hide and needle and thread—she could make a warm hat for little Gertie.

Martin leaned against a crooked apple tree to catch his breath. The snow swirled around him, limiting his visibility, making him feel strangely disoriented. Which way was home?

He heard something behind him—the soft whoosh of footsteps moving rapidly through the snow.

He turned. There was no one there. It was only the wind. He bit down on his lip, touched the warm ring in his pocket.

Ten yards ahead of him, a gnarled old apple tree moved. He squinted through the blowing snow and saw that it wasn't a tree, but an old woman hunched over. She was dressed in animal skins, her hair tangled like a nest of serpents.

"Hello?" he called.

She turned, looked at Martin, and flashed him a smile, showing pointed brown teeth. Martin blinked, and it was a tree again, gently swaying under a heavy coat of snow.

The fox darted out from behind it, half a chicken still in its mouth. It froze, looking at Martin, its gold eyes flickering. He held his breath, shouldered the gun, and sighted the fox, which now looked up and watched him, its eyes like little rings of fire.

The fox looked at him; suddenly, for two whole seconds, it wasn't the animal's eyes that gazed dispassionately at him, but Sara's.

Martin Shea, you are the one I shall marry.

One day, we'll have a little girl.

Martin blinked, trying to push this image from his mind—this was no trickster fox from a fairy tale. It was just his imagination, the result of a childhood spent absorbed in all those books.

The fox, now an ordinary fox with ordinary eyes once more, turned, dropped the chicken, and leapt away just as Martin squeezed the trigger.

"Damn it!" Martin shouted, realizing he'd missed.

He took off running in the fox's direction and saw there was fresh blood on the ground. He'd hit the animal after all. Martin reached down; his fingertips brushed the snowy tracks and came away red. He raised them to his lips and tasted. It was sharp and salty and made his mouth water. Then, gun at the ready, he followed the trail through the orchard, up over the rocky ridge, past the Devil's Hand, and down into the woods below, until he could only see a faint red every few paces. The beeches and maples, all stripped bare of leaves and shrouded in snow, looked unfamiliar. For an hour or more, he moved on through thickets of dense growth, last year's raspberry canes lashing out at him, home farther and farther away. The woods grew darker. He began to wonder if he had made the right choice, coming out here in the storm.

"Too late to turn back now," he told himself, foot aching as he pushed himself forward.

He didn't allow himself to think of the accident very often. When he did, it was at times like this—when he felt as if the world he inhabited was against him in some profound way.

He'd been up on the hill cutting firewood. It was a pleasant late-summer morning a year after he and Sara were married. He'd found a clearing full of deadfalls, already dried out, and was cutting them into stove-sized pieces and loading them onto the cart. He worked all morning, went home for lunch, then returned to the woods, pleased with how much he'd accomplished. He'd told Sara to keep supper warm—he'd work until either the wagon was full or it grew too dark. She'd frowned, never liking it when he was in the woods after nightfall.

"Don't be too late," she'd said.

But the work was going so well, with the wagon almost full, that dusk came and went, and Martin kept sawing. His shoulders and back ached, but it was a good kind of ache. At last, he could get no more wood on the wagon. He gathered his saws and ax, hitched the horse back up to the cart, and began the slow and careful descent of the hill. It was quite dark by then, and he walked beside the horse, guiding her around rocks, over roots and gullies. When they were just past the Devil's Hand, the horse froze.

"Come on, girl," he urged, pulling the reins and giving her a gentle swat. But she refused to budge, her eyes focused straight ahead, ears pricked up at attention. She took a step backward, whinnied nervously. Martin heard a twig snap in the darkness ahead of them. He gave the horse a reassuring pat on the neck.

"Steady, girl," he said, then stepped forward into the shadows to investigate.

He never could say what had been out in the woods that night. When Lucius asked him about it later, Martin claimed that he hadn't seen anything, that the horse had been spooked by a sound.

"That old mare you've got is as steady as they come," Lucius had said. "Must have been a bear. Or a catamount. There had to be something that frightened her like that."

Martin nodded, and didn't tell his brother, or even Sara, what he'd really seen: a flash of pale white, like an owl, only much, much larger. It had been in a low branch and swooped down onto the forest floor, making a strange sort of hiss in flight. It had looked . . . almost human. But no person could move that way—it was too quick, too fluid. And there had been a smell, a terrible burning-fat sort of reek.

This was too much for the horse, who instantly bolted straight ahead, right for Martin. He saw her coming, knew what he had to do, but his brain was spinning in circles from fear, and he couldn't seem to make his body move. His eyes were locked on the horse's eyes, which bulged with panic. At last, Martin dove to get out of her way, but not in time, not far enough. The horse knocked him down and trampled his legs, breaking his left femur with an audible snap. His temple caught the edge of a large rock on the way down, and the world got darker and his vision blurred. The cart ran over his left foot, crushing it from the ankle down. He could feel the bones grinding under the wheel. The pain, though excruciating, felt far away, almost as if it were happening to someone else. Behind him, a twig snapped. He turned, and saw the pale figure move off into the shadows just before he lost consciousness.

The cart broke apart halfway down the hill, and the horse arrived back at the barn, dragging what remained of the shaft and front axle, the wheels smashed to pieces. Afterward, he learned that when Sara saw this, she gathered a lantern and went looking for him.

"I was sure I would find you dead," she told him later. "I almost couldn't bring myself to climb the hill. I didn't want to see."

She found him alive but unconscious, crushed and bleeding. Sara managed to lash together a stretcher from two saplings and Martin's coat and dragged him down the hill by herself.

In the weeks of Martin's recovery, during which Lucius reset his bones as best he could and Sara wrapped his leg and foot in poultices to speed the healing, he would ask her again and again how she, so tiny, had managed to get him down the hill.

"I suppose God helped me," she told him.

On he trudged, following the animal's small tracks, unsure of where he was or how much time had passed. He searched for the sun in the sky, but there was too much snow, too much gray, for him even to see it. Though he knew the woods around the farm well from his years of hunting and gathering firewood and maple sap, he didn't recognize a single landmark. The trees around him seemed gangly and monsterlike as they fought their way up toward the light. The snow was falling too hard, too thickly, covering everything familiar. He followed the tracks, the only thing he was sure of, and was relieved when they circled back toward the rocks. He was exhausted. Hungry. His foot ached, and his mouth was dry. He sucked on clumps of snow, but it did little to quench his thirst.

Crisscrossing what remained of his footprints from earlier, he climbed back up the hill, slipping and sliding on the steep parts, grabbing hold of poplars and beech trees, and came, at last, to the Devil's Hand—a collection of enormous rocks that seemed to reach straight upward, wearing a fresh glove of pure white snow. But there, in the shadow of the center finger, right where the tracks led, the snow had been pushed away, and there was a little opening he'd never noticed before. The small mouth of a cave.

Martin crept to the entrance. It was quite narrow, barely large enough for a man to crawl through, and didn't appear to be very deep. It seemed a cozy little alcove. The fox rested against the wall, panting, thinking perhaps that it was hidden in the shadows. Martin smiled. She'd been hit in the left flank, the fur blown away, flesh exposed. He could smell the rich iron scent of her blood. Her whole body seemed to tremble as she watched him, waiting.

Martin raised the gun and pointed the barrel into the cave.

He aimed for the head, not wanting to ruin the pelt.

. . .

Where's Gertie?" Sara was running toward the barn as Martin came out. He'd skinned the fox and nailed the pelt up to dry against the north wall of the barn. He'd done a messy job, nothing like what Sara would do, but, still, it was done. He'd succeeded.

Martin blinked at her, the bright snow overwhelming after the darkness of the barn. "Not here," he said. He was tired. Cold. Impatient. Killing the fox should have left him feeling satisfied, but instead it had unsettled him, perhaps because at the end it hadn't been a fair fight, the animal cornered and frightened.

Sara's eyes were wild, frantic. She hadn't put on a coat, and stood shivering in her sweater and housedress. Snow sat in great clumps in her hair and on her shoulders.

"Where have you been?" she asked, her eyes moving over Martin's soaked, muddy pants, his coat stained with fresh blood.

"The fox came back. Killed three hens. I tracked it down and shot it." He raised his head high as he said this. *See what I can do? I can protect what is ours. I have the heart of a hero.*

"I skinned the fox," he said. "I thought you might make Gertie a hat."

Sara reached out and grabbed the sleeve of his coat, fingers working their way into the damp wool. "Gertie wasn't with you?"

"Of course not. She was still in bed when I left."

All Martin wanted was to go inside and change into dry clothes, have some breakfast and a hot cup of coffee. He had little patience for Sara's need to have Gertie by her side at every second, for her near panic whenever the girl was out of sight for more than five minutes.

"She ran after you, Martin! She saw you out in the field and put on her coat to go meet you. She wanted to help you gather eggs."

He shook his head. "I never saw her."

"That was hours ago." Sara's gold-flecked eyes scanned the empty field. The snow had been falling steadily all day, the wind sending it drifting. All the tracks from the morning were covered over. Martin gazed across the yard helplessly, panic now rising.

There was no telling which way the girl had gone.

Martin

He searched the fields and woods for hours. The snow was letting up, but the air was bitterly cold, and the wind was blowing hard, creating great drifts and giving the yard and fields the appearance of a white sea with powdery waves.

How long could a child survive in weather like this? He tried not to let himself think about it, just trudged on, calling Gertie's name. He hadn't eaten all day or had so much as a drink of water. Desperation gnawed at his belly. His head ached, and it was becoming a struggle to think clearly through the rising panic. Most important, he knew, he had to remain calm for Sara, to convince her everything was going to be all right.

Sara stayed close by the house, in case Gertie returned. Martin could hear her, though. Even way up past the ridge, he could hear her desperate voice calling out, "Gertie, Gertie, Gertie . . . ," a strange chant behind the howling wind. His ears played tricks on him. He heard "Dirty, dirty, dirty," then "Birdy, birdy, birdy."

Martin's head pounded. His bad foot throbbed from all the miles he'd gone, trudging along in his duck-foot snowshoes—lift, slide, lift, slide. No sign of the girl.

He stumbled, pulled himself up again.

Birdy. Birdy.

Dirty birdy.

He thought of the fox with the chicken in its mouth.

Dead birdy.

He thought of his little girl, following his footsteps up into the woods.

Dead Gertie.

He covered his ears with his mittened hands and collapsed into the snow. He was supposed to be able to keep his family safe, to fix things when they went wrong. And here he was, soaking wet, half frozen, a man who appeared to be in need of rescue himself.

"Gertie!" he screamed.

Only the wind answered.

At last, exhausted and barely able to put any weight on his ruined left foot, he headed back down the hill, toward the house, as the sun sank low.

As he shuffled across the field in his snowshoes, he spotted Sara coming out of the barn. Wrapped in a light shawl, shivering with cold, she walked in frantic circles around the yard, her voice diminished to a hoarse croak: "Gertie! Gertie! Gertie!" She had no gloves on, and her hands were blue, her fingertips bloody and raw—she picked at her skin when she was nervous.

He recalled those same hands clinging so desperately to Baby Charles, whose body was cold, his lips blue.

I can feel his little heart beating.

If they lost Gertie, Martin knew it would ruin his wife.

She saw him and ran over, eyes enormous, hopeful. "Any sign?"

He shook his head. She stared at him a minute in disbelief.

He thought of the fox with its golden-rimmed eyes, how it had looked at him, through him, before he shot it.

"Martin, there isn't much daylight left. Get the horse and ride to town. Tell Lucius and Sheriff Daye what's happened. Gather people to help us look. Have them bring lanterns. Stop and see if the Bemises might have seen Gertie. She's been over to play with their girl Shirley."

"I'll go right now," he promised, putting a hand on her shoulder. "You go inside. Get warmed up. I'll come back with help."

He was so hungry, so thirsty. But to stop now, to go back to the house for even a cup of water, would be wrong. Not when his little girl was out there, lost in the storm. He'd stop at the creek on the way into town. He'd hunker down and drink like an animal.

"Martin," Sara said, taking his hands. "Pray with me. Please."

Martin had never been a praying man. Sara and Gertie prayed each night before bed, but he never joined them. He went to church every Sunday with them, listened to Reverend Ayers read from the Bible. It wasn't that he didn't believe in God, just that Martin never believed that God might listen to him. With the millions of people who must be praying to him each day, why should God pay attention to Martin Shea in West Hall, Vermont? But now, desperate and running out of hope, he nodded, removed his hat, and bowed his head, standing in the snow outside the barn, Sara's hands with their bloody fingers gripping tightly to his own.

"Please, God," Sara said, voice hoarse. Martin sneaked a look at her; her eyes were clamped shut, her face was blotchy, nose running. "Watch over our Gertie. Bring her back to us. She's a good girl. She's all we have. Keep her safe. Please bring her back. If she's gone, I . . ." Sara's voice broke.

"Amen," Martin said, ending the prayer.

Sara let go of Martin and walked off toward the house, head still bent down, lips moving, as if she was continuing her own private conversation with God, bargaining, begging.

Sliding open the door to the barn, Martin heard the animals letting him know he'd never fed them. The cow hadn't been milked. She gave a mournful wail as he walked by her pen, but she would have to wait. He grabbed the saddle and was lugging it to the horse stalls when something caught his eye, stopped him in his tracks. His heart pounded in his ears; the saddle was heavy and awkward in his hands, now slick with sweat.

The fox pelt was gone.

Hours ago, he'd nailed it up against the north wall of the barn to dry. Then he'd stood back and admired his handiwork, imagined the hat Sara might make for Gertie.

He squinted at the empty wall.

Only it wasn't empty.

No, something else hung there by a nail. Something that glinted in the little bit of light coming in through the window. His breath caught in his throat as he stepped forward to see. The saddle fell from his hands.

There, nailed to the rough wooden boards, was a hank of blond hair.

Gertie's hair.

His stomach cramped up, and he leaned over, retching.

His head felt as if it were being pounded between a hammer and an anvil. He gripped it in both hands, fingertips pressing into his temples.

He looked down, saw the blood on his clothing from skinning the fox.

"Martin?"

He swallowed hard and turned to see Sara in the doorway. She was walking toward him slowly. He jumped up, stood so that he'd block her view of the hair.

"What are you doing?"

"I was . . . getting the saddle."

For the second time that afternoon, he prayed: *Please, God, don't let her see the hair.*

He could not allow Sara to see the hair; it would destroy her. He had to hide it—throw it into the stream, where it would be carried away.

"Hurry," Sara said. "It'll be dark soon." Mercifully, she left the barn.

Martin turned, hands shaking as he reached for the thick rope of blond hair. He pulled it loose from the rusty nail and shoved it into his pocket.

When he had saddled the horse, he led her out of the barn, into the deep snow. It would be slow going, and he hoped they'd rolled the main roads by now.

It was possible, Martin told himself, that an animal had come into the barn and torn down the fox pelt. A coyote or a stray dog. But then he reached into his pocket, felt the thick hank of hair. He could come up with no explanation for Gertie's hair being on that nail.

"Martin?"

There was Sara again, waiting outside, just to the left of the open door, rocking back and forth, picking at the skin around her nails. Her eyes were wild and frantic. "You need to go inside, Sara. You're not dressed to be out in weather like this."

She nodded, turned toward the house, stopped. "Martin?"

"Yes?" A lump formed in his throat. Had she seen the hair?

"It's because of the ring."

"What?"

She was looking not at him but down into the snow at her feet. "The ring you found in the field. The one you tried to give me for Christmas. I know you still have it."

She'd known all along that he'd held on to the ring. That he'd been too selfish to bury it as she'd asked. Now here he was, caught in his lie. He didn't speak.

Sara's breath came out in white puffs of steam. Her skin was pale; her lips were blue with cold. "You were wrong to take it. I warned you never to keep anything you unearth there. You must get rid of it, Martin. You must give it back."

"Give it back?"

"Take it back out to the field and bury it. That's the only way we'll get our Gertie back."

He stared down at her, blinking. Surely she couldn't be serious. But her face told him she was. Sara had always been so strange about the field and woods, warning him to be careful out there, not to plow too close to the rocks, never to keep anything he unearthed. He'd thought it was old family superstitions, passed down. But this idea that Gertie was missing because he kept a ring he found out there—it was preposterous. Mad, even.

"Go do it now, before you go into town. Please, Martin."

He remembered what Lucius had told him back when Sara had her spell after the death of little Charles: "You must never argue with a person experiencing an episode of madness. It will only serve to make matters worse."

Martin nodded at Sara, clicked his tongue, turned his horse in the direction of the fields.

He rode out to the place where he'd found the ring—in the back corner of the far field, right up against the tree line. He dismounted, turned, and looked back toward the house, where Sara stood, watching, just a tiny shadow.

He took off his soaked mittens and reached into the right front pocket of his trousers. The ring wasn't there. His fingers searched frantically. He patted his left pocket. Nothing. His left coat pocket held only a few shotgun shells. Then, in the right coat pocket, his fingers brushed against the coil of hair. He shuddered with revulsion.

The ring had to be there! He'd put it in his pocket this morning. He remembered checking it when he was out hunting the fox. It had been in his pocket then, he was sure of it.

Sara was still watching, arms crossed over her chest. She swayed slightly in the wind, like a piece of tall, dried-out grass.

Sweat coated Martin's forehead in spite of the cold.

He reached back into the right pocket of his wool overcoat, felt the hank of hair curled like a soft snake.

Getting down on his knees, he started to dig with his fingers. He went as deep as he could with his numb fingers, until he hit a layer of crusted ice that he couldn't break through. He kicked at the ice with the toe of his boot, kept digging. When he could go no deeper, he dropped the hair inside, refilled the hole with snow. Wiping his frozen hands on his trousers, he walked back to the trembling horse. She fixed him with a pitiful gaze.

"Did you do it?" Sara asked, when he rode by her on his way into town.

He nodded, but couldn't look her in the eye. "Go inside and get warmed up. I'll come back with help."

{ Visitors from the Other Side

The Secret Diary of Sara Harrison Shea }

January 13, 1908

It was Clarence Bemis who found her, early this morning, nearly twenty-four hours since she crept out of bed to follow her papa.

When the three men—Clarence, Martin, and Lucius—came into the house, tracking in snow, at ten past eight this morning, I knew from their faces. I wanted to send them away. Bolt the door. Tell them there must be a mistake—they had to keep looking, they could not come back until they brought me my little girl, alive and well.

I hated all three men just then: Clarence in his overalls, his hair too long and shaggy and the stink of whiskey on him; Lucius with his earnest face, good shoes, and carefully trimmed mustache; Martin, who limped in, shoulders slumped, looking pathetic and ruined.

Go away, I longed to say. *Get out of my house.*

I wanted to turn back time, keep Gertie wrapped up in my arms, soft and warm under the covers.

Martin took me by the hand, asked me to sit down.

"We found her," he said, and I covered my mouth, thinking I would scream, but no sound came.

All three men stood frozen, hats in their hands, six sad eyes all on me.

.   .   .

*T*here is an old well at the far-eastern edge of the Bemises' property, something that ran dry years ago. I remember Auntie and I went there once, when I was a girl not much older than Gertie, to drop stones down and listen for the sound of them hitting bottom. I leaned against the rough circle of stones and tried to see the bottom, but it was too dark. There was a dank smell coming out of it, and I could almost imagine feeling a cool breeze.

"How far down do you think it goes?" I asked Auntie.

Auntie smiled. "Maybe all the way through to the other side of the world."

"That's impossible," I told her.

"Or maybe," she said, tossing another pebble down, "it leads to another world altogether."

I leaned farther down, desperate to see, and Auntie grabbed the back of my dress and pulled me upright. "Be careful, Sara. Wherever it goes, I don't think it's anywhere you want to be."

*C*larence said Gertie was curled up at its bottom so sweetly, as if she'd just fallen asleep.

"She didn't suffer," Lucius said, his voice low and calm as he put his hand on top of mine. His hand was soft and powdery, not a callus or a scar on it. He was there when they hauled my Gertie out, and this seemed all wrong to me, that Lucius was there when they pulled her out, and not me. They sent Jeremiah Bemis down by rope, and he tied it round her waist. I closed my eyes. Tried not to imagine her small body swinging, banging against the curved wall of the well, as they hoisted her up out of the darkness.

"She died instantly," Lucius said, as if it would be a comfort.

But it is no comfort. Because, over and over, I think of those stones I once dropped, and how long it took for them to reach the bottom.

I imagine what it must have been like, falling.

Surrounded by a circle of stone, falling, falling into the darkness.

January 2

ξ

Present Day

Ruthie

The snowflakes were spinning, drifting, doing their own drunken pirouettes, illuminated by the headlights of Buzz's truck. The studded tires bit into the snow, but he took the corners fast enough that they fishtailed dangerously close to the high snowbanks that lined the single-lane dirt roads.

"Turn off the lights," Ruthie said, because they were close now, and she didn't want her mother knowing she was out past curfew again. She was nineteen years old. Who did her mom think she was anyway, giving Ruthie a goddamn curfew?

Ruthie reached down, grabbed the bottle of peppermint schnapps that Buzz held between his thighs, and took a good slug of it. She rummaged through the pockets of her parka and pulled out the Visine, tilted back her head, and put three drops in each eye.

They'd been out partying at Tracer's barn, finishing up the keg left over from the big New Year's Eve bash. Emily had brought pot, and they'd huddled around the kerosene heater, talking about how much winter sucked and how everything was going to change in the spring. They'd all graduated the June before, and here they were, still stuck in West Freaking Hall, Vermont, the black hole in the center of the universe. All their friends had gone on to college, or moved to big cities in warm places: Miami, Santa Cruz.

It wasn't that Ruthie hadn't tried. She'd applied to schools in California and New Mexico, places with good business-administration programs, but her mother said that it wouldn't work right now, that they just didn't have the money.

They'd always lived pretty close to the bone, making ends meet by selling vegetables and eggs at the farmers' market. Her mom sold hand-knit socks and hats there, too, and at craft shops and shows around the state. Her mother was big into bartering. They never bought anything new, and when something broke, they fixed it rather than replacing it. Ruthie had learned at a young age not to beg for stuff they couldn't afford. Asking for a certain kind of sneaker or jacket just because all the other kids in her class had it earned her serious looks of disapproval and disappointment from her parents, who would remind her that she had perfectly nice things (even if they had come from the thrift store and had some other kid's name written inside).

Ruthie's mom decided it would be best if Ruthie stayed in West Hall and went to community college for a year; she even offered to pay Ruthie to help with the egg business. It was now her job to keep the books, feed the hens each day, gather the eggs, keep the coop clean.

"You want to study business, isn't this a much more practical way to learn?" her mother had asked. ·

"Selling a few dozen eggs at the farmers' market isn't exactly what I had in mind."

"Well, it's a start. And with your father gone, I could use the extra help," her mother had said. "Next year," her mother promised, "you can reapply anywhere you'd like. I'll help pay."

Ruthie argued, said there were student loans, grants, and scholarships she might qualify for, but her mother wouldn't fill out the paperwork, because it was just another way Big Brother was watching. The feds were not to be trusted, even when they were loaning money to college students. They'd get you caught up in the system, the very system her mother and father had worked so hard to stay free from.

"Things would be different if your father were still here," her mother said. And Ruthie knew it was true, though she found it unsettling that whenever her mother spoke of him she made it sound as if he'd gone off on a trip, up and left them on purpose, not dropped dead from a heart attack two years ago. If her father were still alive, she'd be off at college. Her father understood her as no one else had, knew how much she'd wanted to get away. He would have found a way to make it happen.

"Is it so bad?" her mother had asked, smoothing Ruthie's unruly dark hair. "Staying home one more year?"

Yes, Ruthie had wanted to say. *Yes! Yes! Yes!*

But then she thought of Buzz, who hadn't even applied to college and was working for his uncle at the scrap-metal yard. It was shit work, but Buzz always had money and found lots of cool pieces for his sculptures—these amazing monsters, aliens, and robots made from welded-together car parts and broken farm machinery. His uncle's front lot was full of Buzz's creations. He'd even made a little money selling a couple to tourists.

She and Buzz had met senior year at a keg party over at Cranberry Meadow. It was early October, and going to the party had been Emily's idea—she had a huge crush on a boy named Adam who'd graduated the year before, and Emily had heard he'd be there. It turned out Adam had come to the party with his cousin Buzz, and, somehow or other, the four of them ended up drifting away from the bonfire by the pond and going up to the cemetery. Adam and Emily were making out under a granite cross while Ruthie made awkward small talk with Buzz, annoyed at Emily for getting her into this. Buzz said his dad and uncle lived in West Hall, but he was living with his mom in Barre and going to school there. He was enrolled in the Barre Technical Center, in the automotive program.

"Cars are okay," he'd told her with a shrug while they sipped cheap beer out of plastic cups. "I guess I'm pretty good at fixing stuff. I'm on the pit crew for my cousin Adam—he races out at Thunder Road. You ever go out to Thunder Road?"

Ruthie shook her head and started stepping away, thinking she'd leave Emily and go back down to the bonfire. She had no interest in a redneck gearhead, no matter how cute he might be.

"Nah," Buzz said. "Didn't think so. How about the Devil's Hand? You ever been up there?"

This stopped her.

"I live right next to it," she said.

"No shit? It's a damn strange place. It's almost like the rocks were put there by someone, right?" Buzz leaned against a lichen-covered headstone.

Ruthie shrugged. She'd never really thought about it that way before.

"You believe in aliens?" he asked.

"You mean, like, from outer space? Um . . . no."

Buzz looked down into his cup of beer. "Well, personally, that's my theory for how the rocks got there. I go up there all the time. I'm actually making a sculpture of it in my uncle's shop. You should come check it out."

"A sculpture?" she asked, stepping closer again. They spent the rest of the night talking about art, UFOs, the pros and cons of getting a business degree, movies they'd seen, how they both felt they were stuck in families where they were totally misunderstood. They wandered around the cemetery, checking out the names and dates on the stones, trying to imagine what kinds of lives these people might have had, how they'd died.

"Look at this one," Buzz had said, running his fingers over letters on a plain granite marker. "Hester Jameson. She was only nine when she died. Just a kid. Pretty sad, huh?"

They'd been together ever since that night. Staying with him one more year sounded all right—more than all right, maybe, especially in moments like this, when they were side by side in the cab of his truck, stoned, cocooned and warm, careening through the darkness like nothing could stop them.

"You don't think your mom's up, do you?" Buzz asked.

"Hope not," Ruthie said.

"Yeah, she'd have a bird."

Ruthie laughed at the expression, but she knew it was true.

It wasn't just her mother—the whole town was worried, uptight, keeping their kids locked in at night. Back in early December, a sixteen-year-old girl named Willa Luce had disappeared without a trace, walking the half-mile home from a friend's house. Just before that, two sheep and a cow were found with their throats slit. And of course, before that, there had been the other disappearances: a boy who went missing in 1952 after his friends watched him crawl into a cave no one could find again, a hunter back in 1973 who'd been separated from his friends and never returned to camp, and the most famous, the college girl in 1982 who'd gone hiking with her boy-friend. The young man had come out of the woods alone, catatonic, and covered in blood. He was never able to say what had happened, and had been charged with her murder even though no body was ever found. In the end, he was deemed insane and sent to the state hospital.

The West Hall Triangle, people called it. There was talk of satanic cults, a twisted killer, a door to another dimension, and, of course, aliens, like Buzz and his friends believed.

Ruthie thought it was all a crock of shit. She wasn't sure what was up with the livestock, but guessed it was just bored kids screwing around. The little boy and the hunter probably just got lost in the acres and acres of forest. You get lost, you get cold, find someplace warm to curl up, and the next thing you know, your bones are being dragged off by coyotes. The college kid obviously went wacko and killed his sweetie—tragic, but it happens.

And Willa Luce—well, she'd probably just kept right on going that night, walked out to the highway and caught a ride with a trucker going west, going anywhere but here. Hadn't Ruthie herself spent years fantasizing about doing the exact same thing? What kid in West Hall hadn't? There just wasn't anything here that begged you to stick around—the world's smallest grocery store, grungy hardware store, cutesy bookshop, overpriced café, antique shop full of creepy moth-eaten shit, and a run-down dance hall that was mostly used for old ladies playing bingo and the occasional wedding reception. The biggest excitement of the week was the Saturday farmers' market.

She reached over and took Buzz's hand, entwining her fingers with his, which were rough and callused, always stained black with grease, no matter how much he washed them. She studied him in the dim light of the dashboard—baseball hat with the alien's face on it pulled down low, his eyes squinting out at the snowy road, battered Carhartt work jacket with its pockets stuffed full of all things Buzz: smokes, lighter, Leatherman multi-tool, bandanna, mini-binoculars, penlight, and cell phone.

These were her favorite times with him, when they were off

alone in his truck. He'd take her up into the mountains to go UFO hunting. They'd park for hours, sharing a thermos of spiked coffee or a six-pack of Long Trail, while he told her about what he and his best friend, Tracer, had seen once, out behind the Bemis farm. A strange light that winked and pulsated, starting up by the rocks, then moving down to the cornfield. Then he claimed they saw a little creature almost flying through the cornstalks: pale and quick, its movements too fast and erratic for any human.

"I know what I saw," Buzz swore. "It was an alien. A Gray. Tracer was right there with me—he saw it, too. It was real short, like four feet or so, and it had on this kind of dresslike robe that flowed out behind it when it ran. I bet you anything that's what got those sheep and cows. They use livestock for experiments—drain all their blood, remove their organs with surgical precision—no animal can do anything like that."

Tracer was a good guy, but Ruthie didn't understand how one individual could smoke the amount of pot he did and still function. She had no doubt they'd seen the little Gray alien after doing copious bong hits in Buzz's truck.

Still, even without Buzz's story, there was plenty of creepy talk about the woods and the Devil's Hand.

"Uh-oh," Buzz said when he pulled up to the bottom of Ruthie's driveway.

"Great," Ruthie slurred, looking up to see that the kitchen and living room were illuminated, the light streaming through the uncurtained windows. Her mother was awake. Ruthie reached into her pocket again for the roll of breath mints and chewed up three of them. She pushed up her sleeve, held down the button on her big digital watch, and blinked at the tiny screen: 1:12 A.M. JAN 2. She was screwed.

Ruthie leaned over and gave Buzz a sloppy kiss. He tasted like weed and schnapps. "Wish me luck," she said.

"Luck," he told her, winking. "Call me tomorrow and let me know how bad the fallout is."

Ruthie opened the door and jumped down out of the cab, her boots sinking into the fresh four inches of snow. She did a slow walk toward the house, stepping with the great care of a drunk trying not to stagger, taking great gulps of cold, woodsmoke-scented air. She shouldn't have had all the schnapps on top of the beer. Emily's killer weed hadn't helped, either. She slapped at her face with her mittened hands. *Sober up. Sober up. Sober up.*

Her mother was going to eat her alive. She'd be grounded. Not allowed to see Buzz for a month.

Ruthie made her way to the front door, keeping her eyes on the windows. She saw no movement inside. No way would her mother go up to bed without turning off the lights—wasting electricity was a serious offense in their house.

She took in one last deep breath and opened the front door slowly, stepped into the entryway, and eased the door shut behind her, bracing herself for attack. But there was no mother waiting to pounce.

She froze, listening.

No footsteps. No *Do you have any idea what time it is, young lady?* Just the sleeping house. So far, so good.

Ruthie shrugged off her parka and kicked off her boots. She shuffled into the kitchen, got herself a glass of water, and chugged it, leaning heavily on the counter, blinking in the harsh overhead light.

The dinner dishes were washed and put away, but there was a full cup of tea on the table. She touched it. Stone cold. Beside the tea was a slice of apple pie with one bite missing, the fork left resting on the plate. Never one to pass up a piece of her mother's pie, Ruthie gobbled it down and set the dish in the sink.

She switched off the lights and went into the living room to turn off that light, too. The woodstove had burned down to coals. She threw on a couple of logs, banked it down for the night, and headed for bed.

As she crept up the steps, as quietly as she could, using the banister to keep her balance, head swimming from booze, one happy thought rose up above everything else: she was home free. She almost laughed aloud in triumph.

Halfway up, she stepped in a small puddle and stopped. There were several dirty puddles on the wooden stairs. It looked like someone had come up without taking their boots off. Annoyed about her wet socks, Ruthie climbed the rest of the stairs to the carpeted hall.

The door to her mother's room was closed, no light underneath. Fawn's door was open, and she could hear her little sister sigh in her sleep. Roscoe came out of Fawn's room and trotted over to Ruthie, purring, his big fluffy tail waving in the air like a please-love-me flag.

Ruthie smiled down at the ash-gray cat, whispered, "Come on, old man," and slipped into her room, the cat right behind her. The bed was unmade, her desk a messy pile of textbooks and papers from the semester that had just ended: English Composition, Intro to Sociology, Calculus I, Microcomputer Applications I. Though they hadn't posted grades yet, she knew she'd aced all the classes, even if they had been as boring as shit.

"It's so easy a trained rat could get a 4.0 GPA. It's a subpar education," she'd complained to her mother. "Is that what you want for me?"

"It's just for one year," her mother had said, a now familiar mantra.

Right.

Ruthie closed the door, pulled off her jeans and damp socks, and crawled into bed. Roscoe settled in beside her, kneading the blankets, circling once, twice, three times, before lying down and closing his eyes.

She dreamed of Fitzgerald's again. A small bakery with steamy windows that smelled of fresh-baked bread and coffee. There was a long counter with a glass front that she stood in front of for what felt like hours, staring at rows of cupcakes, apple turnovers, cookies dusted with colored sugar that sparkled like jewels.

"What do you choose, Dove?" asked her mother. She held Ruthie's small hand firmly in her own. Her mother wore smooth calfskin gloves. Ruthie pointed her other hand, chubby little-girl fingers smearing the glass.

A cupcake with pink sculpted icing.

Then Ruthie looked up to see her mother smiling down—only this was where the dream always went funny, because the woman standing over her wasn't her mother at all. She was a tall, thin woman with heavy tortoiseshell glasses shaped like cat's eyes.

"Good choice, Dove," the woman said, ruffling her hair.

Then the dream changed, as it often did, and she was in a tiny dark room with a flickering light. There was someone else there with her—a little girl with blond hair and a dirty face. The room seemed to get smaller and smaller and there wasn't enough air; Ruthie was gasping for breath, sobbing.

Ruthie opened her eyes. Roscoe was smothering her, his warm, heavy body draped over her nose and mouth.

"Get off me, you big lug," Ruthie mumbled peevishly, shoving at him.

But it wasn't the cat. It was her sister's arm, clad in fleecy pajamas. Ruthie's head pounded, and her mouth tasted like cat shit. She was in no mood for a visitor this early.

"What are you doing in here?" Ruthie snapped. Her twin bed was crowded enough without her little sister, who did acrobatics in her sleep, often waking up with her head down at the foot of her bed. Fawn sometimes crawled in with her mother in the night, but hadn't gotten into Ruthie's bed in ages.

Fawn didn't answer. Ruthie rolled over to find that the mattress was warm and damp.

"Oh my God!" she yelped. "Did you pee in my bed?" She reached down. The mattress was soaked. So were her little sister's fleece pajamas. Fawn kept her eyes closed tight, pretending to be asleep. Ruthie shoved at her, trying to roll her out of the bed.

"Go wake up Mom," she said.

Fawn rolled over onto her belly, her face buried in the pillow. "Aacaaat," she mumbled.

"What?" Ruthie asked, rolling her sister over to face her.

"I said, *I can't.*" Fawn's face was flushed and sweaty. The urine smell hit Ruthie hard, making her stomach flip.

"Why not?"

"She's not here. She's gone."

Ruthie glanced over Fawn to the alarm clock. It was six-thirty in the morning. Her mother was rarely up before seven, much less out of the house. She needed a good three cups of coffee before she'd even speak most mornings.

"What do you mean, *gone?*"

Fawn was quiet for a minute, then looked up at Ruthie with huge, saucer eyes. "Sometimes it just happens," she said.

"You've gotta be kidding," Ruthie said, rolling out of the damp bed. Her bare feet hit the floor, which was freezing cold. The fire had gone out. She threw a sweater over her shoulders, pulled on some sweatpants.

Ruthie marched down the hall to her mother's room. She felt queasy, and when she burped, she still tasted schnapps. She half wondered if she was still a little drunk and stoned, which contributed to the this-can't-really-be-happening sort of feeling that was washing over her. She put her hand on the knob and opened it slowly, not wanting the squeak of hinges to wake her mother. But when the door swung open, she saw only the bed, neatly made.

"I told you," Fawn whispered. She'd come up behind Ruthie in the hall.

"Go get cleaned up and changed," Ruthie said, her eyes locked on her mother's empty bed. She stood a minute, swaying slightly, while her sister crept off down the hall.

"What the hell?" she said. It was six-thirty in the morning. Where was Mom?

She went down the steep, narrow wooden stairs, counting them, like she'd done when she was little, for luck. There were thirteen, but she never counted the bottom one, jumping over it like it didn't exist, so that she'd have a nice even twelve.

"Mom?" she called. The full cup of tea was still on the table. Ruthie went into the living room to discover that the logs she'd put on the stove last night had never caught. It was a big soapstone stove set up against the brick hearth of the old, original farmhouse fireplace. The stove was their only source of heat—her parents refused to buy fossil fuels.

She bent over, head pounding, and hauled the unburnt logs out of the stove so she could scoop the ashes into the can next to it. Then she started a fire from scratch: wadded-up newspaper, cardboard, kindling.

Fawn padded down the steps, dressed in red corduroy overalls and a red turtleneck, her mother's hand-knit thick wool socks on her feet. Red, of course.

"You're looking very monochromatic," Ruthie said, closing the glass door of the woodstove, the fire inside already crackling and popping.

"Huh?" Fawn said. Her eyes looked funny—all glassy and far away, like they looked when she was sick.

"Forget it," Ruthie said, staring at her odd little sister.

Fawn had been born at home and delivered by a midwife, just like Ruthie.

Ruthie had been homeschooled until third grade, when her parents finally gave in and agreed to send her to West Hall Union School after she wore them down with her pleading. As much as she wanted to be there, the transition was difficult and painful— she was behind academically, and the kids teased her for the garish hand-knit clothing she wore, for not knowing any multiplication. Ruthie had worked hard to catch up and blend in, and soon excelled at school, getting top marks in the class year after year.

When Fawn turned five, Ruthie insisted on having her enrolled in kindergarten.

"There's no way Fawn's going to be a complete social misfit, Mom. She's going to school. It's the normal thing to do."

Her mom had looked at her for a long time, then asked, "And what's so great about normal?"

In the end, Mom had given in and enrolled Fawn in school. Ruthie watched Fawn worriedly last year, peeking out through the senior-class windows to the kindergarten playground, where Fawn always sat alone, drawing in the dirt, talking animatedly to herself. She didn't seem to have any friends. When Ruthie gently brought this up with Fawn, her little sister said other kids asked her to play all the time.

"So why don't you ever join them?" Ruthie had asked.

"Because I'm busy."

"Doing what?"

"Playing with the friends I already have," Fawn had said, running off before Ruthie could ask what friends she meant—ants? pebbles?

Fawn stuck her hands deep into the pockets of her red overalls, and stared vacantly into the fire.

"So when's the last time you saw Mom?" Ruthie asked, collapsing onto the couch and rubbing at her temples in a pathetic attempt to stop the pounding headache.

"We ate supper together. Lentil soup. Then Mom came up and tucked me in. She read me a story." Fawn sounded like a robot running low on batteries. "'Little Red Riding Hood.'"

Ruthie nodded. Maybe that explained Fawn's choice of clothing. She took stories very seriously. She got on these kicks where only one story would do, and you'd have to read it to her over and over until she had every word memorized. And then, when she wasn't being read to, it was like a part of her stayed stuck inside the story. She'd leave trails of breadcrumbs around the house; build little houses out of mud, sticks, and bricks; and she would constantly be whispering to herself and her old rag doll, Mimi, about which way the wolf had gone, or if the frog really could be a handsome prince.

"What are we going to do?" Fawn's voice was faint.

"I'll go check outside. See if the truck's there. Then I'll check the barn."

"Mimi says we won't find her."

Ruthie took in a deep breath, then let the air come hissing out. "I don't really care what your doll thinks right now, okay, Fawn?"

Fawn's head slumped down, and Ruthie realized now wasn't the time to be a complete shit, killer hangover and missing mother or not. Fawn was only six. She deserved better.

"Hey," Ruthie said, crouching down and lifting Fawn's chin. "I'm sorry, kiddo. I'm just really tired and a wee bit overwhelmed. Why don't you go upstairs and get Mimi. Bring her down, and when I come back inside I'll make us a big breakfast. Bacon and eggs and hot chocolate. How does that sound?"

Fawn didn't answer. She looked small and pale. Her skin felt feverish.

"Hey, Little Deer," Ruthie said, using Mom's pet name for Fawn. "It's going to be okay. We'll find her. I promise."

Fawn nodded and backed away, heading up the stairs.

Then, absurdly, Ruthie thought of Willa Luce. Of how search teams had scoured the entire town—the whole state of Vermont, even—and not found a single trace.

How was it possible to disappear so completely, to be here one minute, gone the next?

Sometimes it just happens, Fawn had said.

Ruthie shook her head. She didn't buy it. People didn't just disappear without a trace. Not Willa Luce, and most certainly not boring old Alice Washburne, who had two girls at home, chickens to feed, and only ventured to town two days each week: to sell eggs and knitting at the farmers' market on Saturday mornings, and to go grocery shopping each Wednesday, when the Shop and Save had double-coupon day.

This was all, obviously, a big mistake. Their mother would turn up at any moment, and they'd all have a good belly laugh about the idea that she, of all people, would go missing.

Ruthie

Ruthie spent nearly an hour searching the house, yard, and barn, but found no sign of her mother. Though her boots and coat were missing, the truck was still in the barn, keys tucked in the visor. There were no footsteps in the snow (of course, it was entirely possible that there had been and they were now buried).

Ruthie stood in the barn, gazing helplessly around at the broken-down lawn tractor, stack of summer tires, screen doors and windows, sacks of chicken feed. Nothing was out of place. Everything seemed normal.

She closed her eyes, pictured her mother looking at her over the tops of her drugstore reading glasses, her gray hair pulled back in a braid, one of her chunky hand-knit sweaters on. "Part of the trick to finding a lost thing," her mother once told her, "is discovering all the places it's not."

Ruthie smiled. "Okay, then. Let's find out where you're not."

Ruthie walked around to the back of the barn to check on the chickens. They were in a big wooden coop with an enclosed run of wire mesh. She unhitched the gate, walked through, and unlatched the coop.

"Hey, girls," she whispered, voice low and soothing. "How was your night, huh?" The chickens gave anxious little coos and clucks. Ruthie tossed them cracked corn from the bucket outside, made sure their food and heated water dispensers were full.

"You didn't happen to see where Mom went, did you?"

More clucking.

"Didn't think so," she said, backing out of the coop.

She left the barn and looked out across the yard, into the woods. It had snowed more in the night, covering the yard in a flat moonscape of white.

Ruthie mentally ticked off all the places her mother was not: the house, the yard, the barn, the chicken coop. And she didn't take the truck.

"Mom!" she called as loud as she could. Ridiculous, really. The snowy landscape seemed to absorb all sound; it felt as if she were yelling into cotton batting.

Ruthie looked across the yard to where the woods began. The idea of her mother traipsing off into the woods in the dark of a winter's night was absurd—as far as Ruthie knew, her mother *never* set foot in the woods. She had her set routes for chores—paths led to and from the woodpile, the barn, the chicken coop, the compost pile near the vegetable garden—from which she never deviated. Her mother believed in efficiency. Going off the path, exploring, aimless walks—these were wastes of time and energy that could be better spent on keeping warm, producing food.

But still, she might as well rule out all possibilities, however unlikely. She headed back into the barn, grabbed a pair of snowshoes, and strapped them on.

Slowly, reluctantly, she crossed the yard and headed for the woods. Like it or not, she was going to have to do it: pass by the place where she'd found her dad.

Once, the whole area north and east of the house and barn had been open farmland, but now it was grown over with poplars, maples, and a stand of white pine. Over the years, the woods had been encroaching on the house and yard, moving closer bit by bit, threatening to overtake their little white farmhouse. The trees were too close together, it was harder to navigate here, the path a tangle of roots and saplings and large rocks poking through the snow to catch her snowshoes. Their land was covered in rocks; it never ceased to amaze Ruthie, the way they would surface each spring in their yard and garden, countless wheelbarrowfuls that they dumped out in the woods, or piled up on the stone wall that ran along the eastern edge of the yard.

Ruthie had always hated being in the woods and had rarely come out this way, even as a young child. Back then she had been sure that the hillside was full of witches and monsters—an evil enchanted forest straight out of a fairy tale.

It didn't help that her own parents encouraged her fears, telling her stories of wolves and bears, of bad things that could happen to little girls who got lost in the woods.

"Could I get eaten up?" Ruthie had asked.

"Oh yes," her mother had said. "There are things in the woods with terrible teeth. And do you know what they're hungriest for?" she asked with a smile, taking Ruthie's hand in hers. "Little girls," she said, gently gobbling at Ruthie's fingers.

This made Ruthie cry, and her mother pulled her tight.

"Stay in the yard and you'll be okay," her mother promised, wiping Ruthie's tears away.

And hadn't she gotten lost in the woods once, back when she was very little? She struggled to remember the details. She remembered being someplace dark and cold, seeing something so terrible that she had to look away. Hadn't she lost something, too, or had something taken? The only thing she was certain of was that her father had found her, carried her home. She remembered being in his arms, her chin resting on the scratchy wool of his coat, as she looked back up at the hill and towering rocks they were moving rapidly away from.

"It was just a bad dream," her father had said once they were back home, smoothing her hair. Her mother made her a cup of herbal tea that had a floral aroma but a strange medicinal undertaste. They were in her father's office; it smelled of old books, leather, and damp wool. "It was just a bad dream," her father repeated. "You're safe now."

Snowshoes gliding over the top of the snow, Ruthie crossed the overgrown field behind the barn and found the seldom-used path that led up the hill to the Devil's Hand. She took a deep breath, stepped into the trees, and began following the narrow path. She was surprised by how easy the path had been to find—for some reason, the way had been kept clear. The brush and branches were recently trimmed. By whom, though? Surely not Ruthie's mother.

She carefully scanned the woods on either side of the path for her mother's orange parka, footprints, any clue at all. There was nothing.

Ruthie moved on, step by step. The path grew steeper. A squirrel chattered a warning from a nearby maple tree. Off in the distance, she heard the drumming of a woodpecker.

It felt crazy, coming out here so early in the morning, hungover, going on less than five hours of sleep. She wanted to turn back, and let herself imagine doing just that: she would go home and find her mother there, safe in their warm kitchen, waiting for Ruthie with a cup of coffee and cinnamon rolls in the oven.

But her mother was not waiting for her at home. She thought of Fawn, imagined her asking, "Did you find her?" and Ruthie knew she had to keep looking. She couldn't return to Fawn until she'd looked everywhere, even up by the Devil's Hand.

Ruthie followed the steep path for ten minutes, then came to the abandoned orchard, row after row of apple and pear trees bent and broken, branches tangled together, leaning like old people wearing shawls of snow. The neglected orchard had brambles and skinny poplar trees growing up between the rows where once there had been neat paths. Ruthie's father had tried, for a time, to revive the orchard—carefully pruning each tree, spraying for bugs and blight, cutting back all the scrawny wild saplings—but the only fruit they ever got was malformed and too bitter to eat. It fell to the ground and lay rotting there, food for the deer or occasional bear who wandered through.

Ruthie stopped to catch her breath and had the sudden sense that she wasn't alone.

"Mom?" she called, her voice high and strained.

She scanned the trees, looking for any sign of movement.

Snow thudded off the branches of one of the apples trees, making Ruthie jump. Had something else moved, something deep in the shadows? She held her breath, waiting. The stillness made her ears ring. Where had the birds and squirrels gone?

There were no tracks of any sort—not even a snowshoe hare, chickadee, or field mouse. It was as if she was all alone in the world.

Ruthie didn't often let herself think about what had happened to her father.

A little over two years ago, he had been out cutting firewood and didn't come back for supper. Ruthie went out to look for him just as it was getting dark.

"Silly old man can't keep track of the time anymore," her mother had said. "Doesn't have the sense to pay attention to his own stomach rumbling, either, evidently."

It had been a damp fall, and the ground was slick with mud and rotting leaves. She slipped several times on her way up the path, slamming her knees down on the rocks, getting scratched by thorns.

She'd found him just north of the orchard. There was a neat pile of cut wood ten feet away with a saw beside it. He was lying on his side, his ax clasped firmly in his hands. His eyes were open but strangely glassy. His lips were blue.

Ruthie had taken first aid at school, and so she dropped to her knees and began CPR while screaming herself hoarse, hoping her voice would carry all the way down to the house. She pushed and pushed for what felt like hours but may only have been minutes, elbows locked, counting fast under her breath—*one-AND-two-AND-three-AND-four*—like she'd done on the plastic dummy in class. At last, her mother came, then rushed off again to call for an ambulance. Ruthie continued the chest compressions until the West Hall Volunteer Fire Department ambulance crew arrived. Her arms and shoulders were shaking, muscles spent, but still she kept going, until her mother gently pulled her away.

It was when she was on her way back out of the clearing that she noticed it: her father's boot prints in the mud, impressions of the last steps he would ever take. But there, beside them, was another set of tracks, much smaller.

She asked Fawn about it later. "Did you go up in the woods to see Daddy today?"

Fawn shook her head hard, hugged her doll against her chest.

"Mimi and me don't go in the woods. Not ever. We don't want to get eaten."

Ruthie got a chill now, thinking of her little sister's words, her mother's long-ago warnings.

"Mama?" Ruthie's voice came out squeaky and little-girl-ish. She hurried through the orchard, doing an awkward shuffle-run in the snowshoes now. The apple and pear trees ended, and Ruthie continued uphill, into the dark forest. The beech, poplar, and maple trees looked more skeletal than ever, bare and coated with fresh snow. She was sure she could feel eyes looking back at her as she climbed up, the trail growing steeper.

Her parents had always warned her about hiking up here alone: too many places to break an ankle. Once, her father had found an old well, way out in the woods, past the Devil's Hand—a hidden circle of stones that went down so deep he claimed he couldn't see the bottom. "I dropped in a stone, and I swear I never heard it hit."

Some said there was a cave where an old witch lived. That was supposed to be where the boy in 1952 had gone in and never come out. When his friends came back later with help, they couldn't even find the entrance again—just a blank face of rock where the opening had been. When Willa Luce went missing last month, a search party had combed through these woods but found nothing.

Everyone in town had a story about the Devil's Hand, and though the stories differed in detail, one fact remained the same: it was an evil place, and bad luck to go there. Kids went on dares, sometimes even spent the night, bringing along a few six-packs for liquid courage. Buzz and his friends went up to smoke pot and watch for UFOs.

Ruthie's skin prickled. She couldn't shake the feeling she wasn't alone out here.

"Hello?"

Stupid, she knew, but she moved faster anyway, trying to get the search over with. She'd go up to the rocks, then circle back.

She was out of breath by the time she reached the Devil's Hand, partly from the effort of the climb, but mostly because she was moving so damn fast—she wanted to get this done.

The huge dark rocks jutted up from the ground as if they'd grown there, sprung up like jagged mutant mushrooms. There were five stones—the five fingers—jutting up from the earth, leaning back as if the hand were open, waiting to catch something (or someone, she thought). The stones that formed the palm were low and covered with snow, but the taller ones stuck out, looking to Ruthie not like fingers but more like dark, pointed teeth.

My, what big teeth you have.

All the better to eat you with, my dear.

Standing in the shadow of the tallest stone—the central finger, which rose nearly twenty feet into the air—she yelled for her mother one more time. "Mom!"

She waited, listening to the sound of her own breath until it seemed so loud it was as if the forest were breathing with her.

Ruthie tightened the straps on her snowshoes and hurried back down to the house, slipping and sliding, falling several times; she moved as quickly as she could, trying to ignore the sense that she was being chased.

Did she take the truck?" Fawn asked.

Ruthie shook her head. She'd stopped back at the coop after putting the snowshoes away and grabbed some eggs from the nesting boxes. She carefully took them from her pockets and set them on the counter. She was cold, exhausted. Her legs and lungs burned from her snowshoe adventure up the hill.

"Where's Mom?" Fawn asked, chin quivering, eyes damp and bulging like a frog's.

"I don't know," Ruthie admitted.

"Shouldn't we call someone?" Fawn asked.

"What, like the police? I'm pretty sure you can't even report a missing person until they've been gone for twenty-four hours. She hasn't even been gone for twelve hours. And Mom would freak, Fawn. You know that."

"But . . . it's so cold out there. What if she's hurt?"

"I looked everywhere she could possibly go. There's just no way Mom's out there. I promise."

"So what do we do?" Fawn asked.

"We wait. That's what she'd want us to do. If she's not back by tonight, maybe we call the cops then, I'm not sure." She ruffled her little sister's hair and gave her best it's-going-to-be-okay smile. "We'll be fine."

Fawn bit her lip, looked like she was about to start crying. "She wouldn't leave us."

Ruthie put her arm around her little sister, pulled her into a hug. "I know. We'll figure it out. After breakfast, we'll look for clues. People don't disappear without a trace. It'll be like playing Nancy Drew."

"Who?"

"Forget it. Just trust me, okay? We'll be fine. We'll find her. I promise."

Katherine

Sometimes, when Katherine woke in the night, she could almost feel them both there beside her. She imagined the other side of the bed was warm, and if she squinted her eyes just right, the pillow seemed to bear a soft indent where their two heads had lain. She'd roll over in the morning and press the pillow to her face, trying to catch a scent of them.

It wasn't just shampoo, shaving lotion, and motorcycle grease. It was all of that blended together with something intoxicatingly spicy underneath—the essence of Gary. And Austin, he'd smelled like warm milk and honey, a sweet ambrosia that she could drink up and live on forever. In the soft hours of early morning, before the sun came up, she believed it just might be possible to distill everything a person was down to a scent.

Once she was awake, like now, sitting in the kitchen with a cup of French roast in her hand and still wearing one of Gary's old T-shirts, she realized how silly the thought was, knew that their being in bed with her was only a dream, a body memory perhaps. Like a person feeling pain in a phantom limb.

How many mornings had they spent like that, Austin tucked between them in fleecy pajamas telling them grand stories about his dreams: " . . . *and then there was a man who had a magic hat and he could pull anything you asked for out of it—marshmallows, swimming pools, even Sparky, Mama!*" She'd ruffled his hair, thought it sweet that he could bring their dead dog back in his dreams.

The acidic coffee hit her empty belly with a snarl and a toothy bite. She tapped her ring against the mug. Gary had given it to her two weeks before he died. She turned it around her finger, noticing the indentation it was leaving, as if it were slowly working its way into her skin, becoming a part of her.

She should eat something. She'd skipped a proper dinner last night, settling in at her worktable with a jar of olives and a glass of Shiraz. Since Gary's death, she'd pretty much been living on canned soup and crackers. The idea of actually going to the trouble of cooking a proper meal for just herself seemed silly, not worth the effort. If she craved something more elaborate, she could go out. Besides, she'd discovered some pretty fancy canned soups: lobster bisque, butternut squash, roasted red pepper and tomato.

But she hadn't been shopping yet, and the soup-and-cracker cupboard was empty; she'd have to go to the market today. She'd unpacked a few dry goods yesterday—oatmeal, baking soda, flour— but the pots and pans were in boxes. She'd been in the apartment for two days now, and other than setting up her artwork area in the living room and making the bed, she had done little to settle in.

The truth was, she liked the sparse look of bare countertops and shelves; the empty white walls felt like a clean slate. She was even hesitant to hang her clothes in the closet, preferring the vagabond feel of living out of suitcases. What did one really need to live? The thought excited her a little—an experiment in pared-down living.

Katherine looked around at the piles of cardboard boxes, neatly marked KITCHEN with contents written below: mixing bowls, steak knives, ice-cream maker, bread machine. But who on earth really needed an ice-cream maker or a bread machine? These, she decided, along with a great many other things in the boxes, would need to go.

Out in the living room were more boxes: CDs, movies, books, photo albums. The things that made up a life. But now, in their boxes, they seemed strangely unreal. A remnant from another woman's life. The Katherine who had been married to Gary and once had a son; who had wedding china and photo albums and an electric knife sharpener. Now all these objects felt like toys, like she was a child in a playhouse trying to imagine what it was that grown-ups did.

· · ·

Austin had died two years and four months ago—leukemia. He was six years old. And it had only been a little over two months since Gary's death. Sometimes it felt like two days, sometimes twenty years. Her decision to move from Boston to West Hall, Vermont (population 3,163), had seemed absurd—concerning, even—to her family and friends. She claimed she needed a fresh start. After all, she'd just been awarded a Peckham grant: thirty thousand dollars to cover living expenses and art supplies, enabling her to work on her art full-time, to finish the assemblage-box series she'd been working on for the past year. For the first time in her life, she'd be an artist and only an artist—not a wife or a mother or the manager of a gallery. She gave notice on their Boston loft, resigned from her job at the gallery, and moved to a small apartment on the third floor of an old Victorian house on West Hall's Main Street.

She didn't tell anyone the truth.

Almost a month after Gary's accident, she'd received his final American Express bill. The last charge on it, dated October 30, the day he died, was a $31.39 meal at Lou Lou's Café in West Hall, Vermont. For some reason, he'd driven the three hours to Vermont, had a meal, then turned around and headed back to Boston. He'd taken the scenic route back, heading south on Route 5, which snaked its way down beside the interstate, I-91. It was snowing, an early-season squall, and Gary came around a bend too quickly, lost control of the car, and slammed into a ledge of rock. The state troopers told her he'd been killed instantly.

When she took the trip up to the garage in White River Junction to claim any belongings inside Gary's car, she took one look at the deployed airbags, the smashed windshield, and the whole front end crushed like an accordion, and actually fainted. In the end, there wasn't much to claim anyway—some papers from the glove box, an extra pair of sunglasses, Gary's favorite travel mug. The thing that she was really hoping to find—the black backpack he used as his camera bag—was not in the car. She tried to track it down, pestering mechanics at the garage, the insurance adjuster, the state police, and the staff in the emergency room—but everyone denied having seen it.

Gary had left home at ten that morning with his backpack, say-ing he had a wedding to shoot in Cambridge and he'd be home in time for dinner.

Why had he lied?

The question plagued her, ate away at her. She searched through his desk, files, papers, and computer and found nothing out of the ordinary. She called his friends, asked if they knew of any buddies Gary had in Vermont—any reason he might go up there.

No, they all said, they couldn't think of anyone. They told her he'd probably heard about a great antique shop, or just wanted a drive. "You know Gary," his best friend, Ray, had said, choking up a bit, "a spur-of-the-moment guy. Always up for an adventure."

As soon as she opened the bill with the charge from the café in West Hall, Katherine got in the car and started driving north. She found West Hall, Vermont, about fifty miles north of where Gary had had his accident.

It was the quintessential New England small town: a downtown with three church steeples, a granite library, a town green with a gazebo in the middle. Beyond the town green, she passed by the West Hall Union School, where small children in winter coats and hats were out on the playground tossing balls and climbing on an elaborate, brightly colored play structure. She thought of Austin— how much he loved to climb and showed no fear, going up to the top of any structure and hollering, "I'm King of the Mountain!" For half a second, she almost believed she could see him there, the wiry boy with the curly hair perched on top. Then she blinked, and it was someone else's child.

She followed the road, which took her past the Cranberry Meadow Cemetery—full of old, leaning stones and enclosed with a rusted wrought-iron fence. She looped back around toward the downtown area and found Lou Lou's Café on Main Street, tucked between a bookstore and a bank, all of them sharing the same big brick building. She went in, ordered a coffee, and looked out the large plate-glass window at the street, thinking, *This was what Gary looked at while he ate his last meal.*

She had a clear view of the town green. It was a bright, cloudless

November day. The trees that lined the green were bare now, but back when Gary was here, they might have been glowing red and orange, leaves falling as storm clouds gathered.

"But what were you doing here?" she asked out loud.

Glancing at the prices on the menu, she decided he must have met someone. The entrées were no higher than twelve dollars—even if he'd ordered a beer, he couldn't have eaten a thirty-one-dollar meal here by himself.

"Excuse me," Katherine called as the waitress passed by. "I'm wondering if you can help." She pulled out the little photo of Gary she kept in her wallet. "I wonder if you might recognize him. He was in here last month."

The waitress, a young woman with dyed-blue bangs and a yin-yang tattoo on the back of her hand, shook her head. "You should ask Lou Lou," she said, nodding in the direction of the woman behind the counter. "She remembers customers real well."

Katherine thanked her, got up, and approached the owner—Lou Lou herself, who was dripping with silver-and-turquoise jewelry and had short bright-red hair.

Lou Lou recognized Gary immediately. "Yeah, he was here, can't say when, but not all that long ago."

"Did he meet someone?"

Lou Lou gave her a quizzical look, and Katherine thought of breaking down, explaining everything: *He was my husband, he was killed in an accident only hours after he sat in here eating a sandwich and soup or whatever, I've never even heard of this place, why was he here, please, I need to know.*

Instead, she stood up straight, said only, "Please. It's important."

Lou Lou nodded. "He was with a woman. I don't know her name, but she's local. I've seen her around, but can't place where."

"What did she look like?"

Was she pretty? Prettier than me?

Lou Lou thought a minute. "Older. Long salt-and-pepper hair in a braid. Like I said, I've seen her around. I know her from some-where. I don't forget faces."

Katherine spent nearly two hours in Lou Lou's, having coffee, then soup and a sandwich, then a slice of red-velvet cake. All the while, she wondered what Gary had eaten, which table he'd sat at. She felt close to him, like he was right there beside her, sharing a secret in between bites of cake.

Who was she, Gary? Who was the woman with the braid?

She watched the people coming and going along the sidewalk: people in fleece jackets and wool sweaters, a couple of men in red plaid hunting jackets, two kids with hoodies on skateboards. She didn't see one person in a suit, or even a tie or high heels. So different from Boston. People actually smiled and said hello to each other on the street. Gary must have loved it.

They used to talk about leaving the city, moving to a small town like this, how it would be so much better for Austin. Gary had grown up in a small town in Idaho and said it was kid heaven—there was room to breathe, to explore, you knew your neighbors, and your parents didn't mind if you were out late because bad things never happened there. You were safe.

Katherine stopped at a bulletin board in the hall on the way out of Lou Lou's Café. She glanced at the notices on it: Trek mountain bike for sale, Bikram yoga classes, a flyer announcing that the farmers' market would be in the high-school gymnasium during the winter months, a poster looking for fellow believers to join a UFO-hunting group. And there, right in the middle, a no-nonsense sign: *Apartment for rent. Downtown in renovated Victorian. One bedroom. No pets. $700 includes heat.* There were little tabs at the bottom with the phone number to call.

Then she felt it again: Gary standing beside her, putting his arm around her, whispering, *Go ahead and take one.* Without thinking, she tore off one of the phone numbers and tucked it in the pocket of her jeans.

Good girl, Gary whispered, a gentle hiss in her right ear.

Isn't it about time to get to work? Gary asked her now, voice teasing, soothingly familiar, as she sat at the kitchen table in her new apartment. Katherine stood up, went over to the counter to refill her coffee cup, then made her way into the living room, between its stacks of boxes, and over to the art table. It was an old farmhouse kitchen table that she'd had since graduating from college, three feet wide and five feet long, made from thick pine planks. It was scarred with saw, knife, and drill marks, splattered with years' worth of paint drops and smudges. There was a vise set up on the right side, which was also where she kept her tools: hammer, saws, Dremel, soldering iron, tin snips, drill and bits, along with a plastic toolbox full of various nails, screws, and hinges. In the middle, at the back, was a coffee can full of paintbrushes, X-Acto knives, pens, and markers. In a carefully labeled wooden cabinet to the left of the table were all her paints and finishes.

There, in the center of the table, was the latest box, the one she'd stayed up late into the night working on. A four-by-six-inch wooden box, it was titled *The Wedding Vows*. On the front were two double doors, styled like church windows with stained-glass designs. When you opened these, there was the wooden altar with a tiny photo of Katherine and Gary on their wedding day, both looking impossibly young and happy, not noticing the shadowy crow that peeked out at them from behind the curtain. *Until Death Do Us Part* was written in neat calligraphy, a promise held in the air like a sweet cloud above their heads. But down in the shadows below their feet were miniature skid marks on a narrow winding road, and over at stage left, half of a ruined matchbox car poked its way through the side of the box, its front end smashed. At the very bottom, two simple lines in quotation marks: "I've got a wedding to shoot in Cambridge. I should be home in time for dinner."

This morning, she'd put the finishing touches on this box—a bit of silver trim around the windows, gold paint for the cross on top— then coat the whole thing with matte varnish. After that, she'd start work on the next in the series: *His Final Meal*. She didn't have the details for this one worked out at all, only that the door would open onto a scene in Lou Lou's Café: Gary and the mystery woman. She was counting on Gary to help out, to lead her along and show her what details to add. Gary as Muse.

Sometimes, only sometimes, when she was good and lost in her art, if she closed her eyes, Gary was right beside her again, whispering his secrets in her ear. She could almost see him: his dark-brown hair with the funny cowlicks, the freckles across his nose and cheeks that multiplied when he was out in the sun too long.

Gary, who loved a good ghost story. Gary, who once teased her by saying, "You better hope you're the one to die first, babe, 'cause if I do I'm gonna come back here and haunt your ass."

She smiled now, thinking of it. She picked up the blue pack of American Spirits—the last of the carton she'd found in Gary's studio. She hadn't smoked since college, and was always hounding Gary to quit, always complaining of the smell on his clothes and hair. Now she found the smell of cigarette smoke comforting, and allowed herself one cigarette a day. Sometimes two. She shook one out of the pack and lit up, knowing it was a little early, not caring.

"What were you doing here, Gary?" she asked out loud, watching the smoke drift up; she secretly hoped that if she started building the next box, adding in details, the answers might come. "Who's the woman with the braid? And where can I find her?"

Ruthie

"Eighteen, nineteen, twenty," Ruthie shouted out, hands covering her face. She opened her eyes, stood up from the couch, and hollered, "Ready or not, here I come!"

Hide-and-seek was Fawn's favorite game, and they'd been playing for nearly an hour now, starting just after they'd washed and put away the breakfast dishes. Ruthie thought it might help take Fawn's mind off Mom's being gone. She also decided that it was an efficient, even fun, way for them to search the house for clues. There were always two rules when they played hide-and-seek. The first was that Mom's room, the basement, and outside were off limits. The second rule was that Fawn always hid. Ruthie was claustrophobic and couldn't stand fitting herself into tight, dark places. Fawn loved hiding, and she was really good at it; a few times, Ruthie even had to shout that she gave up, so Fawn would come popping out of some unlikely place—the laundry hamper, the cabinet under the kitchen sink.

"Where can she be?" Ruthie asked loudly as she searched the living room. She peered behind the couch, then went into the front hall and looked in the closet. From there, she moved on to the kitchen, where she carefully checked each cupboard. Nothing. Surely Fawn couldn't fit herself into one of the drawers? Ruthie checked anyway. "Have you turned into a little mouse and crawled somewhere I'll never find you?" Ruthie called.

This was also part of the game, the constant silly banter that sometimes made Fawn giggle and give herself away.

For twenty minutes, Ruthie searched the house, looking in all of Fawn's favorite places, but found no sign of her sister.

"Are you under Daddy's desk? Nope. Have you turned into a speck of dust and blown away?"

Fawn wasn't in any of the closets, under any bed or table, or lying in the bathtub with the shower curtain drawn around her. Ruthie even checked under the old claw-foot tub, remembering that once she'd found her sister crammed in there on her belly.

Usually when she couldn't find her sister, Ruthie just got annoyed. Today she felt panic rising, growing stronger as she checked each empty hiding place.

What if Fawn really was gone? What if whatever happened to their mom had happened to her?

Stop it, she told herself. *It's only a game.*

"Fawn?" Ruthie called out. "I give up! Game's over! Come out!"

But Fawn did not appear. Ruthie went from room to room, calling out, listening intently for a giggle or a rustle, as a cold sweat gathered between her shoulder blades. She ended up back in the living room, right where she'd started, on her knees, looking behind the couch.

"Boo!"

Ruthie screamed. Fawn was right behind her.

"Where *were* you?" Ruthie asked, relief flooding through her.

"Hiding with Mimi." The doll dangled limply from Fawn's hand.

"Where?"

Fawn shrugged. "It's a secret. Are we done playing now?"

"I've got a new game," Ruthie said. "Come on." She led her sister up the stairs to Mom's room.

"What are we doing in here?" Fawn asked. Mom was big into "respecting each other's private spaces," which meant: don't enter without knocking, and no snooping when no one was there. Ruthie couldn't remember the last time she'd even set foot in her mother's bedroom—back when her father was alive, maybe.

It was the largest bedroom in the house, but seemed larger still because of its sparseness: white walls with ancient cracks in the plaster; only a bed, a dresser, and one bedside table; no art on the walls; no clutter. Not even a stray sock on the old pine floors, just a couple of hand-loomed wool throw rugs on either side of the bed.

Her mother had the best view in the house, too, the window beside the bed looking north out across the yard and to the wooded hillside. In the fall and winter, when the leaves were off the trees, you could see all the way out to the Devil's Hand, at the top of the hill. Ruthie stared out that way now, catching only a glimpse of rock peeking through the blanket of thick snow. Then, for a split second, she caught a glimpse of movement—a shadow sliding out from behind the rocks, and back. There, then gone. A trick of the light, she told herself, turning away.

"We're playing a new game," Ruthie told her little sister. Fawn's eyes widened.

"What kind of game?"

"A searching game."

"Like hide-and-seek?"

"A little. Only we're not looking for each other, we're looking for clues."

"Oooh, clues!" Fawn squealed. Then she got serious. "What kind of clues?"

"We're looking for anything out of the ordinary, anything unusual. Anything that might help us figure out where Mom might be."

Fawn nodded enthusiastically. She held Mimi by the arm— something Mom had made. The yellow yarn hair was matted now, the fabric on her hands and feet worn through and patched in places. She had a carefully stitched smile that always kind of creeped Ruthie out and reminded her of a scar, or of lips sewn closed to keep the thing quiet. Mimi was always whispering to Fawn, telling her secrets. When Fawn was very young, they'd find her hiding in the closet with the doll on her lap, deep in conversation.

Ruthie smiled down at her sister. "Are you and Mimi ready to play?"

"Let me see if Mimi is," she said, holding the doll's face up to her ear and listening. Fawn listened for a minute, nodding, then put the doll down. "Mimi says yes, but she wants to know if we can play real hide-and-seek again after."

"Haven't we played hide-and-seek enough for one day?"

"Mimi doesn't think so," Fawn said.

"Okay, we'll play one more round after," Ruthie promised. "Oh, I forgot to tell you the best part about this looking-for-clues game—there are prizes. One chocolate kiss for each clue found."

"From Mom's secret stash?"

Ruthie nodded. Mom kept a bag of Hershey's Kisses hidden away in the back of the freezer, and neither girl was allowed to touch it unless offered, usually as a bribe. Mom didn't approve of the girls' eating refined sugar, so chocolate was always a big treat, especially for Fawn.

"Ready, set, go!" Ruthie called, but Fawn stayed frozen.

"I'm not sure where to look," she said.

"You're a kid! Use your imagination! If you wanted to hide something in here, where would you put it?"

Fawn looked around. "Under the bed?" Her voice came out small and shy.

"Maybe," Ruthie said. "Let's check it out." They both dropped to their knees to peer under the bed. Nothing under there but years' worth of dust bunnies.

Ruthie checked the floor under the bed for loose floorboards. When she was very young, she'd discovered a nice little hiding place under a loose board in her own room, right under the bed. Over time, both she and Fawn had found many little places like this throughout the house: a small hidden door that opened behind the cabinet they kept the plates in; a corner of the doorframe leading from the kitchen to the living room that popped out to reveal a little niche, perfect for hiding a tiny treasure. It seemed likely that there was at least one secret place in Mom's room.

"Kids must have lived here before," Ruthie had told Fawn once. "All these hidey-holes—it's not something a grown-up would do."

"Maybe we'll find something they left behind. A toy, or a note, or something!" Fawn had said, excitedly. But so far, all of the hidden niches they had discovered had been empty.

Ruthie pulled back the mattress and checked between it and the box spring. Nothing. There was a stack of paperback mysteries on top of the bedside table—her mom was a big Ruth Rendell fan. She opened the drawer and found only half a Hershey bar with almonds, a flashlight, and a pen.

There had never been a table on her father's side of the bed—he didn't read at night. He had believed beds were made for sleeping, so he had no table, no lamp. He had done his reading (mostly non-fiction: dense, depressing tomes about global warming or the evils of the pharmaceutical industry; thick, glossy books about gardening and homesteading; slim, antique field guides filled with drawings of New England flora and fauna) in a big leather chair in the office. Her father had loved to read, loved the feel and smell of books—he even used to buy and sell antiquarian books, back before Ruthie was born, before they'd moved to Vermont.

Ruthie didn't know much about her parents' lives before. They'd met in college, at Columbia. Her mother had been an art-history major; her father was studying literature. It was nearly impossible to imagine what her parents might have been like back in college; the very idea of them as young, daring, and idealistic made Ruthie's head spin. After graduation, they'd started the book business in Chicago. They came east to Vermont after reading Scott and Helen Nearing's book *The Good Life,* with the intention of becoming as self-sufficient as possible. They bought the house and land for a song (*They practically gave it away,* her parents always said), got chickens and sheep, planted a huge rambling vegetable garden among the rocks. Ruthie was a little over three when they first moved here. Fawn came along nine years later, when their mother was forty-three, their father forty-six.

"Seriously?" Ruthie had asked when her parents announced that Ruthie would soon have a new baby brother or sister. She'd known something was up—her parents had been whispering and secretive for days, but she'd never imagined this news. When she was little, she'd longed for a baby brother or sister, but now wasn't it too late?

"Aren't you happy about it?" her mother had asked.

"Sure," Ruthie said. "I'm just a little shocked."

Ruthie's mother nodded. "I know, sweetie. Honestly, we were a little surprised, too. But your father and I know this is meant to be, this baby belongs with us, here in our family. You're going to be a wonderful big sister, I know you will."

Up until this new disappearing trick, the most interesting thing about her mother had been her decision to have a second child so late in life, which sounded like it had been more accident than conscious choice.

"I don't like being in here without her," Fawn complained as she looked helplessly around her mother's room. She was on the bed, where she'd been searching through the covers and pillows. Ruthie was running her hands along the rough plaster walls, looking for secret openings but finding nothing.

The truth was, Ruthie felt the same—like she was trespassing and invading her mother's much-loved privacy.

"It's okay," Ruthie said. "I know it's a little weird, but I think Mom would understand that we're doing this because we need to. Because we want to find her."

Ruthie headed toward the closet. Fawn got up off the bed and watched, rocking a little, twisting Mimi's rag-doll arm in her hands.

Roscoe came in, tiptoeing hesitantly, turning his head from side to side, like he didn't know what to expect. This room was even off limits to the cat, because their mother claimed to be slightly allergic and didn't want to sleep on a bed covered in cat dander. Now Roscoe explored cautiously, his big fluffy gray tail up and twitching. He sauntered over to the closet door, gave it a tentative sniff. Immediately he arched his back and jumped back with a loud hiss. Then he bolted from the room.

"You old drama queen," Ruthie called after him.

Ruthie went to the closet door, turned the knob, and pulled. Nothing happened. She yanked harder, then tried pushing. It still didn't budge.

Weird. She stepped back, studied the door, and noticed now that two boards had been attached, one at the top and one at the bottom, screwed into the frame and across the door itself, preventing it from being opened. Why on earth would anyone seal up a closet door like that?

She'd have to go downstairs and get a screwdriver—a crowbar from the barn, maybe.

"I think I found something." Fawn's voice was shaky. Ruthie jumped a little, and then turned to see her sister had pushed back the wool throw rug on the right side of the bed and had pulled open a little trapdoor built into the wide pine floor. Her face was pale.

"What is it?" Ruthie asked, bounding across the room in three leaps.

Fawn didn't answer, just stared down, eyes huge and worried.

Ruthie looked down into the secret hiding place Fawn had discovered. It was about a foot and a half square, and the wooden floorboards had been cut carefully and put back together as a small door with old brass hinges. It was shallow, only about six inches deep. There, right on top, was a small handgun with a wooden handle. Below it, a shoebox. Ruthie blinked in disbelief. Her mom and dad were peace-loving, pacifist hippies; they hated guns. Her dad could bore you to death with handgun statistics—how much more likely it was that a gun would end up killing a family member than an intruder, how many violent crimes were gun-related. When they killed a chicken or a turkey, their mom made them do this elaborate ceremony, thanking the earth and the bird and urging the bird's spirit to move on to a higher plane.

"It can't be Mom's," Ruthie said out loud, sure that there was some mistake. She looked at Fawn, who stood frozen, the doll dangling from her hand, swinging like a pendulum over the open hole in the floor.

"We should cover it back up. Leave it alone," Fawn said.

Ruthie half thought her sister was right. But they had to look, didn't they? What if whatever was in the box held a clue about what might have happened to their mother?

Ruthie got down on her knees, sitting before the hole in the floor in praying position. She reached for the gun, then stopped, her hand hovering just above it.

"Please don't," Fawn said, eyes frantic. "It's dangerous."

"Not unless you pull the trigger. Besides, maybe it isn't even loaded." Ruthie picked up the gun, surprised by its heaviness. Fawn clapped her hands over her ears and squeezed her eyes shut. Ruthie held the weapon gingerly by the metal barrel, not wanting to put her hand anywhere near the trigger. Carefully, she set it down on the floor next to her, making sure it was pointed away from her and

Fawn. She reached back down into the hole and pulled out the box. *Nike,* it said on the side.

Ruthie flipped open the top of the shoebox. There was a Ziploc bag tucked inside. The bag held two wallets: a black leather billfold and a large beige one designed for a woman. Ruthie held the clear plastic bag in her hand, suddenly afraid to open it. A prickling feeling worked its way from her hands up her arms and shoulders, settling in her chest.

This was silly. They were only wallets.

Ruthie opened the bag and pulled out the smaller billfold. It held a Connecticut driver's license and credit cards belonging to a man called Thomas O'Rourke. He had brown hair, hazel eyes, was six feet tall, 170 pounds, and an organ donor. He lived at 231 Kendall Lane, Woodhaven, Connecticut. The woman's wallet belonged to Bridget O'Rourke. There was no driver's license, but she carried a Sears credit card, a MasterCard, and an appointment card for Perry's Hair Salon. Both wallets had a little cash in them. Bridget had change in a special zippered pocket that also contained a small gold bracelet with a broken clasp. Ruthie pulled out the bracelet—it was too tiny to belong to an adult. She dropped it back in.

"Who are they?" Fawn asked.

"No idea."

"But why are their wallets here?"

"I don't know, Fawn. What do I look like—a walking crystal ball?"

Fawn chewed her lip harder.

"Sorry," Ruthie said, feeling like shit. With Mom gone, she was all Fawn had right now.

She knew she hadn't exactly been the best big sister, even from the very beginning. Ruthie had been obliged to be at Fawn's birth. The midwife had handed her a drum—the beat was supposed to help keep her mom focused in labor. Ruthie thumped at it halfheartedly, feeling out of place and awkward. When Fawn came out, she was squalling and scrunch-faced—not at all precious or beautiful, despite what her parents and the midwife said. She'd reminded Ruthie of a grub.

As Fawn grew, Ruthie would occasionally play with her—dolls, dress-up, or hide-and-seek—but only because her parents made her, not out of sisterly love. Not that she didn't love Fawn—she did—but their age difference seemed to put them on entirely different planets.

"All this is just making my head spin, you know?" Ruthie explained. She looked down at Thomas O'Rourke's driver's license again. "This is old. It expired, like, fifteen years ago." She tucked it back into his worn leather billfold, put both wallets back in the bag, then carefully placed the bag right back in the shoebox.

"If Mom gets back, we have to pretend we never found any of this, okay? It has to be our secret."

Fawn looked like she was about to cry.

"Come on," Ruthie said, smiling like a cheerleader. "It's not that hard. You can keep a secret, right? I know you can. You won't even tell me where you and Mimi were hiding."

"You said *if*," Fawn said.

"Huh?"

"You said, '*If* Mom gets back.'" Her chin quivered, and a tear rolled down her left cheek.

Ruthie stood up and took her little sister in her arms, surprised to find her own eyes filling with tears. Fawn felt small and hollow. She was burning hot. Ruthie hugged her tighter, cleared her throat, and shook off the urge to cry. She needed to take Fawn's temperature, get some Tylenol into her if it was as high as it felt. Poor kid. What a shitty time to be sick. Ruthie tried to remember everything Mom did when Fawn was sick—Tylenol, endless cups of her own fever-reducing herbal tea, piling the covers on Fawn, and reading her story after story. It was the same stuff she'd done when Ruthie was little.

"I meant *when*," Ruthie whispered soothingly into Fawn's ear. "*When* she shows up. Because she will." Fawn didn't hug back, just stayed limp in Ruthie's arms.

"What if she doesn't? What if she . . . *can't* or something?"

"She will, Fawn. She *has* to."

She pulled away, looked down into Fawn's face. "You feel okay, Fawn? You have a sore throat or anything?"

But Fawn's glassy eyes were focused down on the secret hole in the floor.

"I think there's something else in there," she said.

Ruthie dropped to her knees and reached in. The edges of the compartment went farther back than she'd thought. Tucked against the far corner was the squared edge of a book. She pulled it out.

Visitors from the Other Side
The Secret Diary of Sara Harrison Shea

It was a worn hardcover with a faded paper jacket.

"Weird," Ruthie said. "Why hide a book?" She picked it up, studied the cover, and started to flip through. Her eye caught on the words in the beginning diary entry: *The first time I saw a sleeper, I was nine years old.*

Ruthie scanned the rest of the entry.

"What's it about?" Fawn asked.

"Seems like this lady thought there was a way to bring dead people back somehow," she said. Kind of creepy, but, still, why would her mother keep it hidden?

"Ruthie," Fawn said, "look at the picture on the back."

There was a blurry black-and-white photo with a caption beneath it: *Sara Harrison Shea at her home in West Hall, Vermont, 1907.*

A woman with wild hair and haunting eyes stood in front of a white clapboard farmhouse that Ruthie recognized immediately.

"No way. It's our house!" Ruthie said. "This lady lived here, in our house."

Katherine

Katherine believed that when the work was going well things just fell into place, as if by magic. It was the artist's job to open herself up, let herself be guided to whatever the next step might be.

Today was not a day when things were going well.

Work on the new box wasn't off to a great start. She was having a hard time making any kind of decisions: Should she use a photo of Gary, or make a little Gary doll to sit at the table with the gray-haired stranger? And what would she put on the table? It seemed a huge responsibility, choosing his last meal. Of all the scenes she'd re-created so far, this one relied the most on her imagination.

All morning, she'd felt Gary's presence so strongly there with her that she was sure he'd been watching over her shoulder, mocking her. She could smell him, almost taste him in the air around her.

What do you think you're doing? he asked as she stared dumbly at the empty wooden box she'd just made.

"Trying to understand why the last thing you ever said to me was a lie," she said out loud, her voice full of bitterness.

It wasn't only that final lie that bothered her—it was everything that had happened in the days leading up to it. Gary had clearly been keeping something from her.

Two weeks before the accident, they'd gone on a weekend trip to the Adirondacks. The trip had given her such hope. It was the middle of October, the leaves were at their peak of color, and the air was full of change. They'd taken the Harley and stayed in a rustic cabin in the woods. It was the first time they'd gone away since

Austin's death, and they'd actually had fun—for once, they weren't completely consumed by grief and fury.

They drank a bottle of wine by the fire, laughed at each other's jokes (Katherine said the man who ran the cabins had a nose like a turnip, and Gary went on to give produce features to everyone they knew—the best was Katherine's sister Hazel, who had a head like an artichoke, spiky hair and all). They laughed until their bellies ached, then made love on the floor. And Katherine had thought that, at last, their heads had come back up above the water, they might not drown. They would find a way to continue on, to make a new life together without Austin. Maybe, just maybe, they'd have another child one day. Gary had even brought it up that last night, face flushed from wine. "Do you think?" he asked.

"Maybe," she'd told him, smiling and crying at the same time. "Maybe."

She'd felt closer to Gary than ever. Like they'd been on this tremendous journey together, had seen each other at their absolute darkest, but here they were, coming out the other side, hand in hand.

On the way home, they'd stopped at a little antique store. Gary had bought a metal file box full of old photos and tintypes to add to his collection. There were some old letters and folded, yellowed pages tucked in among the photos, as well as a couple of envelopes. When he opened up one of the envelopes, he'd discovered the funny little ring, which he'd given to Katherine, slipping it on her finger, saying, "To new beginnings." She'd kissed him then. One of those hungry, dizzying kisses from back in their college days. And she believed, as she turned the little ring on her finger, that they would start over.

But when they got back from the trip, Katherine immediately sensed that something wasn't right. Gary was pulling away again, worse than ever this time. He was staying out late, leaving early, spending hours closed up in his studio—the workspace he'd walled off at the back of their loft. When Katherine asked him what he was working on, he shook his head, said, "Nothing."

She reached out to him every way she could think of—cooking his favorite dinners, suggesting they take another motorcycle trip before the weather got too cold. She even tried asking him to tell her a story about the people in the photos he'd been restoring.

"I'm not working on any restorations right now," he'd told her.

Then what was he doing, hour after hour, in his studio, door locked, music cranked up so high she could feel the pulse of it through the floorboards?

She kept the little ring on that he'd given her, staring at it, willing it to take her back in time to the way things had been at the cabin. But Gary remained distant, secretive.

She feared he was going back into the dark place he'd lived in after Austin died. The place where he was not only a man Katherine couldn't recognize, but one she had actually been frightened of. A fragile man who drank too much, and who was prone to violent physical outbursts in which he would destroy thousands of dollars' worth of camera equipment or smash their large-screen television. Once, perhaps two months after Austin's death, Gary broke all the wineglasses in the kitchen and used a shard to slash at his forearm. The slow leak of blood told Katherine he hadn't hit a major artery, but he might not be so lucky if he tried again.

"Gary," she'd said, her voice as level as she could make it as she stepped slowly toward him. "Put it down, sweetie. Put the glass down."

He looked at her as though he didn't recognize her, and the truth was, she didn't know him in that moment, either. Behind his eyes, there was no trace of the Gary she had fallen in love with and married.

"Gary?" she said again, as though trying to wake him gently from a bad dream.

He raised the jagged edge of broken glass and took a step toward her. She ran out of the apartment, terrified.

She never forgot his eyes: black and hollow, like empty, shadowy sockets.

They started grief counseling the following week. There were tearful, desperate apologies, and the rages gradually became rarer, briefer, more controlled. Eventually they stopped altogether—the boundless anger replaced by simple sadness. Gary was himself again, a mourning version of himself to be sure, but recognizable. Katherine believed they might be okay.

And then, back in October, once they'd returned from their weekend away, it seemed all the warning signs were back. Gary was letting the monster of his own grief take over again. And she wasn't sure how much more she could take.

Then he left one morning to go to a photo shoot, and later that night, she was facedown on the couch, screaming into the cushions, clawing at them until they ripped, because two police officers had knocked on her door.

Unsure of how to move forward with the inside of the *His Final Meal* box, she decided to begin work on the outside, and was giving the box a brick façade, making it look like Lou Lou's Café. But when she went to paint the sign above the door, she couldn't find any of her smallest paintbrushes. They must still be in a box somewhere, but she had already unpacked the cartons labeled ART SUPPLIES. Katherine sighed in frustration.

She spotted Gary's battered red metal tackle box, which he'd used to organize his supplies for cleaning and restoring the old photographs he collected. There should be a small brush in there—he often did retouching by hand. Most people did all their restoration on the computer these days, but not Gary.

She popped open the box and went through it: can of compressed air, white cotton gloves, cotton swabs, soft cleaning brushes and cloths, alcohol, dyes and toners, and there, at the bottom, in a plastic case all their own, were the brushes, including just the one she needed.

Lifting the case out, she saw there was a small hardcover book tucked underneath. How odd.

Visitors from the Other Side
The Secret Diary of Sara Harrison Shea

It felt like a funny joke, a book Gary had planted there for her to find right now: *This is what I've become, a visitor.*

She reached for the book, flipped it open to page 12:

I have been despondent ever since. Bedridden. The truth was, I saw no point in going on. If I'd had the strength to rise up from my bed, I would have gone downstairs, found my husband's rifle, and pulled the trigger with my teeth around the barrel. I saw myself doing just that. I visualized it. Dreamed it. Felt myself floating down those steps, reaching for the rifle, tasting the gunpowder.

I killed myself again and again in my dreams.

I'd wake up weeping, full of sorrow to find myself alive, trapped in my wretched body, in my wretched life. Alone . . .

Leaving the case of brushes, Katherine stepped away from the art table with the strange little book clenched in her hand. She crossed the living room, grabbed the cigarettes and lighter from the coffee table, curled up on the couch, turned back to the very beginning of the book, and continued to read.

Ruthie

"It's definitely loaded," Buzz said, holding the gun they'd found under her mother's floor. He kept his index finger off the trigger, resting it along the metal barrel. They were sitting side by side on her mom's bed. Ruthie was holding a bottle of beer. Buzz had put his down on the bedside table, where it sat abandoned and sweating. Ruthie was worried it would leave a ring in the wood, a telltale sign that they'd been there. She put the bottle on the floor and wiped off the tabletop with her sleeve.

It was ten o'clock, and Fawn was sound asleep. She'd had a fever of 102. Ruthie had been giving her Tylenol every four hours to keep it down. She'd even made up a brew of some of her mother's tea with feverfew and willow bark and had Fawn drink it. Once Fawn was asleep, she called Buzz and asked him to come over. He brought a six-pack of beer.

"See? Here," Buzz said, and held out the gun to show her the inner workings. "The cylinder holds six cartridges. Six shots. It's an older gun, but it's a real beauty, and it's in good shape. Your mom's kept it cleaned and oiled."

"Are you sure?" Ruthie asked, still unable to believe that her mother would even touch a gun.

"Well, someone has. And this is her bedroom, right? It's not so unusual, really, for a woman living alone out here with her kids to want some kind of protection. My dad sells more handguns to women than men."

Ruthie shivered, but moved in for a closer look. "So how's it work?"

"Simple," Buzz said, eyes all lit up. He was loving this—the chance to be an expert in something. Buzz's dad ran Bull's Eye Archery and Ammo out on Route 6. Buzz had grown up around guns and had been hunting since he was eight years old. "What we have here is a Colt single-action revolver. This is the safety latch. You want to push that back. Then use your thumb to pull down on the hammer until it clicks. After that, you just aim and pull the trigger. The trigger releases the hammer, and the gun fires."

Buzz turned the gun in his hand. "If you want, we can try it out tomorrow. I can show you how to fire it."

Ruthie shook her head. "My mom would kill me."

He nodded and put the gun back into the box carefully, respectfully.

"I still can't believe she just disappeared like this," he said, taking off his baseball cap and running a hand through his close-cropped hair.

"I know," Ruthie said. "It's not like her. She's a little odd, but she's so . . . dependable. Stuck in her ways. She barely ever goes to town, and now she's gone and vanished off the face of the freaking earth. It doesn't make sense."

"So what's your plan? I mean, if she doesn't show up?"

"I don't know." Ruthie sighed. "I had been thinking that I'd call the cops if she wasn't back by tonight, but then we found this stuff. Now I truly don't know what the hell to do. What if she's caught up in something . . . illegal?"

Buzz nodded. "Maybe it's a good thing you didn't call the cops. Finding the gun and wallets—it does make you wonder."

"I know," Ruthie said weakly. It seemed impossible—the idea that her mild-mannered, herbal-tea-loving, middle-aged mother was involved in something criminal.

What else didn't Ruthie know? What else might be uncovered if she did call the police?

Buzz was a quiet a minute. "Maybe it's the aliens."

"Goddamn," Ruthie spat. "I am *so* not in the mood for any alien theories right now."

"No, no, really. Alien abduction. It happens all the time. They suck them up in these tractor beams and do experiments and probe them and shit, then let them go, sometimes miles from where they were taken, memories wiped clean. And you know what me and Tracer saw out in the woods, not even a mile from your place."

Ruthie remembered the shadowy woods, the rocks jutting up like teeth that made her feel as if she were on the verge of being swallowed up.

"Come on, Buzz. I could use a little sanity here."

"Okay. But can I just point out something kind of obvious?" Buzz asked.

She shrugged, but didn't protest.

"Well, do you ever think about the way you guys live? You know, you're kind of cut off from the world out here—barely any visitors, unlisted phone number, no-trespassing signs everywhere."

"You know my mom. She's a total hippie freak," Ruthie said. "My dad was the same way, too. That's why they moved out here from Chicago when I was three. They didn't want to be a part of the machine. They wanted to go back to the land, live this happy hippie utopian dream with chickens and an herb garden and fresh whole-grain bread."

"What if it's more than that?" Buzz asked.

"What are you saying?"

"That sometimes, if people don't want to be found, there's a damn good reason for it."

They were quiet a minute.

"I'm gonna go check on Fawn," she said. "When I get back, we can try to get the closet open."

She padded down the hall to Fawn's room. In the soft glow of Fawn's night-light, she found her little sister curled up under a quilt, Roscoe purring contentedly on top of her. Mimi had fallen onto the floor.

"Hey, old man. You looking after Fawn?" Ruthie asked, stroking the cat. "Good boy." She reached down to feel Fawn's forehead. Still warm, but the fever was down. She picked up Mimi, tucked her in right next to Fawn, and pulled the quilt up to cover them both.

"I think her fever's down," she reported to Buzz back in her mom's room.

"That's good news."

"Yeah. Poor kid. It sucks that she's sick now, when Mom's not here."

Buzz smiled. "Fawn has you."

"Yeah, well, Mom better show up soon. I can't take care of a kid. You should have seen me trying to figure out how much Tylenol to give her. I didn't even know what she weighed—I had to ask her."

Buzz took her hands in his. "You're doing just fine," he told her. "Quit being so hard on yourself."

"If you say so," Ruthie said. "Now let's see about that closet."

Buzz grabbed the crowbar Ruthie had found in the barn and went to work. Ruthie stood back and watched, suddenly nervous about what they might find inside. In less than five minutes, Buzz had both the top and bottom boards off.

"You want to do the honors?" he asked, stepping away from the closet door.

Ruthie shook her head. "You go ahead."

"All righty, then," Buzz said. Keeping the heavy metal crowbar in his right hand, just in case, Buzz turned the knob and slowly pulled open the door.

"Nothing." He stuck his head in for a better look. "Just a bunch of clothes." He stepped back and went to sit on the bed with his beer, clearly disappointed.

Ruthie came forward to peer in.

Buzz was right—there was nothing unusual inside. Ruthie flipped through the clothing on hangers: her dad's familiar flannel shirts, her mom's turtlenecks and fleece. There was a stack of sweaters on the shelf above. Clogs and running shoes in neat rows on the floor below.

Her mother had kept most of her dad's clothes after he died, almost as if she was expecting him back. Checking that Buzz wasn't looking, Ruthie buried her face in one of her dad's old plaid shirts hanging in the closet, trying to catch a scent of him. She smelled only cedar and dust.

She didn't like being in the closet, even with the door open. Small, tight places had always freaked her out. In her worst nightmares, she was trapped in tiny rooms, or having to wriggle through narrow passageways she could barely fit through. And she always got stuck and woke up screaming, breathless.

Keeping as much of her body as possible outside the closet now, Ruthie searched through the clothes, thinking how odd it was that her mother had sealed away this stuff. Hadn't she just been wearing this green cardigan last week? Ruthie peered inside all the pockets, even reached into the shoes. All she came up with were a couple of matchbooks and half a roll of Life Savers covered with pocket lint. She pulled out all the shoes, clearing off the floor, and felt around the edges of the floorboards, checking for another secret compartment.

"I still say it's pretty freaking weird," Buzz said, squinting at the closet.

"Yeah, why try to keep people out like that? All she's got in there is a bunch of old shoes and stretched-out turtlenecks."

Buzz shook his head. "That's not what bugs me. What it looks like to me is, she was trying to keep something *in*."

Ruthie forced out a wheezy-sounding laugh, watched Buzz tearing at the label of his beer bottle.

It felt strange and kind of thrilling to have Buzz here, in the house—in her mom's room, even. Mom didn't think much of her relationship with Buzz, and made it clear that she believed Ruthie could do better than the stoner kid who worked at his uncle's scrap-metal yard.

"I mean," her mother told her once, "I see that the boy is handsome, but he's just not who I would picture you with."

"And who *would* you picture me with?" Ruthie had asked, temper flaring.

Her mother thought a minute. "Someone who didn't spend all his time searching the sky for flying saucers. He calls so much attention to himself that way. I saw a flyer at the farmers' market—he's started a UFO-hunting group of some sort. It said on the flyer that he thinks the Devil's Hand is some kind of alien hotspot."

Ruthie shrugged.

"That's all we need," her mother said. "Buzz and his merry band of wackos out roaming our woods."

"They're not *our* woods," Ruthie said.

"Still," her mother said, pursing her lips. "The boy needs to have some sense talked into him."

"You don't know him *at all,*" Ruthie had said, stalking out of the room.

Buzz was the most sensible, stable person she knew. Yeah, he had a few weird ideas, but so what? The guy was rock solid. She understood that her mother was distrustful of people she didn't know, but, still, it pissed Ruthie off that her mother didn't trust her judgment.

But now, with her mom gone, all of this felt silly and little-girl-ish. If her mother got back, Ruthie would do things differently. She'd insist on inviting Buzz to dinner, let her mother see how wonderful and unique he was once you got to know him. She'd even take her mom over to see his sculptures. Who knows, maybe, with all her mom's craft-fair connections, she might have some ideas for ways Buzz could market his art, someday even make a living from it.

She joined Buzz on the bed, picked up *Visitors from the Other Side,* and flipped it over to look at the photo of her house with Sara Harrison Shea.

"It's really bizarre that she lived here," Buzz said. "I mean, I knew she was from West Hall, but—"

"Wait, you've, like, heard of her?"

Buzz sat up straighter. "Sure. Sara Harrison Shea is *kind* of the most famous person who ever lived in West Hall. I even read the book, but that was way before I met you. I guess that's why I never recognized your house. Crazy."

Buzz hadn't done well in school—he was a learn-by-doing kind of guy and, back in high school, always had trouble memorizing things and then spitting them back out for tests. He did great with all the hands-on automotive-technology stuff, but give him a pop quiz and he was screwed. He was a very slow reader, and Ruthie suspected he had some degree of dyslexia, but never brought it up because he was so insecure about people thinking he was stupid.

"So she was famous because of this book?"

"Well, yeah. In certain circles, she's a big name."

Ruthie nodded. Despite his slow reading, Buzz was well read when it came to the supernatural and conspiracy theories. *Of course* he'd know all about the freaky lady who saw dead people.

"You mean, with people who believe in ghosts and stuff? What was she, like, a medium or something?"

"She wasn't just a spiritualist—not in the traditional sense anyway. She claimed that the dead could really come back. Not like ghosts, but with actual flesh-and-blood bodies."

Ruthie got a chill; she looked down at the photo of Sara on the back of the book.

"But I think she's most famous for how she died," Buzz continued. "And the journals her niece published, they read like a goddamn real-life murder mystery."

"All it says in the introduction is something about her having been brutally murdered," Ruthie said.

"I'll say!"

"So what happened?" she asked.

Buzz scowled at her. "Are you sure you want to know?"

Ruthie nodded, seeing that he was clearly bursting to tell her. Besides, how bad could it be?

He took in a breath. "Okay. She was found in the field behind her house—I guess I should say, behind *your* house." He paused for a second here, watching her, knowing he was creeping her out, and enjoying every second.

"She'd been skinned," he said, making his voice as eerily Vincent Price–like as he could. "Peeled like a freaking grape. And you know the most messed-up part? They say her skin was never found."

Ruthie squirmed, fought the instinct to give him a girlish *Ewww!* "I don't believe it," she said, sitting up straight to finish the last swallow of beer. "That's totally made up!"

"No," Buzz said, holding up two fingers, "Scout's honor. They said it was her husband, Martin, who did it. The town doctor, who was also Martin's brother, found him right beside her body, holding a gun, covered in blood and half crazy. He shot himself right in front of his brother."

Buzz's eyes were big and glistening. He was just as excited as when he was telling one of his alien stories.

"There's more, too. My grandpa, he said his dad told him that after she died people would sometimes see Sara walking through town late at night."

"What, like, her ghost?" Ruthie felt the same way about ghosts as she did about UFOs.

"No. Like some actual person all dressed up in her skin!"

"Okay, you've officially crossed the line. That's beyond gross. Not to mention obviously bullshit!"

"It's true! Ask anyone. There were some weird deaths, and people blamed Sara—or whatever it was walking around in her skin. So everyone in the village started leaving gifts out on their porches for her—food and coins, jars of honey. She'd walk through town collecting them late at night. Every full moon, the whole town would put stuff out for her. Some people, old-timers like Sally Jensen out on Bulrush Road? They're still doing it."

Ruthie shook her head in disbelief. "No way!"

"I'll prove it. Next full moon, you and I will take a ride around town. I'll show you the offerings set out here and there on porches and doorsteps."

"So how come I've never heard any of this before?"

He shrugged, set down his empty beer bottle, and leaned back into the bed, hands clasped behind his head. "I guess people don't talk about it all that much. My grandpa only mentioned it once, when he was good and drunk one Thanksgiving. He was legitimately scared."

Ruthie shook her head, lay back in the bed beside Buzz, and closed her eyes. It had been a long, exhausting day. She just needed to rest for a minute.

Suddenly she was back in Fitzgerald's, holding her mother's hand. The fluorescent light was flickering above them, growing steadily dimmer.

"What do you choose, Dove?" asked her mother, who held her hand a little too tightly. The bakery seemed to be shrinking around them, the walls closing in.

Ruthie stared at the rows of cakes and cookies and pointed at the pink cupcake. The ceiling was lower now.

Then she looked up to see her mother smiling down. And it was the stranger again—a tall, thin woman with tortoiseshell-framed glasses shaped like cat's eyes. The bakery wasn't much bigger than a closet now, and everything had gotten very dark. The only source of light was the glass case that held the cupcakes, which seemed to sparkle and glow.

Ruthie felt that old familiar panic at being in such a small, tight place. She was breathing too fast, doing an openmouthed panting like a dog.

"Good choice, Dove," the woman said, then reached around the back of her head and pulled on a zipper. Her whole mommy disguise came peeling off, leaving a sack of red oozing flesh with a hole for a mouth.

Ruthie tried to scream, but couldn't. She gasped herself awake, heart hammering.

She blinked hard. She and Buzz were lying on her mom's bed, on top of the covers. Buzz was snoring softly. The light was still on, glaring down like an eye. She caught movement off to her right side—something in the closet. She turned; a shadow moved. The cat? No, it was too big to be Roscoe. She sat up, drawing in a sharp breath; from the back corner of the closet she saw the glint of two eyes.

Buzz bolted up in bed, body rigid. "Whatisit?"

Ruthie pointed to the closet, hand shaking. "There's something in there," she told him, her throat almost too dry to speak. "Watching us."

Buzz had his feet on the floor in two seconds and the crowbar in his hand. He bounded to the closet, swept back the clothes on hangers.

"Nothing here," he said, after a second.

Ruthie shook her head, rolled out of bed, and approached the closet cautiously. There was nothing but the familiar rows of shoes, her parents' clothing on hangers. But something was different. The air in the closet felt strange—crackling and used up. And there was an odd acrid, burning odor—something familiar to her, but she couldn't say where she'd smelled it before.

"Maybe it was just a bad dream?" Buzz said, ruffling her hair.

"Yeah, maybe," she said, and closed the closet door hard, wishing she could lock it.

1 9 0 8

Visitors from the Other Side

The Secret Diary of Sara Harrison Shea

January 15, 1908

Things have become so very strange—I feel as though I am floating outside my body, watching myself and those around me with the same curiosity as if I were watching actors on a stage. Our kitchen table is piled high with food the women bring: brown bread, baked beans, smoked ham, potpies, potato soup, gingerbread, apple crisp, fruitcake soaked in rum. The smell of the food sickens me. All I can think is how much Gertie would have loved it all—fresh gingerbread topped with whipped cream! But Gertie is gone, and the food keeps coming.

I see myself nod, shake people's hands, accept their hugs and food and kind gestures. Claudia Bemis has cleaned the house from top to bottom and kept the coffeepot full. The men have split kindling, carried in bundles of firewood, kept the dooryard shoveled.

Lucius has stayed right by Martin's side. The two of them spent much of yesterday in the barn together, building Gertie's coffin.

These past two days, so many people have come to pay respects, to say how sorry they are. Their words are hollow. Empty. Soundless bubbles rising to the surface of the water.

Gertie is with the angels now.

We're praying for you.

The schoolteacher, Delilah Banks, came calling. "Gertie had the most fanciful thoughts," she said through tears. "I can't tell you how very much I will miss her."

One teary-eyed face after another, a chorus of voices low and somber: *So sorry. We're so, so very sorry.*

I do not wish for their sympathy—what I want is my Gertie back, and if no one can give me that, then, as far as I'm concerned, the world can just go away and take their tears and potpies and gingerbread with them.

Poor old Shep has taken up residence at the foot of Gertie's chair in the kitchen. He lies there all day, looking hopeful each time he hears someone enter the room, only to rest his head mournfully on his front paws when he sees it is not Gertie.

"Poor love," my niece, Amelia, says, getting down on her knees to stroke the dog's head and feed him choice scraps. Amelia has been very kind. She has insisted on staying with us for a few days to help with things. She is twenty-one, very striking, strong-willed.

Last night, she brought me some warm brandy before bed and insisted I drink the whole cup. "Uncle Lucius says it'll do you good," she explained.

Then she took up my brush and began to work the tangles out of my hair. I haven't had my hair brushed for me since I was a little girl.

"Can I tell you a secret?" Amelia asked.

I nodded.

"The dead never really leave us," she whispered to me, her lips so near my ear I could feel the warmth of her breath. "There is a circle of ladies in Montpelier who meet once a month and speak with those who have passed on. I have been several times now, and heard the spirits rapping on the table. You must come with me, Aunt Sara," she said, her voice growing urgent. "As soon as you feel up to it, we will go."

"Martin would not approve," I said.

"Then we won't tell him," she whispered.

*M*artin has been no comfort—he is shy, clumsy, and awkward. Once, I found these things sweetly boyish and endearing; now I find myself wishing that he were a different man, a man more sure of himself. I have come to despise the way he never looks anyone in the eye—how is a man like that to be trusted? There was a time, not all that long ago, I even loved his limp, because in some way it reminded me of everything he'd given our family—his constant drive to keep us warm and fed, to keep the farm going no matter what. Now I loathe the way his bad foot scrapes across the floor so noisily; it is the sound of weakness and failure. I know it's wrong, and it makes me sick, this new seething venom inside me, but I cannot help it.

Deep down, I understand the true cause of these feelings: I blame Martin for what happened to Gertie. If she hadn't followed him into the woods that morning, she would still be here by my side.

"We will see our way through this," he tells me, squeezing my hand in his own, which is as cool and damp as a fish. He gives me a warm, loving smile, but behind it I see his concern.

I do not answer. I do not tell him that I no longer wish to get through it. That what I want most is to sneak away and throw myself down into the bottom of that well so I can be with my Gertie once more.

Even Reverend Ayers can offer no relief.

He came this afternoon to discuss the service and burial arrangements for Gertie. I had been putting off this discussion, but today Martin and Lucius announced that it was time, we had waited long enough.

We sat at the table over cups of coffee that grew cold before us. Reverend Ayers had brought a basket of muffins his wife, Mary, had made. There was some talk of burying Gertie up at the cemetery by Cranberry Meadow with Martin's family, but I wouldn't have it.

"She belongs here," I said. Martin nodded, and Lucius opened his mouth to say something but thought better of it. And so it was decided we would bury her in the small family plot behind the house, beside her tiny brother, my mother and father and brother.

As Reverend Ayers was leaving, he took my hand. "You must remember, Sara, that Gertie is in a better place now. She's with our Lord."

I spat in his face.

I did this without thinking, automatically, as if it were as natural to me as taking a sip of water when thirsty.

Imagine, me spitting in Reverend Ayers's face! I've known the man all my life—he baptized me, married Martin and me, buried our son, Charles. I have struggled all my life to believe his teachings, to live the word of God. But no more.

"Sara!" Lucius said, looking alarmed as he pulled a clean white handkerchief out of the front pocket of his trousers and handed it to the reverend.

Reverend Ayers wiped at his face and stepped back away from me. He looked . . . not angry or worried about me, but frightened of what I might do next.

"If the God you worship and pray to is the one who brought my Gertie to that well, who took her from me, then I want nothing more to do with him," I said. "Please leave my house and take your vicious God with you."

Poor Martin was horrified and stuttered off excuses for me.

"I'm so sorry," he said, as he and Lucius walked Reverend Ayers out. "She's sick with grief. Not in her right mind."

Not in my right mind.

But I am in the same mind I have had all along. Only now there is a piece missing. A Gertie-shaped piece cut from the center of my very being.

And perhaps, with this new grief, I am seeing things clearly for the first time.

I understand now that Martin has never known the real me. There is only one person who ever did—who saw all of me, all the beauty along with the ugliness. And it is that person I long for now.

Auntie.

For so long, I have done my best to push all my memories of her away. I've spent my whole adult life trying to convince myself that she got what she deserved; that her death, terrible as it was, was the consequence of her own actions. But that's never been what I truly believed. What I think about most is how I should have done something to stop it. If I had found a way to save her, I tell myself, maybe my life might have turned out differently. Perhaps all the tragedy and loss I have suffered is somehow linked to what I did that one day when I was nine.

It's funny that she is the person I long for most in times like these, when my heart has been shattered and I see no sense in going on.

She is the only one who might know what to say to me now, who might be able to offer true comfort. And I know, I just know, she would laugh when I told her I spat in the reverend's face!

She'd throw back her head and laugh.

$\mathcal{R}$everend Ayers says there is only one God," I told Auntie once. It was only a few weeks after I'd seen Hester Jameson out in the woods and asked Auntie about sleepers. "And that it is wrong to pray to anyone or anything else."

Auntie laughed, then spat brown tobacco juice onto the ground. We were bumping along in her old wagon, all loaded with animal pelts, for a trip to a dealer in St. Johnsbury. She made the trip four times a year, and he always gave her a fair price for the skins. This was the first time Father had consented to let me make the overnight trip with her. Before leaving, Auntie had sprinkled some tobacco on the ground around the wagon and said a safe-journey prayer to the spirits and the four directions.

"Young Reverend Ayers looks at a lake and sees only his own reflection in it; that is what God is to him. He does not see the creatures that live down deep, the dragonflies that hover, the frog on the lily pad." Auntie's face was full of pity and scorn as she shook her head and spat tobacco juice again. "His heart and mind are closed to the true beauty of the lake, the place where all its magic lies."

Auntie held the reins, guided the horse to pull us along the narrow dirt road that was full of ruts from wagon wheels. Sometimes I doubted Auntie needed the reins at all; it seemed she could get the horse to do just what she wanted by talking to it. She had the amazing ability to communicate with almost any animal; she could call birds to her, bring fish closer to her net. Once, I saw her coax a lynx out of hiding and right into her snare.

We bumped along slowly. The air was warm and sweet and full of birdsong. We were several miles east of town now, surrounded by rolling green hills dotted with cream-colored sheep that bleated contentedly as they ate their fill of fresh spring greens.

"But he's a clever man," I said. "He has studied for years. He reads the Bible every day."

"There are different kinds of cleverness, Sara."

I nodded, understanding just what she meant. Auntie was the cleverest person I knew; people came to her little cabin in the woods from all over town to buy remedies and cures, spells for love and good crops. But no one talked about it or admitted that they'd paid Auntie for a syrup to cure a child's cough, or a charm to wear to attract their heart's desire.

"Reverend Ayers says when we die our souls go on to Heaven, to be with God."

"Is that what you believe?" Auntie asked, her eyes fixed on the rough road ahead.

"It's not what you have taught me," I answered.

"And what is it I have taught you?" She turned toward me, raised her eyebrows.

Auntie was often giving me these little tests, and I knew I had to choose my words carefully—if I answered wrong, she might ignore me for hours, pretend I wasn't there; she might even go so far as not to give me my share of lunch or dinner. I had learned at a young age that disappointing Auntie always meant paying a price, and it was something I worked very hard to avoid.

"You always say that death is not an ending, but a beginning. That the dead cross over to the world of the spirits and are surrounding us still."

Auntie nodded, waiting for more.

"I like that idea," I told her. "That they're all around us, watching."

Auntie smiled at me.

On our left was a narrow stream, and as it was a clear day, we could see Camel's Hump off in the distance. On our right was a neat row of apple trees in bloom, the scent heady and sweet. Bees buzzed from flower to flower, flying drunkenly, weighted down with pollen.

I moved closer to Auntie there in the cart; her hands on the reins were the strongest hands I'd ever known. I felt safe and thrilled, and as if I was right where I belonged.

Later that night, after we'd sold the furs to the merchant in St. Johnsbury, we camped by the river in a grassy clearing under a willow tree. Auntie had made us a little bed in the back of the wagon, out of a bearskin and blankets. She had a fire blazing, and when it died down, we cooked the trout she'd just caught on sticks, turning them gently over the glowing coals. She'd brought out an enameled pot and used it to brew a sweet tea full of herbs and roots, which we drank from tin mugs. After dinner, after the fire had been rekindled, Auntie sucked on the fish bones until she had removed every morsel of meat. She ate nearly every part of the fish, even the eyeballs. The innards she threw to Buckshot, who'd wandered off from camp and come back with his own dinner, a woodchuck that had been too slow to get back into its den.

The moon was not up, and the night was inky black. We couldn't see anything beyond the circle of light that the fire cast. The world beyond had turned to nothing but noises: the babble of the river, which had seemed soothing in daylight and now carried strange eerie-sounding murmurs; the occasional croak of a bullfrog; the far-off hoot of an owl.

"Tell my future," I begged as I plucked at the long, soft grass that grew around me.

Auntie smiled, stretched like a cat. "Not tonight. The moon is not right for such things."

"Please," I pleaded, tugging at her coat as I had when I was a much younger child. I loved that coat. The colorful painted flowers along the bottom, the beads and porcupine quills stitched in neat patterns over the shoulders and down the front.

"Very well," she said, throwing the fish bones into the fire and wiping her greasy hands on her skirt. She reached into the pouch she carried tucked into her belt and withdrew a small amount of finely ground powder.

"What is that?"

"Shh," Auntie said. Then she mumbled something I did not hear—another prayer, I supposed. A wish. An incantation.

She tossed the powder into the fire. It crackled and hissed, made the fire sparkle with shades of blue and green. The drooping branches of the willow above us seemed to catch the light and glow, and they swayed like tiny arms, reaching for us. Out on the water, there was the splash of a bird landing, a duck or heron.

Auntie stared into the flames, searching.

Then—did I imagine it?—Auntie seemed to flinch and look away. There was a sharp intake of breath, as if the fire had dealt her a blow.

"What is it?" I asked, leaning toward her. "What did you see?"

"Nothing," Auntie said, looking away from me, but I knew her well enough to tell that she was lying. Auntie had seen something terrible in my future, something dark enough to make her turn away.

"Tell me," I said, putting my hand on her arm. "Please."

She shook my hand off as if I were a pesky insect. "There is nothing to tell," Auntie snapped.

"Please," I repeated, grabbing her arm again, my hand touching the soft deerskin coat. "I know you saw something."

Her eyes turned dark, and she reached down and gave the back of my hand a hard pinch. I jerked my hand away and drew back.

"As I said, the moon is not right for such things. Maybe next time you will listen."

Auntie gazed back into the fire, which was dying back down, all the bright colors gone. I moved even farther away, wrapped my arms around my knees, and slid closer to the heat. My hand stung where she had pinched it, and I wondered if she had broken the skin, but knew better than to look. Best to ignore the pain, to pretend it hadn't happened.

After a few moments of uneasy silence, she looked my way.

"What I can tell you is this: you are special, Sara Harrison, but you already know this. You have something inside you that makes you different from others." She looked at me with such seriousness that my chest felt heavy. "Something that shines bright, gives you the same gifts I have. The gifts of sight, of magic. It makes you stronger than you know. And, oh, little Sara, let me tell you this." She smiled, rocking forward, throwing another stick onto the fire. It crackled and popped as it caught. "If you ever grow up and have a girl child, the gift will be passed down double to her. That girl will walk between the worlds. She will be as powerful as I am, maybe more. I have seen it in the fire."

. . .

*H*ow I wish Auntie were here now, how I ache for her. There are a thousand questions I would ask. But first I would tell her she was right that night long ago when she stared into the fire—my Gertie was special. She'd seen things others hadn't. Things like the blue dog and the winter people. She'd walked between the worlds.

I am in bed now. A short while ago, Lucius came up to give me my nightly cup of rum. He also delivered a box of ribbon candy.

"This is from Abe Cushing," Lucius said. I nodded, watched him put the candy on my bedside table. Abe runs the general store. He is a man of few words, but he loved Gertie—was always sneaking her lemon drops and toffee when we went in to pick up sugar and flour, or cloth and thread for a new dress.

Lucius looked down at me. His eyes were bright and clear; his shirt was unwrinkled, impeccably white. How did he manage always to look so tidy?

"Where's Amelia?" I asked.

"Downstairs," he said. "I thought I'd come check on you tonight." He laid a hand on my forehead, then placed two fingers on my wrist, feeling for my pulse. "How are you feeling?"

I did not answer. What did he expect me to say?

"Martin is very worried about you," he said. "Your outburst today with Reverend Ayers was inexcusable."

I bit my lip, said nothing.

"Sara," he said, bending over so that his face was right in front of mine. "I understand that you are grieving. We all are. But I'm asking you to make more of an effort."

"An effort?" I asked, puzzled.

"Gertie is gone," he said. "But you and Martin, you've got to go on living."

Then he left me alone with my rum, which I drank in two long swallows as I settled back into the pillows, the weight of the quilt on top of me feeling impossibly heavy.

Gertie is gone, Lucius told me.

But then I hear Amelia's voice in my head: *The dead never really leave us.*

And I think of what Auntie taught me long ago: that death is not an ending, but a beginning. The dead cross over to the world of the spirits and are surrounding us still.

"Gertie," I say aloud. "If you're here, please give me a sign." Then I wait. I lie under the covers and I wait until I ache. I wait for a whisper, the feeling of soft fingers writing letters into my palm, even a few raps on a table, as Amelia described.

But there is nothing.

I am alone.

Visitors from the Other Side

The Secret Diary of Sara Harrison Shea

January 23, 1908

We buried Gertie six days ago. The day before, Martin was out from sunup through sundown, feeding a blazing fire to thaw the soil enough so he could dig the hole for her small coffin. I watched the fire through the kitchen window, the way it lit up Martin's face, the ashes it threw on his clothes and hair. It was a terrible thing, that fire. Like a beacon letting me know that the end had come and there was nothing I could do to stop it: Gertie was dead and we were going to bury her in the ground. Martin looked like a devil, face glowing red and orange as he stood there, feeding it. He was unshaven, his face thin and hollow. I wanted to look away, but could not. I stood by the window all day, watching it burn, watching it consume any shred of hope or happiness I had left.

Most of the town came to see us bury our little girl the next day. Reverend Ayers put on quite a show for them, talking about God's little lambs and the beautiful glory of his Kingdom, but I was only half listening. I wouldn't even look him in the eye. Instead, I stared down at the simple pine box they'd laid my Gertie out in. It was a miserably cold afternoon. I couldn't stop shivering. Martin put his arm around me, but I pushed it off. I took off my coat and used it to cover the coffin, thinking poor Gertie must be terribly cold in there.

I have been despondent ever since. Bedridden. The truth was, I saw no point in going on. If I'd had the strength to rise up from my bed, I would have gone downstairs, found my husband's rifle, and pulled the trigger with my teeth around the barrel. I saw myself doing just that. I visualized it. Dreamed it. Felt myself floating down those steps, reaching for the rifle, tasting the gunpowder.

I killed myself again and again in my dreams.

I'd wake up weeping, full of sorrow to find myself alive, trapped in my wretched body, in my wretched life. Alone in this bedroom with its white walls stained yellow from years of dust, smoke, and grime. Only me and the wooden bed with the feather mattress, the closet where our ragged clothes hang, the nightstand, the dresser full of our underthings, and the chair Martin sits in each night to take off his boots. When Gertie was alive, this room, the whole house, seemed to glow and radiate warmth. Now everything is dim, ugly, cold.

I came to believe that there was no point going on without my little Gertie, my sweet tadpole of a girl. Every time I closed my eyes, she was there, falling down that well, only in my mind it was a fall that went on forever. She went on and on into blackness until she was a tiny speck, and then—nothing at all. And when I opened my eyes, there was only the empty room, empty bed, my empty, aching heart.

I stopped eating. I hadn't the energy to leave the bed. I just lay there, drifting in and out, imagining my own death. Martin came and went. He tried to spoon-feed me, cooing at me as if I were an injured baby bird. When that failed to yield results, he tried yelling, screaming sense into me: "Damn it, woman! It was Gertie who died! Not you. You and I, we've got to carry on living."

Lucius came to see me several times. He brought a tonic that is supposed to help build my strength. It was thick and bitter, and the only way I could get it down was by imagining that it was deadly poison.

My niece, Amelia, tried to rouse me. She came into the room gaily, in a new bright dress, her hair neatly plaited. She brought me tea and shortbread cookies that came in a tin all the way from England.

"I had Abe Cushing order them for me special," she said, prying open the tin and offering me a cookie. I took one and nibbled at the edge. It tasted like sawdust.

While Martin was with us, Amelia chatted about the news from town—there had been a fire at the Wilsons' house, Theodore Grant was fired from the mill for showing up too drunk to work, Minnie Abare was pregnant with her fifth child (she was hoping for a girl, of course, what with four boys already).

After a few minutes, Martin left us alone.

"The dead never really leave us," she whispered, stroking my hair. "I have been to the spiritualist circle in Montpelier," she told me. "Gertie came through. She rapped on the table for us, told us she is fine and misses you very much. The women of the circle want you to join us. They can come here, to West Hall. We'll meet in my house, and you can see for yourself. You can talk to Gertie again."

Liar, I wanted to scream. But all I could do was close my eyes and drift back to sleep.

I woke up, sure Gertie was right there beside me. I could feel her, smell her. Then I opened my eyes and she was gone.

How cruel this life had become. How cold and empty and cruel.

And so I prayed. I prayed for the Lord I had by then forsaken to take me. Take me to join my Gertie. When this did not work, I prayed to the Devil to come and set my soul free.

Then, yesterday morning, Martin came in and kissed my forehead tenderly.

"I'm going into the woods to do some hunting. I was out scouting earlier and saw some nice tracks—a large buck, from the look of them. Amelia is coming by this afternoon. She'll fix you lunch and sit with you until I'm home. I'll be back before dark."

I didn't bother to nod, just rolled over and went back to sleep.

I dreamed Martin was chasing a deer through the woods; then the deer, somehow, had come into the house and was standing at the foot of my bed. I lifted my head for a closer look and discovered it wasn't a deer at all, but Auntie.

She looked older, wiser, but still wore her deerskin coat with the quills, beads, and painted flowers. She smelled like leather, tobacco, and damp, tangled woods. I felt instantly comforted, and believed, for the first time in days, that things would be all right. Auntie was back. And Auntie could fix anything.

Auntie was talking to me. At first I couldn't understand what she was saying, and I thought she was speaking the language of deer, which is silly, because deer are silent animals. The bedroom was dark, full of shadows that moved and twirled around us. The bed felt high up, as if it were floating over the wide pine floorboards, going up higher and higher, Auntie perched at the end like the masthead of a ship.

"Where did you come from?" I asked.

"The closet," she told me plainly. I was relieved that she was speaking words I could understand.

"My Gertie is gone," I told her, beginning to weep. "My little girl."

She nodded and looked at me a long time with her coal-black eyes. "Would you like to see her one more time?" Auntie asked. "Would you like a chance to say goodbye?"

"Yes," I said, sobbing. "Just one moment with her. I would give anything."

"Then you are ready. Do you hear me, Sara Harrison? You are ready."

The bed came floating back down to the floor. The room brightened. Auntie turned and walked back into the closet, shutting the door behind her. I closed my eyes, opened them. I was awake. The room smelled like the air after a lightning storm. Judging by the light, it was still morning. Martin hadn't been gone long.

I lay there a minute, thinking of the dream—of the deer and of Auntie. Remembering what she told me that long-ago afternoon when I first asked her about sleepers:

I will write it all down, everything I know about sleepers. I will fold up the papers, put them in an envelope, and seal it with wax. You will hide it away, and one day, when you are ready, you will open it up.

I leapt from my bed and ran down the hall to Gertie's room, which was my own bedroom when I was growing up. I was weak. My body felt as light and floaty as a bit of dandelion fluff, but was humming with a new, strange energy, a drive such as I had never known before.

I hadn't been in her room since that terrible day, and I hesitated for a second before pulling the door open. Everything was just as she'd left it: the unmade bed, the tangled covers we'd hidden under together on that last morning. Her nightgown was thrown on top of the bed; her closet door was open, and one dress was missing—the dress she put on to follow her father out into the yard and woods.

Look out, Papa. Here comes the biggest cat in the jungle.

The dress she had chosen was her favorite, blue with tiny white flowers. We had made it together when school first started, out of material she'd picked out at the store. She helped cut the pieces and even did some of the sewing herself, pumping the treadle and guiding the fabric through the machine.

It is the dress we buried her in.

Over on the right side of her room, there were shelves that contained a few toys and books and little treasures she'd collected: pretty rocks, the beautiful magnifying glass Amelia had given her, a few funny little animal sculptures she'd made out of clay from the river, a ball and jacks I'd bought her at the general store. (Martin had asked me not to spend money on such things, but how could I help it?)

It took my breath away, being in her room. I could smell her, taste her in the air around me. It was almost too much to bear. Then I remembered what I'd come for.

I pushed the heavy, wood-framed bed aside, found the loose floorboard where the left rear foot of the bed had rested. I dug my fingers into the crack so deeply that I tore a fingernail, but soon I was able to work the board free.

There was Auntie's envelope, right where I had hidden it when I was nine years old, the wax seal unbroken.

I tucked the envelope into my nightgown, pushed back the bed, then returned to my own room. I made a tent of the covers, as Gertie and I used to do, and opened the envelope, hidden. Inside were several pages carefully folded. I had to hold up one side of the blanket to let in enough light to read by.

There was Auntie's familiar scrawl. It sent a wave of memories through me. Auntie teaching me how to write my letters, how to tell a poisonous mushroom from one that was good to eat. I felt her beside me once more, smelled her pine-tree, leather, and tobacco smell; I heard her voice, soft and musical, as she breathed life's lessons into my ear.

My Dearest Sara,

I have promised to tell you everything I know about sleepers. But before you go on, you must understand that this is powerful magic. Only do it if you are sure. Once it is done, there can be no going back.

The sleeper will awaken and return to you. The time this takes is unsure. Sometimes they return in hours, other times, days.

Once awakened, a sleeper will walk for seven days. After that, they are gone from this world forever.

Seven days, I thought to myself, as sinister wheels began to turn. What I wouldn't give to have my Gertie back for seven whole days!

Martin

January 25, 1908

The noise woke him sometime after midnight—a scratching, a scuttling. His eyes shot open, and he lay in the dark, listening.

Pale moonlight came in through the bedroom's frost-covered window, giving everything a bluish glow. He stared up at the plaster ceiling, listening. The fire had died down, and the room was cold. He inhaled, then exhaled, feeling as if the room were breathing with him.

There it was again. The scratching. Nails against wood. He held his breath and listened.

Mice? No. Too big for mice. It sounded like something large trying to claw its way out of the walls. Behind the scrabbling, he heard what sounded like the rustle of flapping wings.

He thought of the chicken he'd found in the woods this morning—another one of their hens taken. Only this time it didn't seem like the work of a fox. He found the carcass up near the rocks. The chicken's neck had been broken, and its chest had been opened up, the heart removed. He didn't know of any animal that would do a thing like that. He'd buried the body in rocks, tried to put it out of his mind.

His own heart thudding now, he felt the bed beside him, expecting to find Sara's warm body, but the bed was cold. Had she gone into Gertie's room again? Were the two of them hidden under the covers, giggling?

No. Gertie was dead. Buried in the ground.

He remembered the way she'd looked when they hauled her body out of the well. Like she was sleeping.

He recalled the feel of her hair in his pocket, coiled softly like a snake.

"Sara?" he called.

He'd been sick with worry over Sara these last days. She had stopped eating, would not leave the bed, would not feed or wash herself. She seemed to get weaker and less responsive with each passing day.

"Honestly, there's nothing we can do but wait," Lucius told him. They had been standing in the kitchen, speaking in hushed voices. "Keep trying to get food and water into her, give her the tonic, offer whatever comfort you can."

"I keep thinking about when we lost Charles," Martin said. "How sick with grief she was." He didn't want to say what he was thinking, not even to his own brother: This time it was worse. This time, he feared, she might not come back to him.

It was one thing to lose poor Gertie, but if he lost Sara, too, his life would be over.

"I don't want to frighten you, Martin," Lucius said. "But if she doesn't come around soon, I think it might be best if we sent her to the state hospital for the insane over in Waterbury."

Martin's whole body went rigid.

"It's not a terrible place," Lucius said. "They have a farm. The patients get outside every day. They would keep her safe."

Martin shook his head. "She'll get better," he vowed. "I'll help her to get better. I'm her husband. I can keep my own wife safe."

But as far as he could tell, Sara was growing worse with each passing hour. And now here it was the middle of the night and she was missing.

"Sara?" he called once more, listening.

And there it was again—the scratching, tapping, fluttering— louder this time, more frantic.

He sat up, scanning the room in the darkness. He could make out the edge of the bed, the dresser to his left, and there, in the right corner, a form hunched, moving slightly, pulsating.

No.

Breathing. It was breathing.

The scream stuck in his throat, coming out as only a hiss.

He looked around frantically for a weapon, something heavy, but then the thing moved, raised its head, and he saw his wife's long auburn hair shine in the dim moonlight.

"Sara?" he gasped. "What are you doing?"

She was sitting on the floor in front of the closet, wearing her thin nightgown, her bare feet as pale as marble against the dark floor. She was shivering.

She did not move, did not seem even to hear him. Worry gnawed at his insides like an ugly rat.

"Come back to bed, darling. Aren't you cold?"

Then he heard it again. The scratching. Claws against wood.

It was coming from inside the closet.

"Sara," he said, standing on shaking legs, blood pounding through his head, making a roaring sound in his ears. The room seemed to shift around him, growing longer. The distance between himself and Sara felt impossibly far. The moonlight hit the closet door. He could see it move slightly, the knob slowly turning.

"Move away from there!" he cried.

But his wife sat still, eyes fixed on the door.

"It's our Gertie," she said calmly. "She's come back to us."

JANUARY 3

~

Present Day

Ruthie

The heater in Buzz's truck was set to full blast, but they still shivered as they navigated the Connecticut suburbs. The floor of the truck was littered with McDonald's bags, coffee cups, and empty bottles of Mountain Dew, Buzz's drink of choice when beer wasn't an option. Fawn sat between them; though her fever was broken, she was still weak and pale. They'd stuffed her into her down parka, then wrapped her up in a wool blanket before leaving home four hours ago.

"Are you sure you're up for a road trip, Little Deer?" Ruthie had asked.

Fawn had nodded eagerly, and so Ruthie said okay, even though she was pretty sure that taking Fawn out in the bitter cold when she was sick was not something Mom would approve of.

It was only day two without Mom, but already Ruthie was starting to realize the million and one things her mother did each day to keep the household running smoothly—cooking, cleaning, laundry, feeding the cat, plowing and shoveling the driveway, bringing in firewood and splitting kindling, taking care of the chickens, giving Fawn medicine and juice. Ruthie didn't get how her mother managed it all and made it seem so effortless. Maybe her mom wasn't as much of a disorganized flake as Ruthie had always thought.

Buzz had borrowed his dad's GPS, and they were using it to find their way to 231 Kendall Lane, Woodhaven, Connecticut, the address on Thomas O'Rourke's driver's license.

Buzz had tried to talk her out of driving down to Connecticut, said they should at least do a little research first.

"It's been a million years, Ruthie," he said. "What are the chances they're even at the same address? I've got my laptop—give me five minutes somewhere with Wi-Fi and I can check it out before we go all the way down there for nothing."

Ruthie was adamant. She insisted they just get in the truck and go.

"It's been *fifteen* years. Maybe they've moved, maybe they haven't. There might be neighbors or relatives who can tell us something."

"It's a hell of a drive for a dead end," Buzz said.

"Look, the wallets have to mean something, my mom saving them all this time, hiding them like that, right? That driver's license is my only clue, and it leads to Woodhaven, Connecticut. I need to go. I'm going."

And so they were on their way, Ruthie silent and deep in thought for most of the ride. She knew Buzz thought she was being ridiculous, but she couldn't shake the feeling that going to Woodhaven was the right thing to do, and she didn't want to waste any more time.

"So what's the plan if we find them?" Buzz asked as he navigated the streets of Woodhaven.

"I'll ask them if they know my mom and dad. Depending on how that goes, I'll show them their wallets and ask if they know why my mom might have them."

"How's that gonna help us find Mom?" Fawn asked.

"I don't know," Ruthie admitted, fiddling with the broken latch on the glove compartment. "But it beats sitting around waiting."

Ruthie was sure she had never been to Connecticut; in fact, she had rarely left Vermont. She was studying the landscape—billboards, chain restaurants and big-box stores, rows of identical houses and condos—with a strange unsettled awe. Her jaw ached from grinding her teeth, a terrible nervous habit she had had since before she could remember.

The streets they'd turned onto now were set up in a neat grid. All the houses were small capes and ranches with barely any yards and sad little hedges marking property lines. The snow lay in filthy clumps along the edges of the streets. She tried to imagine growing up in a place like this—your neighbors so close that you could see into their windows. Maybe her parents were right to keep them removed from the world on their little homestead in Vermont.

"This is Kendall," Buzz announced, as if Ruthie couldn't read the sign herself. He went to gun shows all over the Northeast with his dad and considered himself quite the experienced world traveler. "It'll be on the left side of the street." He scanned house numbers. "Here's 185. 203. Look, there's 229, so the next one's it." The chirpy female voice on the GPS confirmed it.

Buzz put on his turn signal and pulled into the driveway of 231 Kendall Lane—a squat house with yellow vinyl siding that was cracked in places. There was a plastic kiddie pool in the yard, the outline just visible through the newly fallen snow. An old white Pontiac with a crushed rear bumper was parked next to the house. Whoever lived here wasn't rich by any means. But Ruthie knew how it was to be scraping by—buying everything secondhand, living with a couch covered in ugly afghans to hide the stains and holes, and knowing there was never money for things like a trip to Disney World. Or college.

"You guys wait here," Ruthie said, grabbing her bag with the two strangers' wallets tucked inside.

"I'll be watching," Buzz promised.

"Me, too," Fawn said, her tiny face peeking out from under the hood of her pink puffy coat.

Ruthie navigated the ice-covered walk and front steps and pushed the doorbell. She didn't hear it ring. She waited, just in case, then pulled open the storm door and rapped firmly on the wooden one behind it. There was a Happy Easter wreath—a bunny encircled in faded pastel eggs—thumbtacked to the center of the door. Ruthie knocked again. A woman with fried blond hair and bad skin opened it.

"Yeah?" The hallway the woman stood in was tiny and dark. It smelled like cigarettes. Ruthie hoped she wouldn't be invited in.

"Hi." Ruthie gave her biggest smile. "I'm looking for Thomas and Bridget O'Rourke."

"Who?"

"They used to live here. Thomas O'Rourke? And Bridget O'Rourke?"

The woman stared at her blankly.

"Never heard of them. Sorry." She shut the door in Ruthie's face. Undeterred, she tried the neighbors. Most people either weren't home or didn't answer the door. Across the street from 231 Kendall Lane, an old man in a bathrobe told Ruthie he didn't know anybody named O'Rourke. At least he was polite about it.

"Dead end," Ruthie announced as she climbed back up into the cab of the truck. "The lady who lives there now had no idea what I was talking about and the one old neighbor who was home never heard of the O'Rourkes. Maybe we did come all this way for nothing."

"Nothing," Fawn echoed, a voice from inside the hood.

Ruthie gave Buzz a sidelong glance.

He smiled at her. "Wanna try it my way?"

Ruthie shrugged and sank down in the seat.

They drove out of the maze of houses that all looked the same and back to the main road. They passed a fire station, bank, pizza place, and grocery store. Soon the road was lined with shopping plazas on both sides. Ruthie was amazed by how busy they were—cars coming and going in and out of parking lots. Shouldn't people be at work?

Buzz pulled into a Starbucks, then reached in the back for his messenger bag.

"Why are we stopping?" Fawn asked.

"He's gonna search for them online. Like I probably should have let him do before we left home this morning."

"Probably should have," Buzz said cheerfully. "But it's never too late. Come on, let's get some coffee and hot chocolate."

"Can you really do that?" Fawn asked as she followed Ruthie and Buzz out of the truck. "Just look a person up?"

"Sure," Ruthie said. "I think you can find out just about anything if you know what you're doing."

"Wow," Fawn said, her eyes big. "I wish we had a computer."

For the millionth time, Ruthie cursed her parents for not allowing a computer in the house. They claimed that technology wasn't safe, that Big Brother was watching everything, monitoring every e-mail and Web search. Her mom also said wireless Internet and cell towers messed with your body's electricity and could give you cancer. Ruthie had to go into school early and stay late to use the computers to work on reports and essays.

Fawn was only in first grade and hadn't taken any classes in the computer lab yet. It was a magical, mythical realm to her.

Ruthie ordered coffees for her and Buzz and a hot chocolate for Fawn.

"Let it cool off before you take a sip, all right?" Ruthie warned.

"Mom puts milk in to cool it," Fawn said. Ruthie nodded, and dumped in some half-and-half, testing it herself to make sure it wasn't too hot before handing it back to Fawn.

They settled in around a table, and Buzz fired up his laptop, which was covered with stickers of aliens and UFO organizations. He typed for a minute and scowled at the screen. Fawn pulled her chair around for a closer look.

"Do you have games on there?" she asked.

"Tons," Buzz said.

"Can you teach me to play one? Please?"

Buzz smiled. "Later. I promise."

Fawn nodded excitedly and took a sip of hot chocolate, not taking her eyes off the screen. Buzz kept typing, fingers clicking on the keyboard.

"No listing for them in Woodhaven, but I get, like, a zillion hits for Thomas and Bridget O'Rourkes all over the country. We've got doctors, actors, you name it. Picking the two of them out from all these names would be like finding a needle in a haystack." He took a sip of coffee, then typed some more. "But it just so happens that there *are* two O'Rourkes listed here in town, William and Candace. Don't know if they're related to our couple, but I got their addresses and phone numbers. At this point, I'd say they're our best lead."

"Let's go," Ruthie said, hopeful once more.

"I thought I was gonna try a computer game," Fawn said, her face serious.

"When we get back to Vermont," Buzz said. "Right now, we're going to go check out these addresses."

"Because maybe the people can help us find Mom?" Fawn said.

"That's what we're hoping," Ruthie told her. "Slip your coat back on and grab your cocoa."

Buzz jotted down the addresses and closed up his laptop, and they carried their drinks to the truck.

Back on Main Street, waiting at the next traffic light, Ruthie studied the landscape of stores and restaurants in a strip mall up ahead: Woodhaven Liquors, Donny's New York Style Pizza, Pink Flamingo Gifts. There, at the end of the strip, was a closed business with boarded-up windows and a FOR RENT sign out front.

She blinked, bit her tongue to make sure she was awake and not dreaming.

"Stop!" Ruthie yelled, gesturing wildly. "Pull in there, next driveway on the left."

Buzz turned left, pulling into the strip mall parking lot too fast—Ruthie bumped against Fawn, and Fawn leaned into Buzz. Ruthie's coffee spilled all over her lap.

"What the hell?" Buzz said once he'd stopped the truck, but Ruthie was already hopping out of the cab, heading for the closed shop, the faded red sign drawing her in: FITZGERALD'S BAKERY.

She held her breath as she approached it, walking in slow motion, suddenly unsure if she really wanted to do this. She shuffled like a sleepwalker, half of her brain lost in a dream-state, the other half scrambling to make sense of what she was seeing: could this place really be here, existing in the waking world?

She approached cautiously, heart thumping in her ears. Plywood covered the windows, and newspaper was taped to the inside of the glass front door. But a square had fallen away, and Ruthie pressed her face against the glass, hands cupped around her eyes to keep out the glare.

There it was: the long glass-fronted display case that had held rows of cupcakes, cookies, and pies, now empty except for a broken lightbulb and a few forgotten doilies. Even the black-and-white-checked floor was the same. She could practically smell the yeasty warm fragrance of fresh-baked bread, taste the sugar on her tongue, feel her mother's hand wrapped around hers.

What do you choose, Dove?

"No way!" Buzz had come up behind her and caught her enough by surprise that she jumped in alarm. "Is this the bakery you keep dreaming about?"

Ruthie shook her head. "It can't be," she stammered. "Maybe it's just a coincidence?" The words felt hollow. But some part of her brain, the part that held dearly to all that was rational and made sense, couldn't let her accept the truth.

"Coincidence, hell! How many Fitzgerald's Bakeries can there be? Does it look the same inside?"

"I don't know," she said, turning away, the lie making her throat tight, the truth making her dizzy and disoriented. "Come on, let's go check out those addresses."

As they pulled out of the parking lot, Ruthie's eyes stayed on the boarded-up bakery. She grasped for some kind of explanation, but all that came to mind were the sort of crazy theories Buzz might conjure up—a dream from a past life, a psychic link to some other girl—things there was no way she could ever make herself believe in.

She rested her head against the cool glass of the truck window and closed her eyes, thinking.

How was it possible to dream about an actual, physical place you'd never been to?

And if the bakery was real, did that mean the woman with the cat's-eye glasses was, too?

Katherine

Katherine hurried along the slushy sidewalks, realizing how completely inadequate her uninsulated, smooth-soled city boots were. She should have taken the car. But it hadn't seemed like a long walk, and she'd thought the exercise and fresh air would do her good.

She was on her way to the bookstore. After finishing *Visitors from the Other Side* last night, she'd looked up Sara Harrison Shea on her laptop and learned almost nothing. Her hope was that the local bookstore might have something else by or about her.

Surely it wasn't just a coincidence that Gary had a copy of this book hidden away in his things, or that Sara was from West Hall, the same place he visited the day he died.

And then there was the ring: Auntie's ring. When Katherine read Sara's description of Auntie's bone ring as she sat on the couch yesterday, her heart jackhammered. She looked past the book in her hand to the ring she wore on her own finger, the ring Gary had given her. She turned it around, touched the strange, indiscernible carvings. Auntie's ring. Was it even possible?

First the hidden book, then the ring—she wasn't sure what any of this meant, but she hoped to find some answers at the bookstore.

Katherine's apartment was at the north end of Main Street, just before the juncture with Route 6. Her neighborhood consisted of stately old Victorian homes that had been converted to apartments and offices. She passed a dentist, several lawyers, an environmental consulting company, a bed-and-breakfast, and a funeral home.

Farther down Main Street, she walked by a sporting-goods shop with snowshoes, skis, and parkas in the window. There was an old, faded painted sign on the side of the building, just above a window with bicycles hanging in it: JAMESON'S TACK AND FEED.

Next she came to the old junk shop. No doubt it was full of the kind of sepia-toned portraits of strangers long dead that Gary had loved. It was an obsession she'd never understood.

"Each photo is like a novel I can never open," Gary had explained once. "I can hold it in my hand and only begin to imagine what's inside—the lives these people might have led."

Sometimes, if there was a little clue on the photo—a name, date, or place—he'd try to research it, and when they sat down for dinner at night, he'd tell her and Austin excitedly about Zachary Turner, a cooper in Shrewsbury, Massachusetts, who was killed in the Civil War. Austin would listen intently, asking his father questions as if these were people Gary actually once knew: *Did he have a dog, Papa? What color was his horse?* Gary would make up answers, and by the time dinner was finished, they'd created a whole life for this long-dead stranger: a happy life full of horses and dogs and a wife and children he loved very much.

Feet thoroughly soaked now, Katherine paused to look in the junk-shop window: an antique gramophone, a Flexible Flyer sled, a silver trumpet. A fox stole was wrapped around the shoulders of a battered-looking mannequin. The fox had a sunken face, small, pointed teeth, and two scratched glass eyes that stared out at Katherine and seemed, at once, to know all of her secrets.

The bookstore couldn't be more than half a mile away, but it seemed impossibly far. The cold bit at her face and at her hands in their thin gloves. Her eyes teared up, crusting her lashes with ice. She felt like an Antarctic explorer: Ernest Shackleton, trudging across a bleak frozen landscape.

She got to the bridge over the river and stopped to rest along the sidewalk, hands on the rail, staring down into the brown water, half frozen at the edges. Something moved along the right bank, just below the bridge, a sleek dark shape pulling itself along. A beaver or muskrat, maybe—she didn't know the difference. It humped its way across the ice and dove into the water, then was gone.

Katherine turned from the half-frozen river and forced herself to move forward, shuffling across the bridge, continuing down Main Street, her hands and feet numb now, her whole body hollowed out. She thought of the little brown creature, how surely and smoothly it had entered the water, how it had barely made any ripples. It was perfectly adapted to its environment. She, too, would have to find a way to adapt. To move through this new landscape with smooth ease. It would start, she decided, with a trip to the sporting-goods store for proper boots, coat, hat, and gloves.

She passed a yoga studio, an ice-cream shop, and an out-of-business florist. There were signs taped up in all the shopwindows, on lampposts and bulletin boards, showing a photo of a local girl who had gone missing: sixteen-year-old Willa Luce. Last seen wearing a purple-and-white ski jacket. She left her friend's house on December 5 to walk the half-mile home and was never seen again. Katherine looked at the girl's smiling face—short brown hair, a smattering of freckles, the glint of silver braces on her teeth. Maybe she'd turn up. Maybe she wouldn't. Sometimes bad things—terrible things, even—happened.

At last, she arrived at the bookshop. The bell on the door jingled cheerfully. The store was warm and smelled of old paper and wood. She was instantly comforted. The worn floorboards creaked under her feet. She wiggled her fingers, trying to get feeling back.

She passed the front tables of staff suggestions, bestsellers, and new releases, and made her way toward the counter, where a man with a beard and a green wool vest was typing on a computer. But she stopped when she spotted the poetry section. She and Gary used to read poetry out loud to each other in bed on lazy mornings: Rilke, Frank O'Hara, Baudelaire. *All the great dead men,* Gary called them. He loved poetry and had even written a short verse as part of their wedding vows:

> *I used to worry that I dreamed you to life,*
> *then I'd wake with you beside me, and take your hand,*
> *a pale starfish against the indigo sheets,*
> *and press my lips to it,*

tasting salt water, candy apples, freshly ripened plums.
If you are a dream, my love, then it is a dream
I want to live inside forever.

Katherine. Gary again, his voice just behind her now. She spun, thinking if she was quick enough she might catch a glimpse of him, but there was nothing. Not even a shadow.

There was an old photograph on the wall. She stepped closer and saw that it was a picture of the West Hall Inn, dated 1889 at the bottom, a large brick building with white shutters and an awning. It looked strangely familiar.

"This whole block was once the inn," the bearded bookseller said when he noticed her looking at the picture. "Here, where the bookstore is, was the dining room and bar. The windows are all the originals"—he pointed to the front of the store—"though I'm afraid everything else has changed beyond recognition." Katherine glanced from where he was pointing back to the photo, finding the same details there.

"If there's anything I can help you with, just give a holler," the man said.

"As a matter of fact, there is," she said. She pulled her copy of *Visitors from the Other Side* out of her bag.

"Do you have anything else by her? Or about her?"

He shook his head. "Afraid that's it. Though they say there are missing journal pages out there somewhere." He had a little glimmer in his eye. "She's kind of a local legend, and, like all good legends, you can't believe half of what you hear."

"So she lived here in West Hall?"

"She sure did."

"Does she have family around still?"

He scratched his head, seeming slightly puzzled by the increasing intensity with which she spoke. She was wearing her good coat and boots, but her hands were covered in paint and, she realized now, she'd forgotten to brush her hair. If she wasn't careful, word would spread fast through the small town of the madwoman who'd just moved in.

"No family. All the Harrisons and Sheas died off or moved away years ago."

"So there are really no other books about her?"

He gave her a sympathetic shake of the head. "It's surprising, I know. I mean, her story has all the makings of a blockbuster movie—heartbreak, mystery, the undead, gory murder—but the only folks who ever come around asking more are grad students, people who are into the occult, and the occasional oddball drawn to the case because of all the gruesome details." He eyed her as if trying to decide which category she fell in.

"So what else can you tell me about her?" Sara asked.

"What exactly is it you'd like to know?" He had an odd expression, like he was asking her a trick question.

She thought a minute. What *did* she want to know? Why had she taken the trouble to come out in the cold to learn about a woman she'd never heard of until yesterday?

She had that feeling she got when she was doing her art and suddenly discovered the missing piece that ties everything together: a tingling in the back of her neck, a crazy buzzed-rush of a feeling that spread through her whole body. She didn't understand the role that Sara Harrison Shea, the ring Gary had given her, or the book he had hidden would play, but she knew that this was important, and that she had to give herself over to it and see where it might lead.

"It says in the book there were lost pages, the ones she was working on just before her death. Were they ever found?"

He shook his head. "The truth is, they may not have existed. Sara's niece, Amelia Larkin, contended there were diary pages missing, but she was never able to produce them. Supposedly, she tore Sara's house apart looking for them."

He took off his glasses and gave them a quick polish. "Of course, there are all sorts of rumors about those missing pages and what they contained. Some people claim they've seen the pages, that they were secretly auctioned off for over a million dollars back in the eighties."

Katherine laughed. "Why on earth would anyone pay a million dollars for a few pages from a diary?"

The bookseller gave a sly smile. "You've read the book, haven't you? All that about awakening sleepers? Some people think that Sara

Harrison Shea left very specific instructions for bringing the dead back to life."

"Wow."

"I know. Crazy. But I guess people believe what they want to believe, isn't that right? Anyway, if she did have this knowledge, it certainly didn't do her any good. I guess maybe you can't perform the magic on yourself."

"So her husband murdered her?"

"Well, that's debatable," he said.

"Debatable?" Katherine asked, moving closer to the counter.

"There was never a trial. There was never even much of an investigation. All we've got are a few solid facts, the stories from the people who were around back then passed down to their descendants. There's no paper trail—it's all oral history. What we know is that Martin's brother—the town physician, Lucius Shea—arrived for a scheduled visit that evening. Sara had not been well and had been under his care. When he arrived, he found the door wide open, but there was no sign of either Martin or Sara. He went around back and found them out in the field. Sara was . . ." He hesitated, looked down at the painted wooden floorboards.

Katherine gave him a questioning look.

"Go on," she said. "I'm not squeamish."

He took in a breath. "Her skin had been removed. Martin was beside her, covered in blood, holding a gun, babbling incoherently. Do you know what the last thing he said was? He told his brother it wasn't he who had done this—that it was Gertie."

Katherine felt her jaw drop, then snapped it closed. "The daughter? But she was dead, right?"

"Yes. Absolutely true. *Unless*"—he paused for dramatic effect—"unless you believe the rest of the story Sara tells in her diary, of bringing Gertie back to life." He leaned forward, looking like an excited little boy telling a ghost story. He studied her, searching her face to see if she might possibly believe such a thing.

"Unfortunately, Martin shot himself before anyone could ask any further questions."

Katherine's head was spinning. "What do *you* think?"

The man leaned back and laughed. "Me? I'm just a bookseller

who has a fascination with local history. It's probable that Martin killed his wife. But a lot of people who were around back then, and even people these days, they say different."

"What do they say?"

"They think that there's something out there, in the woods at the edge of town, something evil, something that can't be explained. There have been a lot of stories over the years, folks who've gone missing, people who say they see strange lights or hear crying sounds, tales of a pale figure roaming the woods. When I was a boy, I thought I saw something myself one time: a face peering out at me from a crack between the rocks. But I moved closer and it was gone." He made his eyes dramatically wide and gave a little chuckle. "Have I scared you yet?"

Katherine shook her head.

"Well, then, let me add another layer to the story. A lot of odd things happened in town shortly after Sara was murdered."

"What kind of things?"

"Clarence Bemis, the closest neighbor to the Sheas, he had an entire herd of cattle killed—woke up one morning and found their throats slit. The largest steer, he'd been cut right open and had his heart removed. Then—Martin's brother, Lucius?—he dumped a gallon of kerosene over himself early one Sunday morning, walked right to the center of Main Street, and lit a match."

"I don't understand what—"

"Folks said they saw a woman slip out the back door of his house just before he came out and lit himself on fire. The people who saw her swear it was Sara Harrison Shea."

Katherine gave an involuntary shiver.

"A lot of deaths that year. Freak accidents and illnesses. Children falling under wagon wheels. A fire burned down the general store and killed the shopkeeper and his family. And people kept swearing they saw Sara. Or someone who looked just like her." He smiled at her. "That's West Hall history in a nutshell—a lot of ghost stories and legends, very few solid facts."

Katherine was quiet a minute. She studied a display of large paperback books by the register. *Then and Now: West Hall, Vermont, in Pictures.*

"Is this a book on local history?" she asked, picking up a copy.

"It's put together by the Historical Society, but it's mostly just a collection of photos. You won't find anything about Sara in there."

"I'll take it anyway," she said, thinking it was only right to buy something after taking up so much of the man's time. He rang her up and she paid.

"Thank you," he told her, handing her a paper bag with the book inside.

"No, thank *you*. Really. You've helped a lot."

"Anytime," he said, going back to his computer.

She turned to leave, then stopped. "You don't believe any of it, do you? The things Sara wrote about in her diary?"

He smiled, folded his hands together. "I think people see what they want to see. Sara's story is pretty amazing—everything she went through. But think about it: if you'd lost someone you love, wouldn't you give almost anything to have the chance to see them again?"

The bell on the door jingled as Katherine left the shop and headed for home, her coat done up, her thin scarf pulled so tight it was nearly strangling her.

"I've been hoping I'd see you again!"

Katherine jumped.

It was redheaded Lou Lou from the café next door; she had bounded out of its doors and stood blocking Katherine's path in the sidewalk, her silver-and-turquoise jewelry glinting. "Then I just looked through the window and there you were! I remembered!" she said, wrapping her arms around herself. She'd come out without a coat.

"Remembered?"

"Where I'd seen the woman with the braid before. Like I said, I never forget a face. She's the egg lady!"

"The . . . egg lady?" Katherine repeated.

"Yes. I don't know her name, but she's at the farmers' market every week. Sells those blue and green eggs. Easter-egg chickens—that's what she calls the hens that lay them. She sells other stuff, too, things she knits. Baby booties, socks, hats. I bought a scarf from her once. Tomorrow's Saturday—you go to the farmers' market and you'll see her. You can't miss her, really. She's always wearing a sweater or shawl she's knit in these bright, crazy color combinations. If you don't see her, just ask—everyone knows the egg lady."

Lou Lou slipped back into the café, leaving Katherine standing there, dumbstruck.

The egg lady. Gary met the egg lady. Although it wasn't her true name, it was a way to identify her, and already this woman was taking shape in Katherine's imagination. She turned and practically ran back down the sidewalk, feet slipping, as she raced home.

A doll. She'd make a doll of the woman, the egg lady in miniature—an older woman with gray hair in a braid, wearing a brightly colored hand-knit sweater. She'd crochet a tiny sweater with fine yarn. She had a box of yarn and crochet hooks somewhere.

The *His Final Meal* box was all starting to come together, and Katherine's mind hummed, her fingers twitched. She unlocked the door to her apartment, dumped her purse and the paper bag from the bookstore on the coffee table, peeled off her coat and gloves, headed over to her worktable, and started to cut pieces of wire that would form the armature for the tiny papier-mâché doll. When she was finished with the egg lady, she'd make a little Gary doll and put them sitting across from one another at a table in Lou Lou's.

And maybe, just maybe, if she got down in front of the box, put her ear to the open doorway, and listened, she'd know what they might have said that day—understand what had brought Gary to West Hall.

Ruthie

No one was home at William O'Rourke's house. Ruthie scribbled a note saying she was looking for Thomas and Bridget and left Buzz's cell-phone number at the bottom. She stuck it in the mailbox and climbed back into the truck.

None of them spoke as they followed the GPS directions to Candace's house. They were in a new part of town now, one where the houses were bigger and spread out farther and farther apart. The roads had grander-sounding names: Old Stagecoach Road, Westminster Avenue. There were neighborhood-watch signs, signs reminding you to drive slowly and keep an eye out for children. Tasteful Christmas lights still decorated many of the houses, and there were cheerful snowmen in huge yards.

Candace O'Rourke lived in a large white colonial with black shutters.

"Nice place," Buzz said as he pulled into the long driveway. Ruthie hopped out of the truck and rang the doorbell. It played a little song. The house was silent. She pushed the doorbell again.

Just as Ruthie was about to give up and go back to the truck, the heavy wooden door was opened by a frazzled-looking woman in pink-and-black exercise clothes. She had blond hair that was stylishly cut but flattened on one side. Ruthie decided she must have woken the woman up from an afternoon nap.

"Yes?" the woman said, blinking sleepily at Ruthie.

The entryway behind her was bright and open, with white walls and a terra-cotta-tiled floor. There was a neat row of silver coat-hooks on the left, with a bench below it.

"I'm sorry to bother you, but are you Candace O'Rourke?"

"Yes," she said, looking wary.

"Uh, I know it's probably a long shot, but I'm looking for some other O'Rourkes? Thomas and Bridget? They used to live out on Kendall Lane."

The woman's eyes narrowed. "And you are?" she asked, taking a step back.

"My name's Ruthie. Ruthie Washburne."

Candace stared at Ruthie a moment; then it was as if she suddenly woke up, her whole body coming to life. "Of course!" she said, smiling as if being reunited with a long-lost friend. "Of course you are. And I bet I know just why you've come."

"Why I've come?" Ruthie said.

"Why don't you tell me, dear? In your own words."

Confused, Ruthie fumbled onward. "My parents, they were, um, they must have been friends of Thomas and Bridget. I found some old stuff of theirs with my parents' things, and I thought . . ."

"Come inside," the woman said. "Please."

Ruthie stepped in, and the woman shut the door behind her. It was warm inside and smelled slightly musty.

She led Ruthie through the entryway and into a large, open living room with a leather sofa and two matching chairs. The Christmas tree in the corner, which went nearly up to the ceiling, was covered with glorious blue and silver ornaments. Ruthie had never seen such a beautiful Christmas tree. They'd always cut their own trees from the woods: scraggly evergreens decorated with a hodgepodge of homemade ornaments, strings of popcorn, and paper chains.

Candace O'Rourke took a seat on the huge leather couch and gestured for Ruthie to join her. Ruthie felt like she'd stepped into the middle of a glossy catalogue or house magazine: everything in this room was perfect. A kid lived here—the world's luckiest and neatest kid. Fawn would flip if she could see all the toys: an old-fashioned rocking horse, a wooden kitchen set complete with real metal pots and pans, even a large wooden puppet theater set up in the corner. Everything seemed sleek and clean and organized. Unreal.

"Would you like a drink?" Candace asked. "Or something to eat?"

"No, thank you."

"I've got cookies."

"No, thanks."

Candace stood up. "I'll just go get us some cookies. Maybe some tea. Do you want tea?"

"No, really, I'm good. I don't need anything."

"I'll be right back, then."

Ruthie sat perched on the edge of the couch, listening to Candace's footsteps echo off down the hallway. She waited a minute, then stood up to look around. She went first to the Christmas tree and discovered, on closer inspection, that it was not so perfect after all. It had shed a lot of its needles, and was dry as a bone. Many of the ornaments were broken and had been put back together with tape and rubber bands. And the tree itself, Ruthie noticed now, was off kilter, leaning heavily to the left. The star that had been at the top was stuck in a branch below, like a bird fallen from its nest.

Seeing the tree up close gave Ruthie an uneasy feeling. Then she looked down at the toy kitchen and saw that there, in a tiny pot on the stove, was a real orange, shriveled and covered with mold.

She went over to the puppet theater and looked behind it to see a tangled pile of broken puppets: a king missing his crown, a headless frog, and a naked princess whose face had been colored with blue Magic Marker and who had a pencil jammed into her stomach like a yellow spear.

Ruthie turned and left the living room, heading back down the hall, away from the front door and toward where she guessed the kitchen must be. She heard the sound of cabinet doors being opened and closed. All along the walls of the hallway were picture hooks, but no pictures.

At last, she reached the kitchen, where Candace stood in front of a large gas range. The countertops were granite, the cabinets some dark wood polished to a shine. But something was wrong. There was nothing on the counters—no loaf of bread or bowl of fruit, no coffeemaker or toaster. The cabinets that Candace had left open were nearly empty—some crackers, a can of tuna, a box of Crystal Light.

"I know there are cookies here somewhere. Fig Newtons. They're Luke's favorite."

"Luke?"

"My son," she said, running a hand through her messy hair.

Ruthie thought of the puppet with the pencil through its belly and wasn't sure she wanted to meet the kid who was responsible.

"He's with his father," Candace said, still playing with her hair, wrapping a strand around her index finger and giving it a tug. "We're divorced, you see, and Randall has full custody now. He's . . . Well, never mind about that. Let's sit down, shall we?"

They sat at the large wooden table. It was covered with a film of dust.

"You said your parents were friends with Tom and Bridget?"

"Yeah." Ruthie fiddled with the clasp on her bag, reached in to touch the wallets. "So you know them, right?" Ruthie's heart started to beat faster. "Maybe you can help me? I know it's crazy, but my mom, she kind of . . . vanished."

"Vanished?" Candace bobbed forward.

Ruthie nodded vigorously. "Yeah. And while we were looking through her stuff to try to figure it out, we found these." She pulled out the wallets, handed them over.

Candace took the wallets and opened them up with shaking hands. Her eyes filled with tears.

"I'm sorry. It's just that it's been so long. Tom was—or is—my brother. He and his wife, they disappeared sixteen years ago. Along with their daughter."

"Daughter?" Ruthie's throat tightened.

"Wait here. Just a minute."

Candace hurried from the room, the soles of her running shoes squeaking on the tile floor.

Ruthie's sense of unease grew. A voice in the back of her mind hissed out a warning: *Leave this place. Run.*

She was standing up, hesitating, when Candace came back with a photo in a gold frame. "This is them," she said, thrusting the framed picture at Ruthie.

Ruthie looked down at the now familiar face of Thomas, identical to his driver's-license photo. The air felt thin and strange. The room seemed to get smaller and darker. Ruthie took an extra gulp of air as she stared down at the photo.

Beside Thomas was a woman with tortoiseshell cat's-eye glasses and curly hair.

The woman from Fitzgerald's.

What do you choose, Dove?

Between the couple, a toddler with dark hair and eyes who had her hand clamped around her mother's. She wore a burgundy velvet dress and matching headband. On her wrist was a tiny gold bracelet. Her hair was neat and combed, her cheeks were pink, and she wore a smile that said she was the happiest kid on the planet.

Ruthie couldn't breathe.

"I've gotta go," she whispered, stepping away on shaky legs and running from the kitchen, back down the hall with its empty picture hooks, to the huge paneled wooden front door.

"Wait," Candace shouted after her. "You can't go yet!"

But Ruthie was out the door, jogging to the truck. She hopped in and slammed the door. "Punch it," she said, gasping for breath.

"What happened? Did she know something?" Buzz asked.

"The lady's nuts. She can't help us."

She watched in the rearview mirror as Candace came down the driveway, chased after them on foot, flailing her arms, yelling, "There's something you need to know!"

Ruthie

"What are you even looking for?" Buzz asked.

"I'm not sure exactly," Ruthie told him.

It was just past eight, and they were back at home. Ruthie was tearing through bookcases, drawers, and shelves while Fawn and Buzz watched from the kitchen table, where they'd set themselves up with his laptop. Buzz was teaching Fawn how to play an alien-hunting game. Fawn was a quick learner and was using the arrow keys to guide her own spacecraft through the galaxy, shooting lasers with the SHIFT key.

"Oops! No, Fawn, the green aliens are the good guys. You don't want to shoot them. They're our allies. There's a red one—blast it!"

Ruthie gave Buzz a warm smile. "Thank you," Ruthie mouthed, and Buzz smiled back. She meant it. He'd taken the day off of work to drive her to Connecticut, and now here he was, still hanging out with them, entertaining Fawn.

Ruthie found the family's one photo album and several shoe-boxes full of pictures, and brought them all back to the table.

"Hit F6 and you go to hyperspace," Buzz said.

"What's hyperspace?" Fawn asked.

"It's where you go really fast. You can outrun just about anything."

Ruthie flipped through the album, which began with baby pictures of Fawn, then moved forward: Fawn's first steps, first tricycle, first lost tooth. Mom and Dad were there, too, along with Ruthie, but clearly Fawn was the star of the show. She flipped back to the first page, showing Mom and Dad each holding Fawn as a new-born. She had a red, scrunched face, and her big wise-owl eyes were wide open, taking everything in. And there, in the bottom corner, was Ruthie—a scowling twelve-year-old with one of her mother's famously bad home haircuts.

The only people in the photos were the four of them. Mom and Dad had no living relatives, so there was no grandma's house to go to on Thanksgiving, no cousins to fight with at Christmas.

Ruthie dumped out the shoeboxes.

"Are you looking for pictures of the O'Rourkes?" Buzz asked, looking up from the computer. Fawn kept her eyes on the screen, fingers punching keys.

Ruthie didn't answer. She flipped through photo after photo, pulling many of them from the drugstore envelopes they'd never been taken out of, passing over one blurry shot after another, passing badly framed pictures where the tops of the girls' heads had been cut off. Here were the girls in front of misshapen Christmas trees, playing in the snow, digging in the garden, holding chickens. And some of a younger Ruthie: Here she was at ten, wearing a baseball cap on her first camping trip with Mom and Dad. Modeling a matching set of sweaters with Mom at fourteen. The two of them looked so odd together—Ruthie tall and skinny with dark hair and eyes, her mother short and round with bright-blue eyes and tangled gray hair. Here she was at eight, with the chemistry set she'd begged for at Christmas. Her father was beside her in this one, showing her a picture of the periodic table, explaining how everything on earth, everything in the universe, even—people, starfish, cement, bicycles, and far-off planets—was made up of a combination of these elements.

"Isn't it amazing to think of, Ruthie?" he'd asked.

Ruthie had found the idea that we were only a series of neatly constructed puzzle pieces or building blocks vaguely unsettling—even at eight, she wanted there to be more to it than that.

Ruthie shuffled back through to the earliest photo of herself she could find: standing in the driveway, holding a green stuffed bear. She guessed she was about three in the photo. It was taken in the driveway one spring. There were still clumps of snow clinging to the grass, but Ruthie could see crocuses poking through. She was wearing a stiff-looking dress and a little peacoat, her hair in two neat pigtails.

She remembered the bear suddenly: Piney Boy. He went everywhere with her. What happened to that old bear? Most of her stuffed animals had been passed down to Fawn, but she hadn't seen Piney in ages. Suddenly she missed the stupid bear so much her eyes began to water.

"Buzz?" she said, clearing her throat and rubbing hard at her eyes. "Would you say there are more pictures of you or your sister?"

He seemed puzzled by the question. "Um, Sophie, definitely. She was the first kid, you know. They got pictures of everything she did—like, *every thing*—including her first poop in the big-girl potty. By the time I came along, things like the first poop weren't quite as exciting. There are pictures of me, sure, but not half as many as they took of Sophie."

Ruthie nodded. That's exactly what she'd been thinking.

"Where are your baby pictures?" Fawn asked, looking as owl-eyed as ever as she studied her sister over the top of the computer.

"There aren't any," Ruthie admitted.

Fawn bit her lip. "Oh," she said, the word a disappointed sigh. She went back to looking at the screen, but didn't seem to be playing anymore.

"Maybe they're just in a different place," Buzz suggested.

Ruthie shook her head. "I've never seen any. Once in a while, especially when I was younger, I'd ask, and Mom always said, 'Oh, we've got pictures around here somewhere,' but I never saw one. This photo of me with the bear is the earliest I can find. I'm guessing I'm maybe three years old here."

Ruthie glanced back down at the picture. She was smiling happily into the camera, her right arm wrapped around the bear. Her coat and dress looked clean and new. She longed to travel back in time, to sit down with that little girl and ask for her story. "What do you remember?" she would ask. "Where have you been up until now?"

She closed her eyes, tried to think back to her earliest memories, but came up with nothing new. She remembered riding her bike in the driveway, being chased by one of the roosters, riding in the truck with her dad to the town dump on Saturday mornings. Being warned to stay out of the woods, told that bad things happened to little girls who wandered off and got lost.

And there it was again, the memory of her father finding her out there somewhere, carrying her back home—running down the hill, her face, wet with tears, pressed against the scratchy wool of his coat. "It was just a bad dream," he'd told her later, while her mother soothed her with a cup of herbal tea. "You're safe now."

She looked back at the photos: there she was with her mother in their matching sweaters, her with the chemistry set, her dad showing her the periodic table.

Liars.

Hello?"

"Hi, Ruthie. It's Candace O'Rourke."

Ruthie had put Fawn to bed, and Buzz had gone out to buy them some beer. As soon as he'd pulled away, the phone started to ring. She'd answered quickly, afraid the ringing would wake Fawn.

"You were at my house today," Candace continued when Ruthie stayed quiet, stunned. "With the wallets."

As if Ruthie really needed reminding. She crept outside, easing the front door closed behind her. Cordless phone in hand, she went down the front steps and into the driveway.

"How did you get this number?" Ruthie asked. Their number was unlisted, impossible to find.

"I'm sorry if I did anything to scare you off," Candace said brightly. "I was just so shocked to see the wallets, to hear your story. I'm really glad you answered—there's so much I didn't get a chance to ask you."

The night was cold and clear; the stars were brilliant. Ruthie looked up and saw Orion overhead, remembered her father teaching her to follow the line of stars that made up Orion's belt to find the star Aldebaran, which was the eye of Taurus the bull. Taurus was her father's astrological sign, and though she'd never admit it to anyone, she sometimes imagined it was him up there, looking down on her.

She made out the Big and Little Dippers, the frosty Milky Way stretched out across the middle of the sky.

"Is Alice still missing?" Candace asked.

"Alice?" Ruthie stammered, mind racing.

"Your mother, dear." She spoke slowly, as if Ruthie were a young child. "You said she'd disappeared?"

"But—I didn't tell you her name."

"So she's still gone?" Candace sounded almost hopeful, excited by the prospect.

"I'm going to hang up now," Ruthie said, in full panic mode. "I'm sorry to have bothered you today. I think I made a mistake."

"Oh, it was no mistake," Candace said. "Please don't hang up. There are things I can tell you."

"What things?" Ruthie watched her breath come out in great clouds of steam as she spoke.

"Like about Hannah," Candace said, voice teasing, luring Ruthie in. "My precious girl. There's not a day that's gone by when I haven't thought of her. I know this might sound crazy, but I never believed she was gone. There were times when I could almost feel her out there, waiting to be found. Does that even make sense?"

"Yes," Ruthie found herself saying as she leaned back and looked up at the stars, which made her feel suddenly dizzy. Head spinning, phone clenched in her hand, she thought about chemical elements, pink cupcakes, green bears; about the ways everything was connected. Maybe it wasn't all so random. "Yes."

And then she hung up the phone.

1908

Visitors from the Other Side
The Secret Diary of Sara Harrison Shea

January 25, 1908

Gertie had always loved the closet so. How she enjoyed hiding there, leaping out to surprise me. One time, I discovered her curled up in the back corner, napping on a pile of mending.

"What are you doing in here, love?" I'd asked her.

"I am a bear in a warm cave," she told me. "I am hide-r-nating."

Gertie?" I called to her this morning. "Are you in there?"

I stood before the closet door and knocked gently.

I was still in my nightgown, my bare feet cold on the smooth wooden floor. The sun was just up over the hill, giving the bedroom a soft glow through the window. I caught sight of myself in the mirror atop the dresser. I looked like a madwoman: pale, thin, dark circles under my eyes, tangles in my hair, nightgown tattered and stained.

I held my breath, waiting.

Then Gertie knocked back!

I turned the doorknob, pulling, but she held fast from the other side with a strength that surprised me.

"Won't you please come out and let me see you?"

The door would not budge. There was only a small scuttling sound from inside the closet.

"It's all right. Papa's gone. He went up the hill to hunt."

I knew she would not come out if he was near. Last night, even though I knew she was in there, I obeyed Martin and went back to bed. But I could not sleep. I lay on my side, my eyes fixed on the closet. I saw the door inch open, the glint of an eye looking through the crack. I waved at her in the dark.

Hello, my wave called. *Hello, hello! Welcome back, my dear, sweet girl!*

Martin was up and dressed early.

"It's not even light out," I said when I saw him.

"I'm going to go look for that buck. His tracks are all over the woods. If I can get him, we'll have meat for the rest of the winter. I'll do the chores and head into the woods; then I have some things I need to do in town. I'll be back for supper."

"Do you want breakfast?" I asked, rising out of bed. I thought this would please him—seeing me up and about, offering to cook.

He shook his head. "I'll wrap up some biscuits and salt pork." He limped down the stairs, started a fire, let the dog out, packed up some food, and fetched his gun. At last, the front door opened, then closed.

I watched out the window as he crossed the yard. As soon as he was out of sight, I ran to the closet.

How relieved I was to know for certain that it was not a dream!

I tugged at the door again, but she held tight.

"Fine, darling," I said, stepping back. "We'll just visit like this, then." I settled myself on the floor. "You knock once for yes and twice for no."

But what to ask? There were so many things I longed to know: what she remembered, if she could recall falling, if it had hurt terribly.

Yes and no questions, I reminded myself.

"Are you all right? Are you . . . hurt?"

No answer.

I took a breath. Tried again, deciding not to mention anything about the accident or her final day. There would be time for all of that later.

"May I get you something? Are you . . . are you hungry?"

She knocked once, hard and fast.

"Yes, of course, I'm so sorry, my darling—I'll bring you some food."

I raced down the stairs, quickly gathered a biscuit, jam, and a piece of cheese from the larder. I heated up milk and spooned in honey, just the way she liked. My heart leapt with joy to be preparing food for her once more. I hurried back upstairs, terrified that I would find the closet empty—that I had dreamed it all.

"I'm back," I announced to the closet door. "I'm putting the food right outside the door. Would you like me to go away while you eat?"

One knock.

But, oh, what joy that one knock brought me!

I laid the food down just outside the closet.

"I'll just be out in the hall," I told her, backing away.

I slipped out of the room and closed the bedroom door. Then I held my breath and waited. I picked at the skin around my fingernails, squeezing out tiny drops of blood.

I remembered all the times little Gertie and I had played hide-and-seek around the house and yard. How I would wait like this, eyes clamped shut while I counted out loud to twenty, then called out, "Ready or not, here I come!"

And when I'd find her, I'd take her in my arms and she'd laugh, say, "Aren't I the best hider ever, Mama?"

"Yes, darling. The best ever."

Sometimes the game would start without warning, even when we were in town. We'd be shopping at the general store, and I'd turn, sure she'd just been right behind me, to find her gone. I'd wander the narrow aisles, the wooden floor creaking beneath my feet, searching. I'd look among the shelves of flour, salt, cornmeal, and baking powder. I might find her hiding amid bolts of fabric, behind the barrel of molasses over by the counter, or in the corner near the coal stove, where the old men gathered to warm their hands and talk. I'd search the store, calling Gertie's name, and the other patrons would chuckle—the farmers in their bib overalls, the women who'd stopped in for buttons and thread or a box of soap powder—they were all in on the game, sometimes helping me look, sometimes keeping her hiding place secret by standing right in front of it. Abe Cushing once let her hide behind the counter, under the cash register. He fed her candy from the jars he kept on the counter—bits of licorice, toffee, rock candy—while she waited to be discovered.

But this was a new game we were playing. And I was not yet sure of the rules.

The minutes passed by. I stayed still as a stone, listening.

At last, I heard the squeak of hinges as the closet door opened, the sound of the plate being dragged into the closet. It took all of my will not to open the door and try to catch a glimpse of her. How I longed to set eyes on her again, to prove to myself that she was real!

There was silence for a moment. This was soon followed by the sound of glass smashing. I hurried back into the room just in time to see the closet door slam. The plate had been thrown, its contents strewn across the floor. The glass of milk was shattered.

"I'm so sorry, Gertie," I said, my hand pressed against the door. "But we can try again. We'll find something you like. I'll bake molasses cookies. You'd like that, wouldn't you?"

One weak knock.

I sat back down on the floor amid the collection of rejected food. Spilled milk soaked my dress.

"I'm just so happy you're here. You are here, aren't you?"

One knock.

I laid my hand against the closet door, stroking the wood.

"And you'll stay? You'll stay as long as you can?"

One knock.

I knew what Martin would say if I told him—what anyone in his right mind would say—but I didn't care. I didn't care if I was going mad, or if all of this was a figment of my imagination.

My Gertie was back. Nothing else mattered.

Martin

January 25, 1908

After finishing his chores in the barn, Martin spent the morning hunting in the woods, following the large tracks that seemed to go in circles, taunting him. The hoofprints were a good four inches long—it was a big animal. He never caught sight of the buck. He could almost smell him, though—a deep musky scent carried in the wind. Still, the buck remained out of reach. The whole time he was in the woods, he worried over Sara, and her new belief that Gertie was hiding in the closet. Midday, he went back to the barn to saddle the horse. He glanced at the house, his eyes settling on their bedroom window. He considered checking on Sara, but no, surely she was sleeping. He mustn't disturb her. He mounted the horse and rode into town to see Lucius.

It was nearly three miles to town, but the day was pleasant, and the snow on the roads had been rolled and packed down, making it easy going for the horse. The road was narrow, with woods on either side, chickadees and squirrels calling out from within the branches. A carriage passed, the driver waving. Martin waved back, unsure who the man was—he was wrapped up in a hat and scarf, and Martin didn't recognize him. He passed the Turners' place, the Flints', Lester Jewett's blacksmith shop. He came to the town green, where the gazebo was piled high with snow. He stayed to the left, continuing down Main Street. On the left, across from the green, was the West Hall Inn, run by Carl Gonyea and his wife, Sally. There was a bar downstairs that some of the men in town frequented nightly. It had been a long time since Martin had had the money for that.

Past the inn was Jameson's Tack and Feed. Beside it, Cora Jameson's seamstress shop with an old dress dummy in the window, stabbed full of pins. ALTERATIONS, said the sign. CUSTOM TAILORING. There was a velvet dress with lace trim and tiny mother-of-pearl buttons hanging, the armless sleeves seeming to reach for something just out of grasp. Cora's shop was seldom open, as the poor woman suffered from "ailments." Everyone knew that her only ailment was her taste for whiskey.

Across from the tack-and-feed shop was the general store. William Fleury came out, with his son Jack behind him. Both men had their arms full: rolls of tarpaper, boxes of nails.

"Afternoon, Martin," William called. Martin got off the horse.

"Hello, William, Jack. Looks like you've got a building project."

William nodded. "Wind took one of those old oaks down last night, crushed the corner of the barn."

"Too bad," Martin said. "I'll come by later, see if I can lend a hand."

William shook his head. "No need. The Bemis boys have offered. We'll have it fixed up in no time. How's Sara?" William's eyes were full of concern.

What were people in town saying? Martin could imagine the chain of events: Reverend Ayers telling his wife, Mary, about Sara spitting in his face, Mary telling the ladies in her sewing circle; after that, word would spread like the chatter of grackles.

"She's well, thank you," Martin said. "Quite well." He pictured her last night, on the floor in front of the closet.

It's our Gertie. She's come back to us.

He bit the inside of his cheek, pushed the image away.

William nodded. "Good to see you, Martin," he said. "You take care, now." William and Jack loaded up their wagon, and Martin walked down the street, leading the horse.

"Martin!" a woman's voice called. He turned to see Amelia just coming out of the inn. She was wrapped in a fur coat, her cheeks pink and bright, her eyes sparkling.

"Uncle Martin," she said, kissing his cheek lightly. "I was having lunch with some ladies at the inn and saw you ride by. How is Aunt Sara?"

"Better," he said. "She offered to make me breakfast this morning."

"Oh, that's wonderful!" Amelia said. "I shall pay her a visit soon. Today or tomorrow. Maybe I'll take her out for a bit. Bring her to my house for tea. What do you think?"

Martin nodded. "I think she'd like that very much. It would do her good to get out of the house. I'll tell her you'll come by."

"Yes! Let's make it tomorrow. Tell her I'll come tomorrow. I'll bring her to my house for a luncheon."

Martin nodded, cringing a little. Luncheon was something the wealthy ladies in town did. Ladies with fancy hats and lace handkerchiefs who didn't have cows to milk, bread to bake.

"We'll expect you tomorrow, then," he said, giving her a little bow. She turned and went back down to the inn to rejoin her friends.

Lucius practiced out of an office in his home on Main Street. It was a freshly painted white house with black shutters; a shoveled brick walkway led to the front door, where a sign hung: LUCIUS SHEA, M.D. Martin entered, hung his coat on the rack, and peeked into the front parlor, which had been converted into Lucius's office. The door was open, and Lucius was at the desk, writing. No patient in the room, no one waiting on the chairs in the hall.

"Hello, brother," Martin called.

Lucius looked up, smiled. "Martin! Come on in!"

It was a simple room with a glass-doored cabinet full of supplies: medicines, cotton, jars and bottles, forceps, clamps, wooden tongue depressors. An examination table made of dark wood took up the center of the room. There were shelves full of medical books and more bottles and jars; below these were rows of drawers. On the right side of the room was the large maple desk Lucius worked at. His hair was rumpled, and his eyes were red.

"You look tired," Martin said, sitting down.

"Long night. Bessie Ellison finally had her baby. Breech birth. Damn difficult. They're both fine now, though."

"You should get some rest."

Lucius nodded. "How's Sara?" he asked.

Martin looked down at his hands, fingers knit together tightly. "I'm worried, Lucius," he said. "Very worried."

"Tell me," Lucius said, leaning forward, so that his elbows rested on the desk.

"Last night, I woke up and found her out of bed. She was sitting on the floor in front of the closet. She said . . ." He paused, rubbed his face with his palms. "She said Gertie was in the closet."

Lucius took in a deep breath and exhaled slowly. "And what did you do?"

"I told her to go back to bed."

Lucius was quiet a moment. He stroked his neatly trimmed mustache. "Have you thought any more about the state hospital?"

"She's been through this before. When Charles died. And she came back around."

"I know," Lucius said. "And we're going to hope that she does again. But we need to make a plan for what we'll do if she doesn't come around. If she falls deeper into these morbid fantasies. It's possible that she will get worse, Martin. And it's possible that, if she loses touch with reality completely, she may become dangerous." Lucius stood, went to the wooden drawers, and pulled one open. "I'm going to give you some pills. I want you to grind one up each night and put it in her tea. It'll help her sleep, still her dreams. I'll stop by to see her soon. In the meantime, if she gets worse, you come get me."

Martin nodded.

"I mean it, Martin. Don't think you can do this on your own. Don't think you have to."

Martin arrived home to find Sara working in the kitchen. There was stew simmering, biscuits just out of the oven, and the smell of something sweet—Sara had baked molasses cookies.

"It's nice to see you up," he told her, kissing her cheek. "Supper looks wonderful."

To see her up and cooking—cheeks pink and a little smile on her face—seemed nothing short of miraculous. He wished Lucius were here to see it.

He'd been so worried about her last night. He was sure, in those dark moments, that Sara had slipped away from him completely.

But there *had* been something in that closet, hadn't there? Something scrabbling, trying to get out.

Mice. A squirrel, maybe.

But hadn't he seen the doorknob turn?

A trick of the light, he told himself.

He pushed it all out of his mind. It didn't matter. Sara was back now. Well again. Everything was going to be all right.

"I ran into Amelia in town. She's going to come by tomorrow. She wants to take you to her house for lunch."

"Lovely," Sara said. "That's just lovely."

Martin sat down at the table, put a napkin on his lap, and watched as Sara served him, ladling stew into a bowl, then bringing the biscuits and butter to the table.

There was something odd about Sara's movements: they were quick and jerky, almost puppetlike. She seemed terribly excited, the way she got at holidays. She sat down and began picking at a biscuit, just pulling off flakes of it onto her plate.

"Tell me what our Gertie looked like," Sara said, eyes glimmering in the lamplight.

His skin prickled. "You know what she looked like," he said.

"I don't mean *before*. I mean when you found her at the bottom of the well."

They had not let her see Gertie's body, knowing that she was too fragile, that it would break her into a thousand pieces, never to be put back together again.

"I want to see my little girl!" Sara had cried, but Martin remembered the way she'd clung to Baby Charles, and shook his head.

"No, Sara," he'd told her, voice as firm as he could make it. "It's best if you don't."

"But I need to see her one more time! For God's sake, Martin, you must understand," Sara had begged.

"Sara," Lucius had said, taking her hand firmly in his own. "We want you to remember Gertie the way she was. Not like this. You need to trust us. It's for the best."

Now Martin kept his eyes down on his bowl of stew, as if the image were trapped there. "She looked peaceful. Like Lucius said."

Martin took another spoonful of stew and swallowed.

"Did she have any . . . injuries?"

Martin looked up into Sara's eyes. "Of course she was injured, Sara. She fell fifty feet down a well."

He shut his eyes, pictured Gertie down there, turned on her side, as if she'd just fallen asleep.

Sara nodded, her head bobbing too fast. "But Lucius examined her, didn't he? Did he find anything . . . unusual? Injuries that might not have occurred in the fall?"

Martin looked at her for a long time. "What is it you're asking, Sara?"

She took in a sharp breath, held her head high. "I believe it is possible that Gertie did not fall down that well."

"But, Sara, how do you explain—"

"I believe she may have been murdered."

Martin dropped his spoon, and it clattered to the floor.

"You cannot be serious," he said, once he'd regained his composure.

"Quite serious, Martin."

"And on what basis . . ."

Sara smiled calmly. "Gertie told me," she said.

All the air left his chest, and the room suddenly got dim. Sara seemed far away and small. There she was, across the old pine table from him, an untouched bowl of stew before her. The oil lamp flickered at the center of the table; the fire in the old cast-iron cookstove crackled. The window above the kitchen sink was frost-covered, the night outside blacker than black. He couldn't even see a trace of stars.

Sara's face, pale as the moon, seemed to get smaller still. He reached out for her, his fingertips brushing the edge of the table.

It was as if he were falling, tumbling, spinning, down, down, all the way to the bottom of the well.

Visitors from the Other Side

The Secret Diary of Sara Harrison Shea

January 26, 1908

This morning, I waited until Martin left the house, then hurried to the closet. I knocked on the door—tap, tap, tap—but there was no answer.

"Gertie?" I called out. "It's Mama." Slowly, I turned the knob, which felt cold in my hand. The door creaked open. In the half-light of morning, I saw that she was gone.

I pushed aside my drab dresses, Martin's shirts, but there was no sign of her. No proof that she had ever been there at all.

The closet looked so empty.

"Gertie?" I cried out again. "Where have you gone?"

I searched the house, the barn, the fields and woods. But my Gertie was always so good at hiding, at fitting herself into such tiny, unlikely places, that she really might be anywhere.

Perhaps she is playing a game, I told myself. Hide-and-seek. I kept turning corners, opening doors, looking under furniture, waiting for her to jump out and surprise me.

Boo.

I was hauling everything out of the front-hall closet when Amelia arrived late this morning.

"Aunt Sara," she said, kissing my cheek and glancing at the pile of coats and shoes I'd pulled out. "How delightful to see you up. And you're cleaning?"

"I'm afraid I've lost something," I told her.

"Sometimes things have a way of turning up once we stop looking for them," Amelia said, her eyes dancing with light. "Do you not find that to be true?"

"I suppose you're right."

"Now, you must come to lunch with me! I have a surprise for you—something wonderful. I'll help you put all of this away, and we'll leave at once."

"I don't know," I said. What if my Gertie should return while I was out?

"It'll just be for a couple of hours. I think it'll do you a world of good. Uncle Martin thinks so, too. Though you must promise not to tell him about the surprise—I think he'd be quite upset with me!"

"All right, then," I agreed, reluctant to leave, but curious about the surprise.

The ride into town was pleasant. The sun was out, and Amelia has a lovely new carriage with red leather seats. Amelia fussed over me, making sure my coat was buttoned all the way, covering me up with a blanket as if I were an invalid. She chattered brightly about this and that—girlish gossip I was not listening to. My eyes were fixed on the woods that lined our road, searching for movement in the shadows, some trace of my little Gertie.

"Are you listening, Aunt Sara?"

"Oh yes," I lied. "It's all very lovely."

She gave me an odd look, and I thought that I really must try harder.

*A*melia married Tad Larkin last spring—the son of the mill owner here in West Hall (one of the wealthiest families in town). They live in a big house at the end of Main Street.

When we arrived, we were met by four other ladies, all strangers to me. They were very friendly and enthusiastic. I was quite taken aback. There were a Miss Knapp and Mrs. Cobb from Montpelier, Mrs. Gillespie from Barre, and a very old woman with a birdlike face—Mrs. Willard—but they did not say where she was from. All the women had on lovely dresses and hats trimmed with lace and feathers.

"Amelia has told us so much about you," they chirped as they led me through the parlor, with its ornate furniture and oil paintings on the walls, and into the dining room, where the table with a pressed white tablecloth was all laid out with a fine lunch—little sandwiches cut into triangles, potato salad, pickled beets. The places were set with bone china, crystal glasses full of something that bubbled. The wallpaper was dark blue with flowers that seemed to wink and sparkle.

"She has?" I sat down and began serving myself as food was passed to me, wondering what Amelia had been thinking—how could she imagine I might be up for so much socializing? What I wanted more than anything was to beg to be taken home, to resume my search for Gertie.

"Indeed," said the youngest, Miss Knapp, who couldn't have been much older than eighteen.

I picked up a chicken-salad sandwich, nibbled at the corner. My mouth felt dry, and chewing was difficult. I put down the sandwich, picked up my fork, and tried a bite of the beets; their taste was as sharp and metallic as blood. I felt the eyes of all the women on me. It was simply too much.

"But she's not the only one who has told us things about you," said Mrs. Cobb, pouring tea. She was a plump woman with a ruddy face. "Isn't that right, ladies?" she practically chortled. It was as if they all shared a joke.

They all nodded excitedly.

"I'm afraid I don't understand," I confessed, setting my fork down on the china plate. It made a terrible clanking sound. My hands began to tremble.

It was the old woman, Mrs. Willard, who spoke. She was sitting across from me, staring fixedly at me. "We have a message for you."

"A message?" I asked, dabbing at my lips with a starched napkin. "From whom?"

"From your child," Mrs. Willard said, her dark eyes boring into my own. "Gertie."

"You . . . you've *seen* her?" I asked. Was this where my Gertie had gone? To these ladies? But why?

Mrs. Cobb chuckled, her cheeks growing even more pink.

"Good heavens, no," she said. "The spirits don't manifest themselves to us that way."

"How, then?" I asked.

"Various ways," Amelia said. "We meet once a month and ask any spirits who are present to join us. Sometimes we will request a certain spirit."

"But how do they communicate with you?" I asked.

"Rapping on the table. They can answer questions that way— one knock for yes, two for no."

My throat tightened as I remembered talking with my beloved Gertie this way only yesterday.

"Sometimes they can communicate through Mrs. Willard," Amelia explained. "She's a medium, you see. A very gifted one."

"A medium?" I looked at the old woman, who hadn't taken her eyes off me.

"The dead speak to me. I've been hearing their voices since I was a little girl," she said. Her eyes were so dark, so strangely hypnotic, if I looked into them for too long, I began to feel dizzy.

Parched, I reached for the crystal glass, took a swallow of cloyingly sweet wine.

"The message your Gertie has for you is this," Mrs. Willard said. "She says to tell you the blue dog says hello."

I gasped, put a hand over my mouth.

Mrs. Willard nodded knowingly and continued. "She also says that this thing that you are doing is not right. She doesn't like it at all." Her look turned sharp, almost angry.

I set my glass down carelessly, and it toppled. I stood to blot the spilled wine from the table with my napkin and swayed dizzily, steadying myself on the edge of the table. The room felt dark and airless.

"Aunt Sara, are you all right?" Amelia asked.

"May I have a glass of water?" I asked.

"Yes. Please, sit down. Why, your face has gone white." Amelia hurried over with water, dampened a napkin, and began to dab at my forehead.

"I'm afraid I'm not well," I whispered to her. "Could you please take me home?"

"Of course," Amelia said, helping me to rise and making apologies to the ladies.

Once outside, I took in gulps of cold air until my head felt clearer. The sun was directly overhead, and made the world seem impossibly bright. Amelia helped me into the carriage and laid the blanket over me.

"I'm sorry," she said. "Perhaps it was all too much."

"Perhaps," I told her.

The other luncheon guests crowded together in the open doorway, waving their goodbyes, brows furrowed with concern. As we pulled away and moved down Main Street, I saw other faces watching, too. Abe Cushing peered out from the window of the general store and raised his hand in a wave. Sally Gonyea was wiping down tables in the dining room at the inn. She stopped and watched us pass, her face somber. And across the street, Erwin Jameson watched us from the window of the tack-and-feed store. When he noticed that I saw him, he looked away, pretended to be busy with something near the window.

I know what they are all thinking: *There goes poor Sara Shea. She's no longer in her right mind.*

When we returned home, Amelia insisted on putting me to bed and offered to go find Martin.

"No need," I told her. "I'll just rest awhile. I'm feeling much better, really."

As soon as she left, I jumped out of bed and searched the house again, more frantically than ever.

I kept hearing Mrs. Willard's words: *This thing that you are doing is not right. She doesn't like it at all.*

What had I done wrong? How had I scared my Gertie off?

Unsure of what else to do, I put on my coat and walked through the woods to the old well, but I found no trace of her. It was a miserable sight, looking down into the darkness at the bottom of that circle of stone, like peering down the throat of a hungry giant.

The whole time I was up on the hill, I felt as if I were being watched. As if the trees and rocks themselves had eyes. As if the branches were thin fingers scrabbling against my face, waiting to grab hold of me.

"Gertie?" I cried out from the center of a small clearing just behind the Devil's Hand. "Where are you?"

The great rocks that formed the hand cast shadows over the snow—long, thin shadows that turned the fingers into claws. And there I was, in the middle of them, trapped in their grip.

I heard branches breaking. Footsteps behind me. I held my breath and turned around, arms open wide to catch her, to hold her tight. "Gertie?"

Martin stepped into the clearing. He had a funny worried look in his eyes. He was carrying his rifle. "Gertie's gone, Sara. You simply must accept that." He moved toward me slowly, like I was an animal he was afraid of startling.

"Did you follow me?" I asked, unable to keep the venom from my voice. How dare he?

"I'm worried about you, Sara. You have not been well. You're not . . . yourself."

I laughed. "Not myself?" I tried to recall the Sara I'd been weeks ago, when Gertie was alive. It was true, I had become a different person. The world had shifted. My eyes were open now.

"Let's go back home, get you into bed. I'll get Lucius to come this evening to take a look at you."

He put his arm around me, and I flinched. I flinched at my own husband's touch. He gripped tightly and led me, as if I were an uncooperative horse.

We said nothing as we walked past the Devil's Hand, climbed back down the hill, through the trees and orchard, across the field, and back home. He led me upstairs, to our bedroom.

"I know you haven't been sleeping well at night. A nice rest will do you good," Martin said, his hand clamped tight around my arm. "Perhaps your trip into town for lunch with Amelia was too much for you."

As we entered the bedroom, we saw it.

Martin froze, his fingers digging into my arm. I gasped, childish and fearful.

The closet door stood open. There were piles of clothing strewn all around the room, as if a great storm had passed through. A closer look showed that it was all Martin's clothing. And it had been torn apart, each garment sliced and ruined. Martin's eyes were huge, furious, and disbelieving. I watched as he leaned down to pick up the sleeve of his good white Sunday shirt, clutching it so hard his hand trembled.

"Why would you do this, Sara?"

And I saw what I had become to him: a madwoman, capable of furious destruction.

"It wasn't me," I cried. My eyes searched the closet, finding it empty.

I turned toward the bed, thinking to look under it. There, amid the remains of Martin's ruined overalls, was a note written in childish scrawl:

Ask Him What He berryed in the field.

I picked up the paper, holding it gently, as if it were a wounded butterfly. Martin snatched it from my hand and read it, his face bone white.

"The ring," he stammered, looking at me over the top of the paper. "Just like you told me to."

But there was a little twitch I'd seen before. The same barely recognizable flinch in the muscles around his left eye that he gave after Christmas, when he promised he'd buried the ring back in the field. And here it was again, that little involuntary quiver that told me he was lying.

JANUARY 4

ʒ

Present Day

Katherine

No one knew where the egg lady was.

Katherine walked around the high-school gymnasium several times, but saw no one selling eggs. The wooden floor was covered with rubber mats to protect the surface from wet boots. The gym was horribly crowded, the sound of people talking a deafening buzz in her ears. People in colorful layers jostled her, shouted greetings to one another, hugging and laughing. A whole community connected, and there she was, the stranger in the dark cashmere coat, moving like a shadow among them. She circled the market behind a family—husband, wife, two boys, one of whom looked to be about eight—the age Austin would be if he were alive. The boy begged his father for a cider donut, and his father bought one, then broke it in half, making him share it with his younger brother. The boy scowled beautifully and shoved his half of the donut into his mouth in one glorious bite, letting crumbs dribble down his chin.

Katherine's eye went to the wall of paintings in the left corner, near the double doors in the back of the gym. They were done in vivid colors and were playful, yet haunting. There was a couple dancing on the roof of a barn while a wolf-faced moon stared down at them. Another showed a man with antlers in a rowboat, gazing longingly at the shore. She turned and continued walking around the gym.

A group of teenagers were gathered in front of the back doors, sharing a bag of maple cotton candy and laughing; they all looked nearly identical in their tall boots and bright ski jackets. She passed a wooden-toy maker, a table from a local apiary selling honey and mead, piles of root vegetables and squash, coolers full of hand-stuffed sausage, a display of sweet rolls and breads, and a table of Unitarian Universalists doing a quilt raffle.

The vendors Katherine talked to didn't seem to know a thing about the woman with the braid except that she was the egg lady and she knit beautiful warm socks. Katherine stopped to ask a woman in the corner who was spinning wool into chunky brown yarn.

"Oh, you mean Alice? I don't know where she could be. She's here every week. Never misses a market."

"You don't happen to know her last name, do you?" Katherine asked.

The woman shook her head. "Sorry, I don't. Brenda Pierce, the market manager, would know, but she's gone to Florida to be with her dad for open-heart surgery. Check back next week. I'm sure Alice will be here. I've never known her to miss a market."

Alice," Katherine said, back in her apartment, holding the tiny doll she'd fashioned yesterday from wire and papier-mâché.

"I may not have found you, but at least you have a name now."

She'd given the four-inch-high doll a long gray braid (embroidery floss) and dressed her in tiny blue jeans. She wore a bright sweater that Katherine had crocheted from turquoise and yellow yarn.

Katherine set Alice down in her box and went into the kitchen to find something to eat.

Alice, Alice. Go ask Alice. Alice down the rabbit hole.

Where are you, Alice?

She'd have to wait. She'd go back to the market next week—surely the egg lady would be back by then. If not, she'd talk to the market manager, get Alice's last name, maybe even her phone number, if she got lucky.

She heated up some soup and made a cup of coffee. Outside, the late-afternoon sky darkened, and snow was beginning to fall more steadily.

After finishing her meager meal, Katherine dug around in her purse for her cigarettes, pulled one out, and lit it. She noticed the paper bag under her purse: the book she'd picked up yesterday.

She slid it out and opened it up. The first page showed a map of West Hall in 1850. The page opposite it showed West Hall in the present day. There were a few more streets, new churches and schools, but, really, Katherine was surprised at how little had actually changed. The town green was right where it always was, gazebo in the center.

Gary would have loved this, the maps and photos pulled together to show the history of a town.

She flipped through and found photos of Jameson's Tack and Feed, Cushing's General Store, the West Hall Inn with its stained-glass windows. Next to all of these were photographs of the same buildings in the present day: the sporting-goods store, the antique shop, Lou Lou's Café, the bookstore. It was odd, how recognizable each building was still, though the signs outside had changed, the roads were paved, and there were sidewalks with benches where hitching posts once stood.

Katherine took a drag of her cigarette and continued to page through the book. Here was a team of horses pulling a giant roller to flatten the snow along the roads, and beside it, a present-day picture of the town garage with two huge orange snowplows. Here were two photos that showed different generations of the same family collecting maple sap, one with tin buckets, the other with miles of plastic tubing. Next came a dirty crew of men outside a sawmill that was now a craft gallery; then a sepia-toned photograph of rows of children with serious faces standing in front of a one-room schoolhouse, and beside that a photo of the current school, West Hall Union, a low brick building built in 1979.

She turned the page and came to a photo showing a group of young men and women on a plaid blanket, with a huge rocky outcropping behind them: five stones rising from the earth. *Picnic at the Devil's Hand, June 1898,* read the hand-lettered caption. Beside it, a photo of the same rocks, the woods behind them taller and denser, and without picnickers: *The Devil's Hand today.*

She flipped to the next page. A white farmhouse with a long driveway, a barn behind it, and plowed fields off to the left. In the corner, more hand-lettering: *Harrison Shea house and farm, Beacon Hill Road, 1905.*

Katherine set her cigarette down in the ashtray and reached into her bag again for Gary's copy of *Visitors from the Other Side*. She turned it over to compare the farmhouse Sara stood in front of to the one in the picture from the new book; they were a match.

She looked back down at the book of photographs, her eye on the opposite page: *Harrison Shea house, present day.* The house looked nearly identical: same black shutters, brick chimney, and front steps. The barn still stood, but the fields were overgrown, the woods closer. Just to the left of the driveway, in the front yard, a woman and two girls tended a large vegetable garden. The photo was taken from the road, and it was hard to make out too many details, but the woman, bent over, had a long gray braid and wore a brightly colored shawl.

Katherine's heart pounded. Was her mind playing tricks on her? She blinked and looked over at her worktable, where the Alice doll sat waiting in a tiny version of Lou Lou's Café. Then she turned back to the photo in the book, squinting down, half expecting that the woman with the braid wouldn't be there—that she'd imagined it. But there she was, hunched over next to a little girl in overalls and a taller girl with dark hair. Could this woman between them with her head bent down possibly be Alice, the egg lady?

"Beacon Hill Road," she said out loud, flipping back to the front of the book, where the maps were. There it was. You just had to follow Main Street west out of town, take a right on Lower Road, which took you over the brook, and then the next right was Beacon Hill. On the 1850 map, there was only one farmhouse drawn, though left unlabeled, about halfway down Beacon Hill Road before it intersected with Mountain Road. Just to the north of that single house on Beacon Hill Road was a hill, and at the top of the hill were the words *Devil's Hand.*

She checked the modern map and found Beacon Hill Road in the same place, and there, on the hill beyond, the Devil's Hand. Mountain Road was now Route 6, of course.

It might be a wild leap, but it was something. And, aside from waiting until next week to try the farmers' market again, she really didn't have any other ideas for tracking down the egg lady.

She glanced out the living-room window; it was fully dark now. How was she going to know if it was even the right house? Wouldn't it be better to wait until morning, to do this in the light of day?

No, she decided, reaching for her bag and keys. This was perfect, really. She'd drive out there, and if she found the right house, she'd go and knock on the door, tell them she'd gotten lost in the bad weather, or had had a little car trouble. Find out what she could that way. Maybe it wasn't even Alice's house, but belonged to some other woman with a long gray braid.

One way to find out.

She stood up and went to the closet to get her coat.

Ruthie

It was an uneventful morning, which put Ruthie on edge—
everything felt normal except for the absence of her mother, looming over everything like a hazy film, giving the whole day a blurry,
unreal feeling and a bitter saccharine aftertaste.

It was Saturday, and though Ruthie thought about going to
the farmers' market to sell eggs in her mother's place, she decided
dealing with all the questions she'd get wasn't worth the hundred
or so bucks she'd make. Buzz was working at his uncle's shop and
wouldn't get off until late.

The girls spent the morning puttering around the house, peering anxiously out the windows, Ruthie willing the phone to ring.
Ruthie washed the dishes. Swept the floor. Fed the chickens and
collected eggs. Kept the fire in the woodstove burning. She did all
the things Mom would do, and did them as Mommishly as she knew
how. Fawn followed Ruthie from room to room, never letting her
big sister out of her sight. She hovered right outside the bathroom
door when Ruthie went in to pee.

"I'm not going anywhere, you know," Ruthie told her.

Fawn shrugged, but continued to shadow Ruthie's every move.

At least a dozen times, Ruthie decided she was going to call the
police, but every time, she stopped herself at the last minute. What if
her mother and father *were* involved somehow with the O'Rourkes'
disappearance? What if that crazy lady in Connecticut had already
called the police about Ruthie showing up on her doorstep? And she

would have to tell them about the gun, right? There was no way it was licensed or legal. And Fawn—they would definitely take Fawn away, wouldn't they? No way they'd leave Fawn in this house with illegal guns and no one but Ruthie to care for her. And still she clung to the idea that her mother would just show up, with a perfectly good explanation—"I'm so sorry I worried you, but . . ."—and God, she would be furious if Ruthie had caved and called the police.

Tomorrow morning, Ruthie promised herself. If her mother wasn't home by then, she'd call the police for sure. First thing.

They made a stew with beef from the chest freezer in the basement—Ruthie had been relieved to see there was enough meat in there to last them for months. There were still plenty of potatoes and onions down in the root cellar, too.

But they couldn't go on like this for *months,* could they? As the day crept by, Ruthie allowed herself to wonder what would actually happen to them if Mom never returned. There was nearly two hundred dollars in the coffee can in the basement. Not much, but they wouldn't need much. There was no mortgage on the house—really, they just had to pay for food, utilities, gas for the truck, supplies for the chickens. Ruthie knew she could run the egg business on her own. She had always resented all the work she was forced to do in their huge vegetable garden, but she knew they could get a lot of food out of it—she and Fawn knew how to start seeds in the spring, how to construct a trellis for the peas, when to harvest garlic. Mom had taught both girls to bake bread and can tomatoes and beans. Ruthie could get a part-time job in town. They'd get by. If they had to, they'd find a way.

But they wouldn't have to, would they? Surely this would all be over soon.

The stew simmered on the back of the woodstove, filling the house with a delicious, comforting smell that made Ruthie miss her mother even more.

By midafternoon, Fawn's fever was back. Ruthie gave her more Tylenol and set her up on the couch with her dolls and coloring books.

"How you feeling, Little Deer?"

"Fine," Fawn said, face flushed, hair damp. She had a funny, glazed look in her eyes.

"You just take it easy, okay? No going outside. Try to drink lots, too."

"Mmm-hmm," Fawn said, feeding a sip of imaginary medicine to Mimi, who also had a fever.

"Mimi should take it easy, too," Ruthie said, making the doll a little bed out of a pillow, with a kitchen towel for a blanket. This pleased Fawn, who insisted that Mimi needed a pillow, too, and Ruthie used a ball of her mom's fluffiest yarn to make her one.

Outside, the wind whistled through the trees, pushing the snow in great drifts. Ruthie curled up in the big recliner under one of her mother's bright afghans and read *Visitors from the Other Side*. Sara's book gave Ruthie the creeps, big-time. She kept looking over her shoulder, sure she saw movement in the shadows. What bothered her most was the idea of little sleeper Gertie in what was now her mother's bedroom closet. The same closet her mother had nailed shut.

Toward the end of the book, Sara revealed the origin of the hidey-holes Fawn and Ruthie had found:

> *As a child, I discovered and created dozens of hiding places by loosening bricks and floorboards, making secret compartments behind the walls. There are some hiding places that I am convinced no one could ever find.*

Ruthie glanced over at her sister. She was on the couch, bandaging her doll's leg. Poor Mimi, first a fever, now a broken leg.

"I told you not to go into the woods," Fawn whispered to Mimi. "Bad things happen to little girls who go into the woods."

Fawn looked up, saw Ruthie watching her. "Will you play with me?" Fawn's eyes reflected the firelight from the glass-fronted woodstove.

"Sure," she said, setting down the book. "What do you want to play?"

"Hide-and-seek."

"Can't we play something else? Dolls or cards or something?"

Fawn shook her head, then lifted up Mimi, who shook her head as well, the scratched button eyes looking right at Ruthie.

"Mimi will only play hide-and-seek. She has a new favorite place to hide."

"But last time, I couldn't find you."

"So maybe try harder," Fawn said, grinning impishly.

"Okay," Ruthie sighed, "but if I say I give up, you have to come out. Deal?"

"Deal," Fawn said.

Ruthie covered her eyes and counted out loud. "One, two, three . . ." she shouted, listening closely, trying to hear which way her sister's footsteps went. Down the hall.

She thought of Sara and Gertie playing hide-and-seek here in this house. How good little Gertie was at hiding. And Sara must have been good at hiding, too. At hiding papers, at least.

"Ten, eleven, twelve . . ."

She heard the closet door in the front hall open, then close. But Fawn did stuff like this to fake her out, to lead her the wrong way. She was a clever kid. Too clever sometimes.

"Eighteen, nineteen, twenty. Ready or not, here I come!"

She rose from the couch, listening hard. The fire popped. The cat thumped down the stairs, coming to see what all the noise was about.

"Where'd she go, Roscoe? Did you see her?"

The cat rubbed against Ruthie's leg, gave her a *m-m-mur-r-r-l?*

Trick or not, she went right for the hall closet, pulled the door open, pushed aside the jackets and coats, and pawed through the jumbled pile of boots and shoes on the floor.

"Hmm, not in the hall closet," she said loudly. She turned and looked out the window in the front door. It had gotten dark. She flipped on the light, saw that it was snowing heavily. Ruthie hadn't heard a forecast. Keeping track of the weather had always been her mother's job. Ruthie relied on her each morning to know how cold it was going to be, if it would rain or snow.

"Where, oh, where can my lost little lamb be?" she asked, moving into the living room, the office, then the kitchen. She went to the downstairs bathroom and flipped on the light. The pink tiles glowed as Ruthie pulled back the shower curtain to find the old claw-foot tub empty except for her mother's chamomile shampoo and a lonely yellow rubber duck.

"Not here," she said, making her way to the stairs, tired of the game already. She'd do a quick once-over of the upstairs, then call it off.

She looked halfheartedly through her room, Fawn's room, the upstairs bathroom, announcing her location, wondering aloud where Fawn could be. Finally, she entered her mother's room, though she doubted Fawn would ever hide there. Fawn wasn't under the bed. The only other place in there to hide was the closet. She stood before the door, hesitant. Stupidly, she knocked. Nothing knocked back. She yanked open the door and was grateful to find it empty.

"Fawn?" she called out. "I give up!" She listened. Nothing. She went from room to room again, calling, then headed back down the stairs.

There it was again: the familiar panic. Fawn was missing. Really missing this time. Ruthie should never have agreed to play hide-and-seek again. Not in this house, where Sara Harrison Shea had called her little dead daughter back to her.

"Fawn!" she called, voice edgier now. "If you don't come out right now, I'm never going to play hide-and-seek with you again!"

She was down in the office. Her father had kept it so tidy, the old mahogany desk clear, books carefully arranged on shelves, nothing on the floor but a woven rug. Now that it was her mother's realm, chaos reigned. Papers, books, knitting patterns, poultry catalogues, and mail were piled in stacks on the desk and floor; there were tote bags full of wool and knitting projects in various stages of completion. Ruthie sat down in the chair and reached into one of the bags to pull out the hat her mother had been making when Ruthie last saw her.

It was New Year's Day, and she was sitting on the couch knitting a hat on circular needles, using chunky yarn in bright colors: fuchsia, lemon yellow, and neon blue.

"Where are you off to?" she'd asked when she saw Ruthie head

into the hall and pull on her parka. She didn't stop knitting, the
needles clinking away in her hands while her eyes were on Ruthie.

"Buzz is picking me up. We're going to hang out with some
friends."

The needles continued to move, stitch after stitch in the round.

"Be back before curfew," her mom said, looking back down at
her knitting.

Ruthie hadn't answered. Hadn't even said goodbye. She just
opened the door and headed out into the cold, down the driveway
to the road, to wait for Buzz.

A hand touched her shoulder. She saw it out of the corner of her
eye—a tiny, filthy, flipperlike hand.

She flinched, and spun to see it was just Mimi the doll. Fawn
laughed, hugged Mimi to her chest.

"Jesus, Fawn! Not funny. You were supposed to come out when
I called you," she snapped. "Those are the rules. Now, where were
you?"

"Hiding," Fawn said.

"Show me where," Ruthie said. It was the second time Fawn
had pulled this, and Ruthie wasn't going to let her keep her new
hiding place a secret any longer.

"No way," Fawn said.

"I swear, Fawn, if you don't show me, I will never play hide-
and-seek with you again."

Fawn stared at her for a moment, gauging her sister's sincerity.
She whispered in Mimi's ear, then held the doll's mouth against her
own ear, nodding.

"Okay," she said. "We'll show you."

Fawn led the way across the living room to the front hall and
flung open the closet door.

"But I looked in here!" Ruthie said.

Fawn pushed aside the hanging coats and parkas and pulled out
the winter boots.

"Here," she said, showing the wooden panels that made up the
back wall of the closet. There were four panels, and they looked as
solid as could be. "This one pops out," she explained, working her

small fingers into the groove of the one on the bottom left, wiggling it until it came free.

"Holy shit," Ruthie said. "How did I not know about this?"

She'd opened the closet door just about every day of her life, grabbing jackets and shoes and umbrellas. How many other secret hiding places did she walk past each day without realizing it?

"It goes way back," Fawn said, sticking her head into the deep, shadowy hole.

"Let me see." As Ruthie stepped into the closet, her claustrophobia kicked in right away. Her palms got sweaty, and her heart beat faster. Her mind screamed, *Get yourself out of here—now!*

Ridiculous, she told herself. It was only a closet. The same closet she hung her coat in every day.

"Let's get a flashlight," Ruthie said. Fawn nodded and ran into the kitchen, pleased to be given an important mission. Ruthie heard her pull open a drawer, rummage around, then come thumping back down the hall.

"Here," she said, flashing the beam of light right into Ruthie's eyes.

"Quit that," Ruthie said, squinting. "Hand it over." She took the light and aimed into the darkness.

"Hey, there's something in there, stuffed way back."

It was hard to make out much in the dark, but there, in the back left corner of the secret compartment, was some kind of bundle.

"Huh?" Fawn said, squinting in.

"Can you go see what it is?"

"Sure," Fawn said, crawling into the space and reaching for the bundle. Ruthie, suddenly afraid, wanted to tell her to stop, hold on a minute. Who knew what Fawn might find? After she found the gun and wallets upstairs, anything seemed possible.

"It's a backpack," Fawn called out, pulling it over to Ruthie.

Ruthie reached for one of the straps and dragged it out into the open, relieved to be in the hallway once again. It was black, and heavier than she expected, with several pockets and zippers covering the outside. It wasn't anything either of the girls recognized.

Fawn bit her lip. "What do you think's in it?"

"One way to find out," Ruthie said. She hauled the bag to the living room, set it on the coffee table, and stared at it for a minute, fingers pinching the zipper. Her mind went to all sorts of terrible places when she imagined what might be inside: cocaine, more guns, snuff films, body parts.

She shook herself out like a wet dog, trying to drive all those thoughts away.

It was just a backpack.

She took a deep breath and yanked on the zipper. Fawn turned away.

"It's camera stuff," she reported, relief in her voice. The backpack was divided into small, padded compartments. She started pulling things out of the bag: Nikon digital SLR, three lenses, a light meter, a flash attachment, an extra battery pack, and a collapsible tripod. She'd messed around with Buzz's camera and video equipment enough to know that this was the real deal—expensive stuff.

The only cameras she'd ever seen her parents use were the disposable ones you could get developed at the drugstore.

Fawn wandered off, dragging her doll.

"I think it came from the woods," Fawn whispered to Mimi.

"What's that, Little Deer?" Ruthie asked.

"Nothing. Just talking to Mimi."

Ruthie picked up the Nikon, flipped the switch to ON, and looked at the screen. Nothing happened. She turned the camera in her hands, looking for some other switch, thinking maybe there was a trick to it—she'd have to have Buzz come take a look tomorrow.

"Ruthie?" Fawn said, her face pressed against the living-room window.

"Yeah?"

"There's someone outside. Coming this way."

Ruthie

"He's coming closer."

Fawn's voice was strangely calm and matter-of-fact as she looked out the window—as if they had visitors all the time.

Ruthie hurried over to join her sister at the window, hoping against hope that it might be their mom. She imagined her mother walking through the door, shaking off the snow, and taking the girls in her arms. "I didn't worry you, did I?" Ruthie could almost feel those arms around her, smell the damp wool of her mother's shawl.

Ruthie put her arm around Fawn and squinted out the window, past the mirrored reflection of her and Fawn huddled together.

It was dark now, but Ruthie could make out a figure crossing the snow-covered yard. Whoever it was wore a bulky coat with the hood up and was hunched over a little, maybe from walking into the cold wind, or from the effort of wading through the deep snow. There was a scarf wrapped around his face, which gave him the appearance of being faceless, bandaged like the Invisible Man. Could it be their mother? No. Ruthie was sure she'd recognize her own mother's walk. This person took small, almost cautious steps. Their mother did everything, including walking, with a bustling, determined sureness that Ruthie could sense a mile off.

"Who is it?" Fawn asked.

Ruthie only shook her head.

"And where did he come from?" her little sister asked.

There was no sign of a car. And this person wasn't coming down the driveway—he was coming across the yard. He left a jagged trail through the snow behind him, a trail that seemed to lead out of the woods.

"Don't know," Ruthie mumbled.

Fawn squinted up at her sister, waiting expectantly to be told what they should do. Ruthie felt the overwhelming need to protect her sister. It hit her hard in the sternum: *Save Fawn. Do not let this man near her.*

The stranger had reached the front door. The first knock made Ruthie's heart skip a beat. It was a loud and determined I'm-not-going-away kind of knock.

"Do you want me to get it?" Fawn asked. She was closer to the door.

"No." Ruthie bit her lip. *Think.* What should she do? Her parents had always taught them never to open the door to a stranger. But her parents were gone now—her father dead, her mother missing. And what if this was a stranger with information, some kind of clue about where her mother might have gone?

But why had he come from the woods?

"Are we just gonna ignore him?" Fawn asked, hunkering down low, the way her parents had taught them to do when a stranger came. Ignore it. Stay down so they can't see you. Eventually, they'll go away.

And why, exactly, had her parents encouraged them to hide?

"If you ever see anyone you don't know come out of those woods, you get inside, you lock the door, and you hide," their mother had told them, again and again.

Never open the door. Even if it looks like someone nice, someone harmless, keep the door locked, and hide.

It was as if her mother had been expecting someone all along—someone dangerous and evil.

But the reality was, they'd had few visitors over the years: the occasional Mormon or Jehovah's Witness, census takers, a man checking facts for the town assessor's office.

Ruthie checked her watch. It was nearly six on a Saturday evening. No one with official business would be out now, not in this weather, not without a car.

She thought of *Visitors from the Other Side,* the idea that the dead could be awakened. Absurd, wasn't it?

Maybe that's what the man knocking on their door was— a sleeper from up in the woods. Maybe it was the ghost of Martin Shea, searching for his wife and daughter.

Stop it, Ruthie told herself. *There's no such thing as ghosts or sleepers.*

"Maybe he's lost?" Fawn whispered.

The man knocked harder, louder. Called out, "Hello in there!"

Only it wasn't a man's voice. It was a woman's.

"Ruthie? It's Candace O'Rourke."

"Oh, *shit,*" Ruthie breathed.

"Should I get it?" Fawn asked, moving right up to the door, putting her hand on the deadbolt.

"No," Ruthie whispered harshly. How had Candace found them?

"I think I might have an idea about what happened to your mother. I've come to help you find her."

Before Ruthie could stop her, Fawn undid the deadbolt and yanked open the door.

A gust of cold wind slapped them in the face.

"Hi, Ruthie," Candace said, flipping back her hood and unwrapping the scarf from her face. Her cheeks were bright pink. "It's so good to see you again. May I come in?" Behind the shock of wind, Ruthie caught the scent of expensive perfume, cigarettes, and booze. Without waiting for an answer, Candace crossed the threshold and stepped into the hallway.

She looked down at Fawn, who had scuttled back. "Hello there," Candace said with a huge smile. "What's *your* name?"

Fawn didn't answer. She clutched Mimi tight against her, then slipped away back down the hall.

"Oh, she's *shy!*" Candace said with amusement.

Ruthie shrugged. *Or she's realizing that she just let a crazy person into our house,* she thought.

"It's freezing out there," Candace said, shivering for emphasis. She looked around the hall. "No sign of your mother yet?"

Ruthie stood still, not answering.

"I see there's a truck in the barn. Is that your family's only vehicle?"

Ruthie was determined not to tell this woman anything. Not until she got some answers of her own.

"Where did you come from?" Ruthie asked. "How did you find us?"

Candace only smiled and unzipped her coat.

Ruthie tried again. "You said you had an idea what happened to my mom?"

Candace smiled an all-in-good-time smile and stepped farther inside, moving right past Ruthie. "This is so nice," she said, going straight for the woodstove in the living room, peeling off her gloves to warm her hands. "Really cozy." She looked all around the room. Ruthie tried to imagine how it must appear to someone like Candace—the rough-hewn floorboards, the faded rugs, the beat-up couch and coffee table.

"Look, however you found us, this really isn't a good time," Ruthie said, following her into the living room.

Candace had tracked in snow on her boots, leaving great puddles across the old pine floor. It was a house rule to take your shoes off in the hall. Ruthie's mother would have a conniption if she were here.

"Hello again," Candace said, as Fawn peeked at her from around the corner. "If you don't want to tell me your name, that's okay. But how about your dolly, she must have a name, right?"

Fawn only stared. Her cheeks were flushed from her fever, and she'd been in the same dirty red overalls for days. Her hair was in tangles. Ruthie realized she looked like a feral child, a little girl raised by wolves.

"I have a boy about your age," Candace said. "His name is Luke. Let me guess, you're six, right?"

Fawn gave a tentative nod.

"My Luke—you know what his favorite thing in the world is? He has a stuffed platypus. Can you guess what he named it?"

Fawn shook her head.

"Spike," Candace said, laughing a little.

Fawn laughed, too, stepping into the living room, coming to join Candace and Ruthie near the woodstove.

"Silly, huh?" asked Candace. "Who names a platypus Spike?"

"Where is he now?" Fawn asked. "Luke?"

Candace's smile faded. "He's with his father. We're divorced, you see, and Luke's father, he's one of those men who always get their own way. Luke lives with him now." Candace ran a hand through her hair. "But, with any luck, that will be changing soon. He hasn't heard the last from me. It isn't right, is it, keeping a boy from his own mother?"

Fawn gave her a sympathetic look. "This is Mimi," she said, holding the doll up for inspection. "And my name is Fawn. I'm six and a half."

"Six and a half is very big indeed. I can tell you're a big girl. And very smart. So let me ask you, where do you think your mother has gone?"

Fawn thought a minute. "Away. Far away."

"Fawn," Ruthie interrupted, "why don't you go up to your room?"

"You poor thing," Candace said to Fawn, ignoring Ruthie completely. "It must be hard to have your mother gone like this. You really have no idea where she might be?"

Fawn shook her head, looked down at her doll.

"I know you found Tom and Bridget's wallets somewhere in the house. Tell me, Fawn, did you find anything else with them?"

Fawn's eyes shot up to Ruthie's, her look a question: *Should we tell?*

Ruthie gave the slightest little shake of her head, hoping it was enough. Ruthie didn't know what the hidden wallets and gun meant, but she knew Buzz was right—they made it look like her mother might be involved in something dark, something criminal. She didn't want Candace O'Rourke to know about any of that.

"There was nothing else," Ruthie said, stepping forward.

But Candace continued to ignore Ruthie, keeping her eyes on Fawn.

"Sometimes big brothers and sisters and grown-ups, they don't tell the truth. It doesn't make them bad people—they're just doing what they believe is right. But you, Fawn, you always tell the truth,

I can tell. Was there anything else with the wallets? Any papers? Anything at all?"

"I told you, there was nothing else!" Ruthie had had enough. "I'm sorry, but you need to leave now."

"And *I'm* sorry, Ruthie, but I simply don't believe you," Candace said. She looked up from Fawn finally, and stared coldly at Ruthie.

"Do I need to call the police?" Ruthie asked.

Candace shook her head with evident disappointment. Keeping her eyes on Ruthie, she opened up her coat to reveal a holster strapped to her chest. She pulled a handgun out of it, slowly, almost awkwardly. The gun was smaller and more square than the one they'd found upstairs; this barrel was silver, the grip black. Candace was clearly not a pro at this, more like an actress with a prop she hadn't had much practice with.

"I was hoping it wouldn't come to this," Candace said with a sigh.

Shit.

Ruthie thought again of all her mother's warnings throughout the years—*Never open the door.* She thought of Little Red Riding Hood being tricked by the wolf in Granny's clothes.

Fawn's eyes got huge. "Are you the police?" she asked.

Candace laughed. "Hardly. Look, I really hate guns. I do. And I'd *really* hate to have to use it," she warned, turning to Ruthie, then back to Fawn. "So here's what's going to happen: You two are going to tell me everything you can about your parents and Tom and Bridget O'Rourke. You're going to show me just where you found the wallets and everything else you found with them."

Ruthie looked at Candace and at the gun, trying to keep a rising sense of panic under control. She didn't think Candace would actually shoot them, at least not on purpose. But she was obviously a wacko—who knew what she was capable of? "If you hate guns so much, why did you bring it?" Fawn asked.

"Because I can't leave here without getting what I came for. I really can't. You need to understand that." The gun dangled from her right hand, pointed toward the ground. She plucked at her hair with her left.

"What is it you're looking for?" Ruthie asked.

Candace scowled at Ruthie. "Something Tom and Bridget had, and I think that your mother, wherever she is, has it right now. So I need you to start answering my questions. Okay?"

Neither of them spoke. Fawn looked petrified, and Ruthie's mind wasn't working fast enough. She was too busy staring at the gun.

"Please don't make me point this at either one of you," Candace said, raising the gun, her finger on the trigger. "So are you ready to cooperate? Because, really, I think we all want the same thing, right? We want to find your mother, don't we?"

Fawn moved closer to Ruthie, snuggled right up against her. Candace waved the gun at them, pointing it first at Fawn, then at Ruthie. "Don't we?" she repeated.

"Yes," both girls sang out. "Yes."

"Good." Candace smiled and lowered the gun, looking relieved. "I can see you're two smart girls. And now that we're all on the same side, I think we're really going to get somewhere. I really do."

Katherine

The snow moved in a furious whirlwind around the Jeep, flying through the air in ways Katherine had never seen. It came down from the sky and shot sideways, the wind blasting it against Katherine's windshield and over the towering banks on the side of the road. It was as if nature itself was somehow against her getting to Sara's house.

It was pure stupidity, driving around on such a night, but Katherine had come this far, was already on Beacon Hill Road. She crept along in low gear, clutching the steering wheel, and at last saw the lights of a house down on the right. It was hard to get a good look from the main road in the dark, especially through the blinding snow. Was that the right house? It could be. The driveway was long and hadn't been plowed recently. But the lights burned bright. Behind the house, she saw the dark outline of a barn.

Just turn around and come back tomorrow, in the light of day, for Christ's sake. She tried to reason with herself, to talk some sense.

Katherine continued down the road, searching for another driveway, just in case there was another house. Half a mile later, she came to a pull-off on the right. There was a Blazer with Connecticut plates parked there, and footprints leading up a trail into the woods. That must be the path to the Devil's Hand. It was a hell of a night for a hike. But maybe it was just kids out partying; she imagined them lying on their backs in the snow, passing a joint and a bottle, looking up into the sky, and imagining it was the end of the world. A nuclear winter. Or that they were lost in space, frozen stars falling all around them.

It was something she and Gary might have done back in college—lying in the snow, hand in hand, imagining they were the only two living beings in the universe, astronauts tethered to one another and nothing else.

She did a poorly executed K-turn, nearly getting stuck in a snowbank, then headed back to what must be Sara's house. As she got to the driveway, she leaned forward, squinting through the snow, trying to get a better look, to see more details, but it was no good.

"I'll come back tomorrow," she said aloud, driving on; it was the sensible, grown-up thing to do.

Five hundred feet from the driveway, she pulled over, turned off her headlights, and cut the engine.

Idiot. What do you think you're doing?

She buttoned her coat and jumped out of the Jeep, her feet sinking in the snow. She'd try to get a look in the windows first; then, if she still thought this might be Alice's house, she'd knock on the door and say she was having car trouble and ask to use a phone. She'd tell them she didn't have a cell. She took the cell phone out of her purse and stuck it in the Jeep's glove compartment, happy with herself for thinking of this detail. Then she locked the car with a mechanical chirp and headed back up the road toward the driveway.

No cars passed. There was no sound at all. The muffled silence of the snowy landscape seemed so unnatural, as if the world had been draped in cotton. The only things she heard were the wind and the sound of her own footsteps squeaking through the fluffy snow.

She pressed on, wanting—needing—to get a little closer. To see the house where a woman with a braid and two girls kept a garden. The house where Sara Harrison Shea had called her Gertie back to her.

Katherine trudged down the middle of the driveway, feet pushing through the snow like awkward canoes. The details of the house suddenly emerged from the darkness. This was it! She recognized it from the photos—a small farmhouse with three windows downstairs and three upstairs. A few brick steps leading up to the front door, right in the center of the house. Woodsmoke poured out of the chimney.

She left the driveway and cut across the edge of the yard, staying in shadows. She had a lovely adrenaline buzz—here she was, doing something crazy, something almost criminal—trespassing, spying like a Peeping Tom.

Just one quick look, she promised herself. She imagined peeking in the window, immediately seeing the woman with the braid. Then she'd go straight to the door with her story of car trouble, find out if the woman's name was Alice.

She ran the last few yards, bent over, keeping herself low and under the windows. She got beneath the middle window, the one to the right of the front door, and caught her breath.

Slowly, cautiously, she lifted her head, half imagining she'd look inside and even see Sara in a rocking chair, little Gertie on her lap.

What she saw instead made her clap her hand over her mouth, bite down on the thin, salty leather of her glove.

She was looking into a large living room with wide plank floors and throw rugs in muted earth tones. Against the wall was a large brick hearth with a woodstove burning.

A woman stood in front of it. She had blond hair and wore an ivory-colored sweater. In her right hand, she held a gun. She was waving the weapon at a small girl in red overalls who was clinging to an old rag doll. An older, dark-haired girl stood beside the little girl, her eyes frantic as she nodded in answer to whatever the woman had just said. The girls from the photograph—the ones helping their mother in the garden.

Katherine ducked back down, reached in her purse for her cell phone to call 911, but then remembered she'd left it back in the car.

"Shit!" she hissed in a low whisper.

She couldn't leave these girls. Not like this. She had to do some-. thing.

She had the sudden sense that this was why she'd been led here, why she'd found Sara's book in Gary's toolbox and discovered the photos in the book she'd bought at the store. Why she'd gotten out of the Jeep in the dark blizzard against her better judgment. Some force had drawn her to this place at this time so she could, for the first time in her life maybe, do something truly useful. Something truly great.

She thought of the weeks when she'd sat by Austin's side—holding his hand in the hospital bed, feeding him bites of Jell-O, telling him silly stories—of how powerless she'd been, unable to save him, to stop this terrible thing that was coming. And then there was Gary. Crushed in a car wreck, and she hadn't even been there—hadn't even been given the chance to try to save him. (*Slow down,* she might have said. *The roads are icy.*)

Some things are out of our control. Sometimes terrible things happen and there's not a damn thing we can do to stop them.

But here she was, given a chance to make a difference.

She was going to save those girls.

Ruthie

"Our mom disappeared on New Year's Day. She made dinner, put my sister to bed, made a cup of tea. When I got home later that night, she was gone," Ruthie said.

Candace nodded, slipping the gun back into the holster now that the girls were cooperating.

"Do you know what happened to her?" Fawn asked, looking up at Candace, her huge brown eyes as pleading as Ruthie had ever seen them.

Candace ran a hand through her hair. "I'm not exactly sure, but I might have an idea."

"Please," Ruthie said. "If you know anything, tell us."

Candace smiled. "Don't worry, Ruthie, we're going to find your mother—I'm not leaving here until I do. We need to start with you telling me everything you know about Tom and Bridget."

Ruthie shook her head. "Next to nothing. We'd never heard of them until we found their wallets the other day."

"So your mom never mentioned them?"

"Never," Ruthie said.

"And how did you find the wallets?" Candace asked.

"Just like I told you. We were searching the house, hoping to find some clue about what happened to our mom."

"You never called the police?"

"We thought about it, but no. Not yet. We knew that's not what Mom would want. She hates the cops."

Candace smiled. "Smart woman. So, tell me, where'd you find these wallets?"

Ruthie paused, thinking. "The hall closet. There's a secret compartment behind the back wall." She flashed Fawn a go-along-with-this look.

"Show me," Candace said.

Ruthie led the way to the hall and opened the closet. The back panel was out, resting against the side, where they'd left it.

"Take a look," she said, handing Candace the flashlight to let her see for herself. Candace got down on her hands and knees and shone the beam around in the empty space. Ruthie looked around for something heavy she could hit Candace on the back of the head with while she was in this vulnerable position. All she saw were a couple of flimsy umbrellas. How hard did you have to bean someone to knock them out?

"And there was nothing else back there?" Candace asked, her voice full of suspicion.

"Not a thing," Ruthie said.

Candace came out of the closet, shone the light on Ruthie. "You wouldn't be lying to me, now, would you?"

"Candace, I swear," she said. "All we found was those two wallets sealed up in a Ziploc bag."

"Hey," Candace said, looking around. "Where did your sister go?"

Fawn hadn't followed them to the closet.

Candace stalked back down the hall into the living room, Ruthie following. Fawn wasn't there. Candace hissed out an angry breath.

"Fawn?" Ruthie called. She wouldn't try to escape, would she? Ruthie pictured Fawn running through the snow with a fever, dressed in her overalls and socks, trying to go for help. The nearest neighbors were a couple of miles away, and very few cars ever came down the road this far. Only people going out to the Devil's Hand, and no one would be going there on a night like tonight. Fawn would freeze to death before she could get help.

She thought of little Gertie, wandering off into the woods and falling into the well.

Is that where they'd find Fawn?

Ruthie breathed a sigh of relief when she heard the thump of feet on the stairs and looked over to see Fawn coming down, cradling Mimi the doll.

"You are not to leave my sight," Candace snapped. Her face was quite ruddy now, damp with sweat. "Do you understand?"

Ruthie clasped her hand firmly around Fawn's, determined not to lose her again.

Fawn nodded rapidly. "I just went to get a blanket for Mimi," she said, showing Candace her doll all swaddled in an old baby blanket. "She's sick, you know. She's got a fever. I had to give her medicine. I'm sick, too."

Candace forced a smile, though it was clear her patience was wearing thin. "Sorry to hear that, kiddo. But from now on, you stick with us, okay?"

"I promise," she said, smiling real big. Fawn's smile could melt an iceberg. You just couldn't help smiling back, no matter how mad you were.

Candace rubbed her face, and let her shoulders slump. "Do you have any coffee?"

"Coffee?" Ruthie said. The woman was holding them hostage, and now she wanted refreshments? "Um, sure. I can go put a pot on." This might be her chance—if she could just get into the kitchen alone for a minute, she could call for help, grab a knife . . . something.

"We'll come with you," Candace said, following close behind. "I don't want to lose anyone else tonight."

Candace sat down at the table and watched Ruthie measure and grind the coffee and start the machine. Fawn settled in at her usual place, the chair across from the window, Mimi on her lap.

Ruthie joined the others at the table, sitting beside Fawn. Fawn took Ruthie's hand and held it tight in her own. Fawn's hand was hot. She probably needed Tylenol again.

Candace stared at Ruthie. "When's your birthday?" she asked.

"October thirteenth."

Fawn tugged on Ruthie's hand, guiding it down to her doll, who was resting on Fawn's legs, still all bundled in a thick blanket. Fawn pushed Ruthie's hand against the doll. There was something hard there, under the blankets.

"And how old are you?" Candace asked.

"Nineteen." Ruthie pulled back the blankets slightly, gingerly feeling the outline of the object. She put all her energy into keeping her face blank.

The gun.

Fawn had gotten the gun from its hiding place in their mom's room and wrapped it in the blanket. Ruthie carefully pushed the blanket back into place.

"You're the spitting image of your mother, did you know that?" Candace said to Ruthie.

Fawn laughed and shook her head incredulously. "Ruthie doesn't look *anything* like Mama."

"That's because Alice Washburne is not her mother." Candace let her words drop like bombs, watching their faces as the dust settled.

"The O'Rourkes are my real parents," Ruthie said quietly. It wasn't a question. Her hand was resting on the blanket-covered gun.

She'd known the truth since she first saw the photo at Candace's, hadn't she? Felt it deep down.

It was funny, though—when she was a little kid, she used to have fantasies about Mom and Dad not being her real parents; she'd imagine a rich couple, a king and queen of some far-off country she'd never heard of, coming to claim her as their own and ferry her off into the life she was meant to be leading, a life that didn't involve cleaning out the chicken coop and wearing hand-me-down clothes. But now that she had finally gotten her wish, it didn't feel like a magical new beginning. It felt like a punch in the gut, hard and heavy.

"Like I said, you're a smart girl."

Fawn clutched Ruthie's hand tighter.

"Which makes you . . . my aunt?" Ruthie wasn't sure what else to say. *Pleased to meet you, actual blood relative*—that didn't seem appropriate.

"I don't get it," Fawn whispered, looking from Ruthie to Candace.

"It's confusing, isn't it?" Candace said, giving Fawn a sympathetic look. "To explain, we'd have to go way back, to when Tommy and I were kids. We lived here, in this house. After Sara Harrison Shea died, the house was left to her niece, Amelia Larkin. It stayed in the family. Tommy and I are the great-great-grandchildren of Amelia."

Ruthie took this in. She was a blood relative of Sara Harrison Shea. Whether Sara had been a madwoman or a mystic, there was a piece of her inside Ruthie.

"When we were kids, we found hiding places all over the house—the one in the hall closet, one in our parents' bedroom floor, several here and there behind the walls, and one in the back of one of the kitchen cabinets, right over there," she said, pointing at the cabinet that held the mugs and glasses. "That's where we found the missing pages from Sara Harrison Shea's diary, including instructions for how to make a sleeper walk again. She'd copied them from the letter Auntie had left for her."

"What's a sleeper?" Fawn asked.

Candace's eyes grew big and wolfish. "A dead person brought back to life."

Fawn bit her lip. "But that's not real, right?" She looked at Ruthie.

"Of course not," Ruthie said, but Fawn looked frightened, unconvinced.

"Like aliens?" Fawn asked.

"Yeah, like aliens," Ruthie said, smiling what she hoped was a reassuring smile at Fawn. She turned to Candace. "So you had these missing pages all this time?"

Candace held up her hand. "Not so fast. Let me finish. We had the directions, but there was still a part missing," she explained. "There was a map telling where to go to do the spell, and we couldn't find it anywhere. Our parents had cleared so much out of the house, hauling off box after box to junk shops, wanting to rid themselves of everything associated with crazy Sara. So Tommy and I knew *how* to do it, but not *where* to do it. Sara's papers said there was a portal somewhere close to the house, perhaps even in the house, and that, for the spell to work, you had to go to the portal. But without the map or a description, we were out of luck."

"So what did you do with the pages you'd found?" Ruthie asked.

"We hid them away. Then, when we were adults, Tommy took charge of them. He promised they were worth a great deal of money, even without the map, and once he found a buyer, we would split the profits. He had a friend he'd met in college who dealt in antiquarian books and papers. . . ."

"Our father!" Ruthie said.

"Yes. James Washburne. Tom and Bridget arranged to meet James and his wife, Alice, here at the house one weekend, sixteen years ago. They were going to show them the diary pages and try one more time to find the portal. Then the pages would go up for auction, and we'd all be rich, according to Tommy."

"So what happened?" Ruthie asked.

Candace shook her head, pursed her lips tight. "Tommy and Bridget were killed."

"Killed?" Ruthie gasped. In just a few short minutes, she'd been given new parents, then had them taken away again. "How?"

"Alice and James claimed there was *something* in the woods that got them—a monster of some sort that dragged their bodies off."

Fawn's whole body went rigid.

"There's no such thing as monsters," Ruthie said, taking her little sister's hand firmly in hers and giving it a squeeze.

"I agree completely," Candace said. "In the beginning, I was in such a state of shock that I accepted their story. I wasn't exactly convinced that there was a *monster,* but I thought maybe there had been a terrible accident. But over the years, I've come to see the truth. I can't believe how stupid, how naïve, I was."

"The truth?" Ruthie said.

Candace nodded. "Isn't it obvious? James and Alice murdered my brother and his wife to get the pages. They knew what they were worth and wanted them all for themselves."

Ruthie shook her head vigorously. "My parents aren't killers!" This idea was more absurd to her than the idea of a monster out in the woods.

"Think about it, Ruthie. Couldn't anyone become a killer if the stakes were high enough?" She was silent for several seconds. "If you want proof, you don't have to look far. Here I am, threatening two young girls, one of whom is my long-lost *niece,* with a *gun,* so that I can find those damn missing pages."

"What do you want them so badly for?" Ruthie asked. "You don't actually believe they work, do you?"

Candace laughed. "No. But there are plenty of other people out there who *do* believe. People willing to pay a great deal of money. Money that I, in turn, will pay the fanciest lawyer I can find to get my son back."

Ruthie nodded. It made sense now and worried Ruthie— Candace was clearly an unstable woman with nothing left to lose and everything to gain. "So you really think my mother has these missing diary pages?"

"Yes, I believe so, though your parents always claimed the pages were lost the weekend that Tommy and Bridget were killed. But I've been waiting patiently over the years, sure the pages would surface one day—that your parents would try to sell them. Which is what I think might be happening now. I think that maybe, for some reason, your mother has finally decided the time is right. Maybe she's already sold them. It's possible she took the money and ran."

Fawn shook her head. "She wouldn't leave us."

"Fawn's right," Ruthie said. "She wouldn't. I can believe that if she did have the pages she might try to sell them, but I think if she was doing it, she'd be doing it for us." Ruthie thought of her mother's promise to help with college next year—was this her big plan, to take the one thing of value she had and sell it so Ruthie could go to the school of her choice?

"Maybe you're right." Candace shrugged. "Or maybe your mother tried to sell them and something went wrong. I must admit that, when you showed up at my house and told me she'd disappeared, I was . . . surprised," Candace said, plucking at a strand of her hair. "Alice was very committed to staying here, to raising you as her own child. Both of your parents were. I promised them I'd stay away, would let them raise you, and would never tell you about your real parents. We all decided that was what was best. There was nowhere else for you to go. My husband—my ex-husband—he didn't want an extra mouth to feed, and he just wanted it all to go away. He never . . . approved of how close I was with Tommy, I see that now. And James and Alice wanted to stay on here, to watch over the hill and make sure whatever creature it was they believed lived there wouldn't harm anyone again. They were . . . caught up in the mythology of it all. In Sara and the sleepers. They felt like they'd been led here—like they were part of something bigger than themselves."

Ruthie thought of all the warnings her parents had given her over the years: *Stay out of the woods. It's dangerous up there.*

Was there something up there in those woods?

She remembered the uneasy feeling of being watched she so often had out there; finding her father dead with the ax clenched in his hands; being carried down the hill when she was a little girl, told it was all a bad dream.

Her thoughts were interrupted by a crashing sound from somewhere in the back of the house. Candace pulled out her gun and jumped up so fast she nearly knocked the table over.

"Where'd it come from?" Candace asked, eyes huge and frightened. She held the gun in both hands, pointing up toward the ceiling.

"The bathroom, I think," Ruthie answered.

Candace started to leave the kitchen, then turned back and looked at the girls, who were still in their seats. "Come on," she insisted. "We stay together."

They raced to the bathroom and found the window broken, glass and melting snow covering the tile floor. There were drops of blood splattered here and there. Fawn grabbed Ruthie's hand, held it in a bone-crushing grip, her own small hand hot and surprisingly strong. Her other arm was wrapped tightly around Mimi—still swaddled in the blanket, gun tucked inside.

"Stay behind me," Candace hissed. Slowly, she followed the puddles and drips of blood down the hall and into the living room. Ruthie kept Fawn behind her, listening hard for sounds, but only hearing her own heart pounding. As irrational as it was, one thought kept bubbling its way to the top of her frazzled brain: *It's the monster. The monster is real, and it's here, in the house.*

"Hold it right there," Candace said, raising her gun.

A woman stood, bent over the coffee table, holding in her

hands the Nikon the girls had found in the backpack earlier. She was tall, thin, and very pale, dressed in paint-splattered jeans and an expensive-looking coat. Blood leaked from the thin black glove on her right hand.

"Where did you get this?" she asked, holding out the camera. Her voice was cracked and broken, and her eyes were full of tears. *"Where did you get this?"*

Katherine

"Put the camera down," the blond woman said, her gun aimed right at Katherine. The two girls stood behind her, looking just as frightened as they had when she'd seen them through the window with the woman who was holding the gun.

As soon as she spotted the familiar bag and contents on the coffee table, she'd forgotten everything else—the gun, the girls in danger she was supposed to be saving.

"Is this someone you know?" the blond woman asked the girls.

"No!" said the older girl. "I've never seen her before."

"Maybe she's a sleeper," the smaller girl said, clutching a beat-up rag doll tight.

What was Katherine supposed to say? How could she begin to explain her presence here?

But no. They were the ones with the explaining to do. They had Gary's backpack.

Ask them, Gary whispered in her ear. *Ask them how they got it.*

She clenched the Nikon tighter and waved it in front of them. "This was my husband's. This is all his."

"Put the camera down and step away from the bag," ordered the blond woman, gesturing with her gun. "I'm not going to tell you again."

"My husband's name was Gary," Katherine said to the girls as she set the camera back down on the coffee table, her voice cracking and desperate. "Did you know him? Did he come to your house, maybe?" Both girls shook their heads.

"He's dead," Katherine said, voice shaking. "He was here, in West Hall. Then, on his way home, there was an accident, the roads were icy and . . ." She was unable to go on, her thoughts jumbled, the pain and loss fresh and raw all over again as she looked down at Gary's things.

"I'm sorry," the older girl said.

The woman with the gun looked over at the older girl. "What's the story with the camera stuff, Ruthie?"

"Seriously, I don't know," she said. "We just found it."

"Found it?" Katherine asked.

The woman with the gun made a tsk-tsk sound, tongue against teeth, and shook her head. "These girls seem to have a talent for finding stuff that used to be owned by the dead and the missing," she said. "So where'd you find the bag, girls—was it in the hall closet? Where you just told me there was nothing but the wallets?"

Ruthie shook her head. "It was in my mom's closet. Upstairs. We just found it tonight. I don't know why my mom had it. I tried turning the camera on, but couldn't make it work."

Katherine nodded. "The battery's probably dead."

"Will it still have photos stored?" the blond woman asked. "Could we put new batteries in it to check?"

"We can plug in the charger, get it going, and take a look," Katherine said. "If no one's erased them, it should have the last photos he took on it."

The last photos Gary took. Katherine's hands were trembling.

The woman nodded. "Let's do that. I think we're all a little curious." She kept the gun pointed at Katherine. "I'll take the bag and camera into the kitchen, and we'll get the battery charging. While we're waiting, you can tell us just who you are and how the hell you figured out your dead husband's camera stuff would be in this house."

"I'm not sure where to start," Katherine confessed once they were all at the table. The blond woman had ordered the older girl to get them coffee and now sat with her gun pointed at Katherine. It was all very bizarre, being held at gunpoint while coffee was being served—"Cream or sugar?" the teenaged girl asked politely. It felt like she'd stepped into a scene from some art house film, the kind she and Gary might have gone to see back in college.

"At the beginning," the woman ordered.

"Okay," Katherine said, taking in a breath and trying not to think about the gun pointed at her chest. She began by telling how Gary was killed in a car accident, how she got the last credit-card bill, how that led her to West Hall.

"So you really moved to West Hall just because that was the last place Gary visited?" the older girl—Ruthie—asked, disbelieving. "I mean, no one ever moves to West Hall. Not willingly."

"Don't interrupt her," the blond woman said, then gestured at Katherine with the gun. "Go on," she ordered. "And don't leave anything out. You never know what might be important."

Katherine told them about finding *Visitors from the Other Side* hidden away in Gary's toolbox, and Lou Lou's telling her about Gary's lunch with the egg lady.

"Egg lady?" Now it was the little girl who spoke, her eyes two huge brown saucers. "You mean our mom?"

So she'd been right! These were the daughters of the egg lady. But where was she? And what was her connection to Gary?

"I guess so. Lou Lou didn't know anything about her—just that she sold eggs every Saturday at the farmers' market. I went today looking for her, but she wasn't there. Then I found pictures of your house in a book I picked up at the bookstore."

"That Historical Society book? Oh God, Mom was so pissed that our picture was in there," Ruthie said. "She tried to get them to take it out, but they'd already printed hundreds of copies."

Katherine went on. "When I saw that picture of you three in the garden, I wondered if the gray-haired lady could possibly be the egg lady I've been looking for, so I decided to take a ride out. I parked by the road and came in on foot to get closer. I saw you holding a gun on these girls," she said, eyeing the woman with the gun, "and knew I had to act."

The woman laughed. "You did one hell of a job, lady," she said.

The girls stared at her, wide-eyed. Katherine was sure she saw a trace of disappointment there. *You? You were our last chance! And look what happened.*

"But why would this lady's photographer husband be meeting Mom at Lou Lou's?" asked Ruthie. She rubbed her eyes, which had dark circles beneath them. "And why does Mom have his bag? It doesn't make any sense."

"He had his backpack with him when he left the house the day he was killed," Katherine told them. "It wasn't in the car after the crash. I asked the police and paramedics, but no one remembered seeing it."

There was silence. They all looked down into their cups of untouched coffee. The little girl clutched her bundled doll tight against her chest.

"So the camera will have a record of the last pictures taken?" the woman with the gun asked.

"Yes," Katherine explained. "They'll be stored there. Unless someone wiped it clean."

"Well, let's turn on the camera and check it out," the woman said.

"What is it you think might be on the camera?" Katherine asked.

"I don't know. Maybe a clue about where Alice Washburne has gone and what she's done with the pages."

"Pages?"

"Candace here thinks my mother has some of the missing diary pages of Sara Harrison Shea," Ruthie said. "The written instructions for how to bring the dead back to life."

Katherine replaced the charged batteries and turned the camera on. The others gathered around as she navigated the menu and pulled up photos onto the camera's display screen.

"We're in luck," she said. "No one's deleted them."

She clicked quickly through the saved photos. There were a series of her sitting on Gary's motorcycle, ones taken on their weekend trip to the Adirondacks two weeks before he was killed. She had on jeans and a leather jacket, her hair was pulled back in a loose ponytail, and she looked so happy, smiling at Gary and his camera. She'd held on to the handlebars and pretended to be riding with the wind in her face, singing "Born to Be Wild." Gary had laughed and said, "Be careful. You know I have a thing for biker chicks."

There was one of her in front of the cabin they'd stayed in, and another beside a little roadside shop they'd stopped at, where Gary had bought the box of photos and papers—and the little bone ring he'd given her—for seven dollars. ANTIQUES AND ODDITIES, said the sign.

To new beginnings.

Katherine arrowed through to the next pictures: shadowy photos of pages of tiny, neat cursive.

"What's this?" she asked out loud.

Ruthie squinted down at the camera. "It's a diary entry, I think. Wait, I can zoom in. Look, there's a date: January 31, 1908."

Katherine scanned the first page:

There are doorways, gates, between this world and the world of the spirits. One of these doorways is right here in West Hall.

"Oh my God," Ruthie said, leaning in for a closer look. "I think it's one of the missing diary pages!"

Katherine arrowed through to the next photo. "It's a map of some kind," she said. Crudely drawn, it showed a house, fields, and a path through the woods that wound up a hill and to the Devil's Hand. All around the Devil's Hand was tiny, illegible script. Below, taking up the bottom half of the paper, was another drawing: a network of lines and circles that could have depicted anything—a waterway or paths, perhaps? This, too, was marked with small, impossible-to-read notations.

"Let me see," Candace said, grabbing the camera from her. "It's the map showing the way to the portal! It has to be. Can you make it bigger?"

Katherine shook her head. "That's as big as it gets on the camera. If you have a computer, we could enlarge it, even print things out."

"We don't have a computer," Fawn reported. "Mom doesn't believe in them."

"Jesus *Christ.* Of course she doesn't," Candace muttered. She squinted at the display. "I can't make out the writing," Candace said, "but it looks like the portal is up at the Devil's Hand. But what's this at the bottom?"

"Some kind of blowup or detail of where the actual portal is, maybe?" Ruthie suggested.

"What other pictures are on here?"

Katherine showed her the button that advanced the pictures.

"Looks like more diary pages," Candace said, squinting down at the screen. "Look at this! There's even a picture of the original letter Auntie wrote Sara about the sleepers. But where'd Gary find them?"

"May I?" Katherine asked, taking the camera back. She scanned through the photos. The little black metal box and tintypes were in the background of some of the pictures Gary had taken of the journal entries.

"Two weeks before he was killed, Gary bought a box of old papers and photos at an antique store in the Adirondacks. He collected old photos—he was kind of obsessed with them. I guess it just so happened that pages of the diary were mixed in with the photos he bought that weekend."

"And you never saw them? He never mentioned it?" Ruthie asked.

"No," Katherine said, her mind spinning. "But he started to act odd. Like he was keeping some kind of secret. He was out of the house a lot and had lame excuses for where he'd been. I think . . ." Her voice broke off. "We had a son. Austin. He died two years ago. He was six."

Her hands shook. She held the camera, Gary's camera, tighter.

She remembered Gary holding her while she wept one night, saying, "I'd do anything to have him back. Sell my soul, make a deal with the Devil, but we aren't given chances like that, Katherine. It's not the way the world works."

But what if he was wrong?

Katherine imagined it, Gary discovering these pages, probably thinking they were pure bullshit at first. But then, as he got more deeply into it and did research on Sara Harrison Shea, maybe he started to wonder, *What if . . . ?*

That's what brought him to Vermont. The idea, the hope, that maybe, just maybe, there was a way to bring Austin back.

Sure enough, the next photos on the camera showed the farmhouse, barn, and fields. Then the woods. Close-ups of a path, of gnarled old apple trees, of rocks jutting up into the sky.

"He was here," Ruthie said. "That's the Devil's Hand. It's up on the hill behind our house."

Gary had been here. Had visited this place on the last day of his life. She flipped through the pictures of the rocks quickly.

"Wait," Candace said. "Go back."

She arrowed back through.

"There," Candace said, jabbing her finger at the screen on the back of the camera. "What does that look like to you?"

Katherine stared down. It was a close-up of one of the large finger-shaped rocks that made up the hand formation. Gary had taken the photo in low light, and it was hard to make out what she was seeing.

"There's something there," Ruthie said, pointing to what appeared to be a squarish hole just along the left edge of the finger.

"It's an opening of some kind," Candace agreed. "A cave, maybe? That map at the bottom of the page, it could be tunnels, right?"

"There's no cave up there," Ruthie said, moving closer for a better look. "Not that I ever heard of."

The next set of four pictures were dark and blurry.

"Jesus, did he go down into it?" Candace said. "Is that why the pictures are so dark?"

"I can't tell," Katherine said. "Like I said, with a computer I could play around and enhance them so we could get a better look."

"We don't need a computer," Candace announced. "Our next move is pretty obvious, isn't it?"

They all looked at her, waiting. She still held the gun, but it was down by her side.

"We're going into the woods. If there's some kind of secret door or cave or something back there, we've got to check it out. Who knows, maybe that's where your mother is; if not, maybe we'll find a clue about where to find her. And if we can find her, there's a chance she's still got all the missing pages—not just the ones Tom and I found, but maybe the ones from Gary as well. Then we'll all get what we want, right? I'll get the pages, you girls just may find your mom there, and Katherine will find out what Gary did here in West Hall."

"I don't think—" Ruthie started to say.

Candace cut her off. "You don't have a choice. We're all going."

"But my sister's been sick," Ruthie protested. "She has a fever."

Candace glanced at Fawn. "She looks fine now. You're well enough, aren't you, Fawn? Don't you want to go up into the woods and see if we can find your mom?"

The little girl gave an enthusiastic nod.

"We're not leaving anyone behind," Candace said, looking right at Ruthie.

Katherine knew Candace was right—the answers they were all seeking might well be out there, under those rocks. She thumbed through the last few blurry photos stored on Gary's camera.

"So what are we waiting for?" Candace barked, raising the gun to remind them that she was in charge. "Everyone—coats and boots—let's go! We'll need flashlights, headlamps, whatever you've got. Maybe some rope. And I saw some snowshoes and skis out in the barn—the snow's pretty deep out there. Let's move. And remember, everyone needs to stay where I can see them. No surprises or I start shooting."

Katherine got to the final photo. Ruthie leaned in, pointed. "There's something there."

The picture was dark and blurry, but definitely taken outside. It was focused right at the little hole in the shadows beneath one of the finger rocks.

But this time, there was someone else in the photo. Someone crouched in the opening in the earth beneath the rock.

"What the hell is that?" Candace asked, squinting down.

The figure was small and fuzzy around the edges.

"Why, it looks like a little girl," Katherine said.

1908

ʒ

{ Visitors from the Other Side

The Secret Diary of Sara Harrison Shea }

January 27, 1908

"Where are you going?" Martin asked when he caught me putting on my coat and boots this morning.

"Out walking. I thought the fresh air would do me some good."

He gave me a strange little half-nod. It almost seemed as though
he was frightened of me.

Perhaps it is I who should be frightened of him.

Over and over, I think of the note we found on the bed:

Ask Him What He berryed in the field.

Martin has been acting very odd ever since—he doesn't look me
in the eye and seems to jump at every sound. Last night, he tossed
and turned in bed, finally giving up on sleep and going down to sit
in front of the fire hours before dawn. I heard him down there, getting up from time to time to throw another log on or pace around
the room. At last, as the sun came up, I listened to him feed Shep and
coax the old boy into going out to the barn with him to do chores.

I have been all through the house a thousand times and seen no
sign of Gertie, so I thought it best to resume my search outdoors. I
knew right away where I was heading—to a place I had not visited
since I was a little girl. Still, I knew the way by heart.

The morning was clear and cold. The sun lit up the fields and
woods, making the light snowfall glitter as if the world had been

draped with diamonds overnight. I imagined Gertie out there some-where—a sparkling gem all her own, just waiting to be found.

I pulled my old wool coat around me tighter and made my way across the field and up into the woods on snowshoes. Up and up I climbed, through the orchard with its bent and broken trees, over rocks and fallen trees, past the Devil's Hand, and through the woods to the north on a little path that was all but grown over with brambles and saplings poking their way through the heavy layer of snow. It was the sort of path no one would notice who had not walked it before, as I used to, many times a week. The path wound through the dense woods like a snake. The day warmed. I undid the top button of my coat and stopped to rest, watching a flock of crossbills settled in a nearby hemlock, chattering away as they pulled seeds from cones with their funny little overlapping beaks.

I continued on and at last arrived in the small clearing, which seemed smaller than it did in my memory. And there, in spite of the heavy snow and the years of trees, brambles, and weeds encroaching, I could still make out the outline of the charred remains of a small building on the ground.

Auntie's cabin.

Martin had asked me about Auntie once, shortly after we were married: "Wasn't there a woman who lived with you when you were young? And didn't something happen to her—did she drown?"

"Where did you hear such a thing?" I asked.

"Here and there, from people in town. My own father even mentioned her once, said she lived out in the woods behind your place. He said the women used to climb the hill to buy remedies from her."

"You've been out in those woods, Martin. There's no cabin," I told him, smiling gently, as if at his simplemindedness. "The stories you heard, they're just stories. People in town love their stories, you know that as well as I do. It was just Father, Constance, Jacob, and I. There was no woman in the woods."

The lie caught in my throat and thrashed there some before I swallowed it back down.

There was no woman in the woods.

As if undoing Auntie's existence would be such a simple act.

Martin had accepted it so easily. He never asked about her again.

I kicked at the snow that I knew covered the coals of her old home, remembering how she kept the front door painted green, explaining that only good spirits would enter through a green door. As though you could keep evil at bay so easily.

It was not only the burnt remains of wood and nails and clothing and pots and a bed that I stood over now. Somewhere in all of this were Auntie's remains. That is, if anything was even left of her after all these years—after the animals, the crows, the endless winters followed by summers. Was there a skull, a few teeth? And what was I hoping to find?

The truth was, I had come up the hill hoping to find nothing at all. Because part of me worried that when Martin dug her old ring up, maybe he'd called her spirit back. And I could only imagine how angry, how vengeful, her spirit might be.

Vengeful enough, perhaps, to lure a little girl into the woods and push her down a well.

*M*y mother died only hours after giving birth to me. Auntie was the midwife who helped bring me into the world. She was also there to guide my mother out of it.

My sister, Constance, was twelve then. My brother, Jacob, eight. They told me later that our mother was not fond of Auntie but Father insisted she accept Auntie's help.

"I don't trust her," Mother had confessed to Constance and Jacob.

Father told my older siblings that Mother's suspicions were unfounded.

"Your mother," he informed them, "has a weak constitution. Auntie has helped plenty of women bring healthy babies into this world, and she will help your mother, too." Father thought she needed all the help she could get, particularly since this pregnancy had happened so late in life—my mother was nearly forty. Auntie made her tonics and teas to help with the pregnancy and labor. My mother, Jacob once confessed, believed Auntie was trying to poison her.

"Please," she'd begged her children, "you've got to help me. The woman wants me dead."

"But why would she want that, Mother?" Constance had asked. Constance shared my father's belief that the pregnancy had affected my mother in some profound way, making her distrustful, even slightly mad.

"She has her reasons," Mother had said.

My mother, who spoke fluent French, had her own name for Auntie: La Sorcière—the Witch. Auntie spoke French, too, and Father thought it would be a comfort for my mother to have some-one to converse with her in her native language. But Constance and Jacob reported there had not been much conversation between them, and neither they nor my father knew what words they did speak, in hushed, sometimes ominous tones.

I used to ask Auntie about my mother—questions I could never bring myself to ask Father. What color eyes did she have? What was her voice like? (Brown ringed with gold, said Auntie. And she sang like a lark.) That was the thing about Auntie: she would tell you whatever you wanted to know. She did not believe it necessary to keep things from children. She saw me as her pupil, her protégée, even, and did everything she could to educate me—to teach me to hunt mushrooms, to plant by the moon cycles, to use flowers and bark to stop a fever.

"How did my mother die?" I asked her once. I was seven or eight years old. We were sitting together in her cabin, and she was teaching me how to embroider. I was making a little pillow with a daisy at the center. There was a fire burning in Auntie's potbelly stove, and a pot of venison stew was simmering on top, filling the cabin with a wonderful, homey smell.

"She bled to death," Auntie said without emotion. "Sometimes, after a difficult birth, there is no way to stop the blood."

Some nights, I would dream of my own birth: of little squalling me coming into this world in a sea of blood, of Auntie's strong hands lifting me up and out of it.

Constance was engaged at nineteen, saying yes to a suitor she only half cared for, because she couldn't wait to leave our house.

She never dared say it out loud, but I knew she had come to loathe Auntie. I'd see the way she glared at Auntie, the false smiles she gave when Father was around. I heard her sometimes using the name my mother had: La Sorcière.

Jacob, on the other hand, worshipped Auntie. He went out of his way to please her, did all he could to spend time with her. Auntie taught us both to hunt and trap, how to skin any animal and tan the hide. Jacob took to it, making his own snares and pit traps, carving a hunting bow and arrows, always eager for Auntie's approval.

"Like this, Auntie?" he asked, sliding a chipped stone arrowhead into a straight shaft he'd carved from a beech branch.

"Perfect," she said, patting his shoulder. "That arrow will fly straight into the heart of a buck."

Jacob all but glowed.

She loved us both as one would love her own children.

My mother's sister, Prudence, was still alive then and came to visit us on a regular basis, often bringing gifts: new dresses for Constance and me, pants and a fine coat for Jacob. It was she who started the fuss about Auntie. She and Father would sit together in the kitchen, talking over coffee. I would crouch down in the hallway, eavesdropping, but could only hear snatches of what she'd say to my father: "Not dignified." "Cannot be allowed to continue." "Filthy heathen witch."

It was Prudence who sent Reverend Ayers and some of the men from town to pay my father a visit after years of her own harsh judgments and threats did little to change my father's mind. I don't know what finally pushed her to call in the men, or how she convinced them to come, but I remember their ominous arrival. It was in the heat of July, only months after I'd seen Hester Jameson up by the Devil's Hand.

"Reverend," Father said when he answered the door, "what brings you out this way?" He looked beyond Reverend Ayers and saw the other men: Abe Cushing; Carl Gonyea, who owned the inn; Ben Dimock, who was foreman at the mill; and old Thaddeus Bemis, patriarch of the huge Bemis family.

"We've come to talk with you," Reverend Ayers said.

My father nodded and held the door open. "Come on into the living room. Sara? Go in the kitchen and fetch the brandy and some glasses, will you?"

They settled in the living room in a circle of chairs pulled around the fireplace. Some of the men took out pipes and smoked. I served them brandy. No one spoke.

"Thank you, Sara," my father said. "Now you and Jacob leave us. Go out and do your chores in the barn. When you're through with that, there's wood to stack."

"Yes, sir," I said.

My brother and I headed out to the barn to do chores. Jacob paced back and forth in front of the horse stalls, wringing his hands.

"What do you suppose it's about?" I asked.

"Auntie. They will try to force him to send her away," he told me.

"They cannot!" I exclaimed. "What right do they have?"

"Father depends on the people in town. They buy our vegetables, our milk and eggs. These men, they have power."

I scoffed. "Auntie's powers are greater."

When the men finally filed out of the house, my father was pale and shaken. He said very little. He poured himself another cup of brandy, which he gulped in two great swallows. Then he had a third.

When Auntie came by later with freshly skinned rabbits to make stew for supper, Father met her outside. They did not come in, and spoke in hushed tones. Soon, however, their voices were raised.

"How dare you!" Auntie yelled.

Eventually, Father came back into the house. "I'm sorry," he said to her before he closed and latched the door. The three of us sat in the living room, listening to Auntie.

"Sorry? You are *sorry*? Open the door! We are not finished!"

I rose from my seat to unlatch the door, but Father pulled me back down and held me there, his fingers digging into my arm. Jacob bit his lip and stared down at the floor, tears in his eyes.

"How dare you!" Auntie shrieked as she watched us through the window beside the door. Her face was as serious and angry as I'd ever seen it. "How dare you shun me? You will pay for this, Joseph Harrison," she hissed. "I promise you that, you will pay."

Later that night, after Father had fallen asleep with the empty bottle of brandy, Jacob crept into my room. "I am going to talk to her," he told me. "I will find a way to get her back." The fierce desperation in his eyes suddenly made me understand how deep his love for her was, how much he needed her. We all needed Auntie. I did not believe our family could get by without her.

I sat up late in my bed, waiting for Jacob to return. Eventually, my eyes grew too tired.

I awoke to Father shaking me. Dawn light streamed in through the window. Father reeked of brandy and had tears streaming down his cheeks. "It's Jacob," he said.

"What?" I asked, jumping out of bed. Father didn't answer, but I followed him out of my room, down the stairs, and out the door. My bare feet padded over the damp, dew-soaked grass. I walked in Father's shadow all the way to the barn, terrified.

Jacob was hanging from one of the rafters, a coarse hemp rope tied neatly around his neck.

Father cut him down, held him in his arms, sobbing. And then, in my shock and sorrow, I did the thing I will always wonder if I should have done—I told him the truth.

"He went out to see Auntie last night," I told him.

Father's eyes clouded over with a storm of thickening rage.

He carried Jacob's body into the house and laid him down in his own bed as if Jacob were a little boy again, being tucked in.

Then Father got his gun and a tin of kerosene.

I followed him across the yard and field and into the woods.

"Turn back," he said fiercely over his shoulder. But I did not listen. I walked farther behind, putting more distance between us. We went through the orchard, the trees hanging with unripe apples and pears, misshapen and spotted with blight. Some of the fruit had fallen and lay rotting on the ground, attracting hornets drawn to its sweetness. The blackflies found us when we were past the Devil's Hand, swarming in tiny little clouds. Toadstools sprouted here and there, inky and poisonous. The path bent and turned, moving downhill.

Father reached Auntie's cabin first—a crooked little house she'd built herself out of hand-hewn logs. Smoke came from her metal chimney. Father didn't knock or call out, he simply threw open the door, stepped inside, and slammed it closed. I crouched behind a tree, waiting, my heart beating as fast as a hummingbird's.

There was shouting, the sound of something being thrown. A window broke. Then—a single gunshot.

Father stepped back through Auntie's green door, carrying the kerosene tin. He turned around, lit a match, and threw it over the threshold.

"No!" I cried, jumping out from my hiding place.

The flames leapt and roared. The heat was so intense that I had to move back.

"Auntie!" I screamed, staring into the flames for signs of movement. There was none. But then, from behind the roar of the fire, I heard a voice. It was Auntie, calling my name.

"Sara," she cried. "Sara." I lunged for the cabin, but Father wrapped his arms around me, pinning me against him, my head close enough to his chest so I could hear his heart hammering.

Black soot snowed down on us, covering my hair and night-gown, Father's flannel shirt.

At last, when it was clear that there was no saving anyone, he let me go and I fell to the ground. Father moved in, stood so close to the flames that he soon had blisters on his face and arms. His eyebrows were singed off and never did grow back right. He stood there, staring into the fire, sobbing, howling like a man who had lost everything.

Behind us, I heard the snapping of twigs. I raised my head, turned, and saw Buckshot, covered in ash. He looked at me, his milky-white ghost eye moving uselessly in its socket.

"Buckshot," I called. "Here, boy." But the dog gave a derisive snort and slipped off into the forest.

Martin

January 28, 1908

Martin was slow to get out of bed, dreading the day before him. Sara had spent the past two days searching the house and woods, barely sleeping, and strangely frantic.

"Did you lose something?" Martin had asked her yesterday morning, when she checked the hall closet for what must have been the twentieth time.

"Maybe," she'd told him.

Yesterday afternoon, Martin had gone into town again to talk with Lucius. Lucius insisted on taking Martin for a drink at the inn. They settled in at the bar, and Carl Gonyea served them each an ale.

"Good to see you, Martin," Carl said, giving him a jovial handshake. "How's Sara doing?"

"Well," Martin said through a tight smile. "She's well, thank you."

"A horrible thing to go through, losing a child like that. My heart goes out to both of you."

"Thank you," Martin said, looking down into his ale. Carl gave him a nod and went to tend to something in a back room.

Martin sipped at his pint and took a look around the room. The dining-room-and-bar area was grand and done in dark wood. Martin could see his reflection in the polished counter. The windows facing Main Street had stained-glass panels at the top that sent patches of colored light to flicker on the polished wooden floor. There were half a dozen tables, laid out with white cloths and silverware, but it was between lunch and dinner, so no one was eating. Martin and Lucius were the only two at the bar. Behind it, bottles of liquor stood on shelves, waiting for the end of the day, when men with more money than Martin had would come in and drink from them.

"Tell me, brother," Lucius said. "Tell me the truth about Sara."

Martin leaned over and filled Lucius in on Sara's condition. He spoke in hushed tones, keeping an eye out for Carl.

He didn't know what he would do without Lucius. Lucius was the only person besides Sara whom Martin ever confided in, and now that he felt he was losing Sara, Lucius was all he had. And Lucius was so patient, so wise. He lent Martin strength, and often, although Sara didn't know it, he'd lent Martin money, too. Just a little here and there, to help them during their darkest times. Martin knew Lucius would give them more—he'd offered, more than once—but Martin didn't feel right taking his brother's money.

Though Lucius agreed that it was a good sign to have Sara out of bed and eating again, he said he was concerned that she seemed still to be experiencing delusional thinking.

"I found her in the woods," Martin explained, "calling out to Gertie, as if she thought Gertie was still out there, lost."

Lucius nodded. "Keep a close watch on her, Martin. Someone with Sara's history . . . who has had episodes of madness before . . . such a person is very susceptible to slipping back into it. As I said, she may even become dangerous. We must prepare to admit her to the state hospital if it proves necessary."

Martin had shivered at the idea of Sara's becoming dangerous.

Now, out of bed and dressed at last, Martin padded down the stairs and found Sara in the kitchen with a fresh pot of coffee. She looked thinner than ever, the dark circles under her eyes more pronounced. Had she even come to bed last night? Martin had the feeling she'd been down here, waiting for him, all night.

"Morning," he mumbled, bracing himself for whatever might come next.

"Do you know where the shovel is?" Sara asked. "I couldn't find it in the barn."

"It's there, lined up with the other tools," Martin said, pouring himself a cup of coffee and peering at her through the steam. "Not enough fresh snow to need to shovel, though."

Besides, that was his job. Was she teasing? Mocking him?

"Oh, I'm not going to shovel snow." She had a curious look on her face, like a child up to no good.

Martin took a swallow of bitter coffee.

"What do you need the shovel for, then?"

"Digging." She paused here, watching Martin's reaction.

He didn't want to ask, didn't want to know, but the words bubbled out of him. "Digging what?"

"I'm going to dig up Gertie's body."

He splashed coffee down his front, burning his chest.

"You're going to . . ." His voice sounded shaky, strange to his own ears.

Sara smiled slyly. "Gertie left me another message," she said, pulling a folded piece of paper from her apron and handing it over to Martin. He unfolded it, and there, in shaky, childish writing, was:

Look in the Poket of the dress I was waring.
You will find somthing that beelongs to the 1 that Kilt me.

He swallowed hard, but the knot in his throat stayed there.

He had a flash of Gertie at the bottom of the well, wearing her wool overcoat and blue dress. Heavy wool stockings bunched up on her legs.

When they pulled her from the well, he saw her hair had been cut. No one but Martin noticed. Martin, who'd carried the hank of hair coiled up in the pocket of his coat, buried it in the snow.

"But Gertie wasn't killed, Sara. She fell." He tried to keep his voice calm and level; his best you've-got-to-see-reason tone, like a parent reprimanding a small child.

But hadn't some part of him been wondering all along if it had truly been an accident? How had Gertie's hair been cut? Who hung it up in the barn?

Sara only smiled. "We buried Gertie in the dress she was wearing when they found her in the well. I need to do this, Martin. I need to know. I need to know if it's her."

"Her? Her who?"

"Auntie. Though Auntie died so long ago . . . The spirit of Auntie. I need to know if she killed our little girl."

"You think Gertie was killed by a *spirit*?"

"I don't know!" she said, exasperated. "That's why we have to dig her up. Don't you see?"

She looked at him long and hard, waiting for a response.

"Don't you, Martin? Don't you need to know the truth?"

He stayed silent.

Gertie had been laid to rest in the small family cemetery behind the house. Beside her were the graves of Sara's parents, her brother, Jacob, and Gertie's tiny infant brother.

"Sara, Gertie's been in the ground for two weeks now. Have you thought about the . . . *condition* her body will be in?" It was dreadful to imagine, and he felt cruel bringing it up, but he had to find a way to stop her.

She nodded. "It's only a body. An empty vessel. The little girl I love is out there still, in the beyond."

Martin took in a breath.

Calm. Be calm.

He felt his face and ears burning, his heart hammering away in his chest.

He remembered seeing Sara come out of the barn the day Gertie disappeared. How he had gone in just after and found the fox pelt gone and the hair hanging in its place.

A terrible possibility began to dawn—something that he hadn't allowed himself to believe in, or even to consider, until now.

Could Sara have killed Gertie?

She may even become dangerous.

He looked down at the note scribbled in childish handwriting. He tried to recall his daughter's penmanship, but could not quite picture it. To his eye, the note Sara had produced looked more like the writing of an adult trying to write like a child.

Was this Sara's way of confessing? Did she know there was something of hers tucked in the pocket of poor Gertie's dress?

The room seemed to tilt slightly, and Martin grabbed onto the table to keep his balance.

He looked at Sara, his beautiful Sara, and wanted to weep and scream and beg her not to leave him, beg her to fight against the madness blossoming inside her.

He remembered handing her the Jupiter marble he'd just won from Lucius when they were children—how she'd been so beautifully radiant that he'd given it over without even thinking; he'd have given her anything then, same as he would now.

She was his great adventure; his love for her had taken him places he'd never dreamed of going.

"If you won't help me, I'll do it on my own," Sara told him now, her body rigid, ready for a fight.

"All right," he sighed, knowing he'd lost. It was over. "But we're going to do it properly. I'm going to go into town to get Lucius. He should be here, don't you think?"

Sara nodded. "The sheriff, too. Bring the sheriff."

"Definitely," he promised, standing to go get his coat and hat. "You just sit and wait. A job like this, it isn't a thing any mother should have to do. We'll take care of it when I get back. We'll take care of everything."

He leaned down and kissed her cheek. It felt hot, dry, and papery, not at all like skin—not at all familiar.

Visitors from the Other Side
The Secret Diary of Sara Harrison Shea

January 31, 1908

For the past three days, I have been a prisoner in my own home.

It was quite a scene when Martin and Lucius came back from town and found me waiting with the shovel over Gertie's grave. The air was frigidly cold. My fingers and toes were numb from standing outside, waiting. Still, I kept firm hold of the shovel as the men climbed out of Lucius's carriage and approached. I was standing right over the place we'd buried her, the wooden cross with Gertie's name carved into it teasing, taunting.

"What are you doing, Sara?" Lucius asked, his voice low and soothing, as if he were talking to a small child.

I explained the situation to him as calmly as I was able. Told him about the note, the crucial clue in Gertie's pocket. Surely he would see reason.

"Put the shovel down, Sara," Lucius said, moving toward me.

"We need to dig her up," I repeated.

"We're not going to do that, Sara." He was closer now. I knew he intended to stop me. So I did the only thing I could think of—I raised the shovel and I swung.

Lucius jumped back; the shovel just grazed his coat. Martin was on me, wrenching the tool from my hands.

It took both men to carry me inside.

"We need to see what's in her pocket!" I cried. "Do you not care that our girl was murdered?"

Lucius ripped up a sheet and tied my arms and legs to the bed-posts. Restrained me like a madwoman. And Martin allowed it, assisted him.

Lucius says I am suffering from acute melancholia. He explained that Gertie's death was too much for me to bear and that it has caused me to lose touch with reality. He said that in this state I am a danger to myself and others. I bit my tongue until it bled, knowing that if I argued it would be a further sign of my supposed madness.

"And these ideas that Gertie is visiting, leaving notes for her?" Martin asked, running his hands through his hair.

"Hallucinations. The sick part of her mind compelled her to write the notes almost as if to convince herself. What she needs is rest. Quiet. And she mustn't get any encouragement that these fantasies are real. Frankly, Martin, I think the best place for her at this point would be the state hospital."

Martin pulled Lucius into the hall, spoke in frantic tones. "Please," I heard him say. "A little while longer. She may still come back to us. She may still get well."

Lucius agreed, but only on the condition that I stay under his watchful eye. Now he comes often to check on me and to give me shots that make me want to sleep all day. Martin comes and spoon-feeds me soup and applesauce.

"You'll get well, Sara. You've got to get well. You rest now."

It's all I can do to fight to stay awake. But I know I must. I know that if I sleep I might miss my Gertie if she chooses to return.

Today is the seventh day since her awakening. There are only hours left before she disappears forever. Please, please, I wish and beg, let her return to me!

"How are you feeling?" Lucius asks when he comes up to see me.

"Better," I tell him. "Much better." Then I close my eyes and drift away.

This afternoon, he untied me from the bed.

"You be a good girl, now," he said, "and we won't have to put these back on."

I am expected to stay confined to my room. I am not allowed to have company. Amelia has come visiting, but Martin won't let her upstairs. Lucius says that it would be too much excitement. Martin warns that if I don't show improvement, if I continue to insist that these visitations are real, I will be sent to the State Hospital for the Insane.

"There will be no more talk of messages from the dead. Or of Gertie having been murdered," Martin says.

I nod like a good, obedient wife. Puppet-on-a-string wife.

"And no more writing in that diary," Martin said. "Give it to me." So I handed him my book and my pen. Luckily, I had foreseen this and was holding an out-of-date diary, full of the trivial details of my life before: entries about baking a pound cake, attending a church supper. Martin did not even think to look through it, and tossed it into the fire before my eyes. I made a show of being upset, and Martin, he looked quite pleased with himself for performing this heroic act to help save his mad wife. But there was something frantic about it at the same time. These last few days, there is something in Martin I've never seen before—this sense of desperation. Of panic. I sense that he is trying so hard, with such determination, not to save me, but to keep me from the truth.

What is it that he does not wish me to know?

Is this delusional thinking, as Martin and Lucius would have me believe, or am I the only one who sees things clearly?

The papers and journals containing all my notes and diary entries since the time of Gertie's death have been safely hidden away. I have a distinct advantage over Martin: I grew up in this house. As a child, I discovered and created dozens of hiding places by loosening bricks and floorboards, making secret compartments behind the walls. There are some hiding places that I am convinced no one could ever find. I have craftily hidden all my writing, scattering it among several hidden niches—that way, if he chances upon one, he won't get everything. And now I only write when he is out in the fields, one eye on Martin through the window, one on my diary.

*A*n amazing thing has happened! Just now, this evening, I was pretending to be fast asleep when Martin popped his head in. Afterward I heard him shuffle down the stairs, get his coat, and go out the front door. It was just getting dark—the bedroom full of long shadows; the bed, dresser, and table barely discernible. I imagined he'd gone to feed the animals and shut them in for the night.

I heard a scraping, scuttling sound from the closet. I turned, held my breath, waiting.

Could it be true? Was my beloved girl back?

"Gertie?" I called, sitting up in bed.

Slowly, the closet door creaked open, and from the darkness within, I saw movement. A flash of a pale face and hands moving deeper into the shadows.

"Don't be frightened, darling," I told her. "Please come out." It took all of my will to stay where I was, not to leap from my bed and run to her.

More scuttling, then the sound of quiet footsteps—bare feet padding along the wooden floor—as she moved out of the closet and into the room.

She moved slowly, almost mechanically, with little stops and starts like a steam engine hiccoughing. The gold in her hair shimmered in the darkness. Her breathing was quick and raspy. And there was that smell I recalled from years ago in the woods with Hester Jameson: a greasy, burning sort of odor.

I nearly fainted with joy when Gertie sat down beside me on the bed! There was no lamp lit and the room was dark, but I'd know her shape anywhere, though she was different somehow.

"Am I mad?" I asked, leaning closer, trying to get a better look. I saw her in profile, and her face was slightly turned away from me. "Am I imagining you?"

She shook her head.

"Tell me the truth," I begged her. "Tell me what really happened. How did you end up in that well?" My fingers ached to touch her, to get lost in her golden hair (was it shorter?). But somehow I knew I mustn't. And perhaps (I'll admit it now, to myself) I was a little afraid.

She turned to me, and in the darkness I could see the flash of a toothy smile.

She rose and went to the window, put her two pale hands against the frosty pane of glass.

I stood up and moved to the window beside her, squinted out

into the darkness. There was a crescent moon rising. Martin was coming out of the barn with a shovel in his hand. He glanced up at the house, and I ducked like a child playing hide-and-seek. He must not have seen me, because he kept walking, crossing the yard.

I knew just where he was going.

I turned to Gertie, to ask her what I was supposed to do next, but she was gone. I looked back to the window, and there were the ghostly imprints of her two hands, left behind in the frost.

Martin

Sweat gathered between his shoulder blades as the shovel bit into the crusty snow. He had to dig through eighteen inches before even hitting dirt. He worked as quickly as he could, scooping and dumping.

His bad foot ached in the cold. His breath came out in great pale clouds. The snowy yard looked blue in the dim moonlight.

Faster, Martin. You've got to do this quickly. You mustn't hesitate. You mustn't be a coward.

"I know," he said out loud.

Behind him, the house watched. Sara slept, dreaming her mad dreams. Over to the left, past the barn, he could see the outline of the hill, the tips of the rocks of the Devil's Hand, dark specks against the snow.

He looked back down at the wooden cross he himself had built, her name carefully carved across the top:

GERTRUDE SHEA
1900–1908
BELOVED DAUGHTER

His hands shook. They were greasy with fear-sweat, the shovel slipping.

Faster.

The slanted shadows of the slate gravestones beside hers watched, seemed to shift impatiently in the moonlight: her infant brother, grandfather, grandmother (for whom Gertie was named), and uncle, watching, wondering, *What are you doing to our little Gertie? She's one of us now. She doesn't belong to you.*

For days now, Martin had stared out at little Gertie's grave, knowing what he must do.

He had to find out what was in her pocket.

Sara had been babbling to Lucius, insisting that Gertie was murdered and that there was proof in the pocket of the dress she'd been buried in, talking nonsense about ghosts and spirits. Who else might she tell, given the chance? How long until someone listened to her and realized that, behind the madness, there might be a horrible, hidden truth? Until Sara was accused of murder? He needed to see what, if anything, was in little Gertie's pocket.

Martin gripped the shovel tighter. The soil was strangely loose and soft under the blanket of snow. The shovel moved through it like a warm knife through butter. It shouldn't be this easy, but it was.

Two weeks ago, he'd lit a fire to thaw the ground enough to dig a hole. He'd stood all day—a father in mourning—feeding it scraps of wood, cut-up deadfalls from the orchard. Shapes had leapt out of the flames at him, taunting: the well, the fox, Gertie's hair hanging from a nail. He threw in one branch after another, trying to feed the hungry flames, trying to burn away the pictures he saw there.

The soil over the grave was still dark with ashes and lumps of charcoal.

How deep down was she? Six feet? Seven?

A foot for each year of her life.

He thought of the warning he'd given Sara days ago: *Have you thought about the . . . condition her body will be in?*

Oh yes. Martin had thought about it. Dreamed about it. Gertie looking up at him, flesh falling away from bones, little teeth still pearly white, mouth open as she breathed the words *Why? Why, Daddy? Why?*

"No choice," Martin said out loud. He redoubled his efforts, digging faster, harder. The pile beside the grave began to grow.

And what was it he hoped to accomplish? If he dug her up, found something of Sara's in her pocket, what would he do?

Hide it? Protect his wife?

Or would he show it to the sheriff, have Sara locked away for good?

Mad or not, Sara was all he had left.

For weeks now, he'd been going over that day in his mind, trying to remember every detail: the fox, the trail of blood through the snow. Had he heard Gertie call him? Had he heard anything at all? Had there been someone else out there in the woods? There was the old woman, but no—that had only been a tree.

Part of him refused to believe that Sara was capable of hurting Gertie, not even in a spell of madness. Gertie was everything to Sara.

His shovel made a clunking sound as it hit wood: the top of Gertie's coffin. The coffin that he and Lucius had made from pine boards he'd been saving to build a new chicken coop in the spring.

"What are you doing, Martin?"

Martin spun. Sara was behind him, shouldering his Winchester rifle, aiming for his chest.

She shook her head, clicked her tongue. She was wearing her nightgown, but had pulled on her overcoat and boots.

He froze, shovel in hand. "Sara," he stammered. "I thought . . . you're supposed to be resting."

"Oh yes. Poor, ill Sara, with her cracked mind, needs her rest, doesn't she? If not, we'll tie her to the bedposts again." She grimaced.

"I . . ." He hesitated, unable to say the words. *I'm sorry. So sorry for all of this.*

"What is it you're looking for, Martin? What do you think is in Gertie's pocket?"

He looked down at the rough wood. "I have no idea."

She grinned, kept the rifle pointed at his chest. "Well, then, let's find out, shall we? Keep digging, Martin. Let us open the coffin and see what we find."

He carefully cleared away the rest of the dirt, brought the lantern close to the edge of the hole, and jumped down into it. Feet straddling the small coffin, he took out his hammer to pry the lid off. But the nails slipped easily out of their holes. His hands trembled so hard that he dropped the hammer before grasping the wooden edges of the top and pulling.

What he saw made him cry out like a little boy. He went cold from the inside out.

Empty. The coffin was empty.

What had Sara done?

Sara smiled down at him, moving her head from side to side like a snake. Her skin glowed in the moonlight, as if she were made of alabaster.

"You see, that's the problem, Martin. If you want to look in Gertie's pocket, you're looking in the wrong place." Holding the rifle in her right hand, she displayed her left, fingers spread. There, above her wedding ring, was the little bone ring. She used her thumb to turn it around her finger, the strange ring she'd once seemed so afraid of.

"Where did you get that?" Martin asked.

"It was in Gertie's pocket."

"Impossible," Martin stammered. He moved toward her, began to climb out of the hole.

"You stay where you are," she warned, keeping the gun aimed at his chest. "I was so sure Auntie's spirit had done this evil thing, but perhaps the truth is simpler; perhaps it's been right in front of my face the whole time, and I just couldn't bring myself to see it."

Sara rocked back on her heels, holding the gun in both hands now, bringing it up high, and sighting down the barrel.

"Was it you, Martin?" she asked quietly. "Did you hurt our Gertie?"

Martin staggered backward and fell against the dirt wall. It was as if she'd already pulled the trigger.

He remembered holding Gertie in his arms when she was a tiny infant, their miracle baby; walking with her, hand in hand, into the woods last month to choose a tree to cut down for Christmas. How she'd found a spruce with a bird's nest in it and insisted they cut that one down. "Aren't we the luckiest people ever, Papa?" she'd asked. "To have a Christmas tree with a bird's nest in it?"

"I . . ." he stuttered, looking at Sara. "I didn't. I *couldn't*. With God as my witness, I swear I would never hurt our little girl."

Sara stared, finger twitching on the trigger. "But the ring was in your pocket when you left the house that morning, was it not?"

"Sara, please. You're not thinking clearly."

She was silent a moment, as though turning the matter over in her mind.

"But it wasn't *your* ring, was it? It was hers. Which means *she* still could have been the one to do it."

"You're not making sense, Sara. You're seeing things that aren't there."

"Am I, now?" Sara said. She lowered the gun, turned, and looked back into the shadows around the house. "Gertie?" Sara called out. "Your father thinks I'm not right in the head. Come show him, darling. Show him the truth."

Martin stood on the empty coffin, peering over the edge of the hole into the darkness. Somewhere in the darkness, a shadow moved toward them, shuffling through the snow.

Oh dear beloved Jesus, no. Please, no. Martin closed his eyes tight, counted to ten, trying to make it all go away.

He opened his eyes and scrambled at the dirt, clawing his way out of the hole, not looking at whatever was moving toward them from the shadows.

"Sara," he said, reaching for the gun, wrapping his fingers around the barrel. The movement startled Sara, and the gun fired.

He heard the sound, saw the flash of light, felt the bullet hit his chest just below his rib cage on the left. He started to run in spite of the searing pain. He clapped a hand over the bloody hole.

"Martin?" Sara called. "Come back! You're hurt!" But he did not turn back.

On he ran, across the yard and toward the woods, hand on his leaking chest, not daring to look back.

Visitors from the Other Side

The Secret Diary of Sara Harrison Shea

(Editor's note: This is the final entry I discovered, though, as you shall see, she makes reference to other pages she had been working on. It is chilling to note that Sara's body was found only hours after she wrote these words.)

January 31, 1908

The dead can return. Not just as spirits, but as living, breathing beings. I have beheld the proof with my own eyes: my beloved Gertie, awakened. And I have made a decision: ours is a story that must be told. I have spent the last hours with papers spread out on the table, oil lamp burning bright, as I wrote down the exact instructions on how to awaken a sleeper. I have copied Auntie's notes and told every detail of my own experience. I have finished at last, and tucked the papers away safely in not one but three separate hiding places.

We are in the house, doors locked, curtains drawn. Shep is stretched out by my feet, his eyes and ears alert. I've got the gun by my side. I do not want to believe that it could be Martin. That this man I thought I knew—this man I cooked for, slept beside each night, told my secrets to—could be such a monster.

Martin was badly injured when the gun went off. He won't make it long out there in the cold with a chest wound. My fear, of course, is that he'll make it to the Bemises' and they'll all come pounding at the door, looking for the madwoman with the gun.

I am pleased that I have had the chance to write down everything that has happened while it is still fresh in my mind. Even more pleased that I have hidden the papers, should they cart me off to the lunatic asylum.

One day, my papers will be found. The world will know the truth about sleepers.

We are nearing the end of the seventh day of Gertie's awakening. And my girl is still hiding in the shadows, here and then not.

When I catch a glimpse of her, she's pale and shadowy. She's dressed in the outfit she wore when she left the house on that last morning: her blue dress, wool tights, her little black coat. Her hair is in tangles now. Dirt is smudged on her cheeks. She gives off the smell of burning fat, a tallow candle just extinguished.

Shep is unsettled by her; he growls into the shadows with hackles raised, his teeth bared.

Since I finished writing down our story, I have been talking to her, singing to her, trying to coax her out into the open. "Remember," I say, "remember?"

"Remember how you and I would stay under the covers all morning, telling each other our dreams?

"Remember Christmas mornings? The time you had the mumps and I never left your side? Your stories of the blue dog? The way you'd run straight for the kitchen when you came home from school and smelled molasses cookies?"

Remember? Remember?

But Gertie has gone again. (Was she ever really here?)

"Please, love," I say. "We have so little time together. Won't you show yourself to me?"

I turn and look for her across the room.

And there, over the fireplace, across the brick hearth, is a message written in black with a charred stick:

Not Papa

And just now, as I'm staring at the words, there's a knock at the door.

A familiar, though impossible, voice calls out my name.

1 8 8 6

May 2, 1886

My Dearest Sara,

I have promised to tell you everything I know about sleepers. But before you go on, you must understand that this is powerful magic. Only do it if you are sure. Once it is done, there can be no going back.

The sleeper will awaken and return to you. The time this takes is unsure. Sometimes they return in hours, other times, days.

Once awakened, a sleeper will walk for seven days. After that, they are gone from this world forever. You cannot bring someone back more than once. It is forbidden and, indeed, impossible.

If you are ready, follow these instructions exactly.

These are the things you will need:

A shovel

A candle

The heart of any living animal (you must remove it no longer than twelve hours before the deed)

An object that belonged to the person you wish to bring back (such as clothing, jewelry, or a tool)

You must take these things to a portal. There are doorways, gates, between this world and the world of the spirits. One of these doorways is right here in West Hall. I have drawn a map showing its location. You must guard this map with your life.

Enter the portal.

Light the candle.

Hold the object that belonged to the person in your hands and say these words seven times: "_____ (person's name), I call you back to me. Sleeper, awaken!"

Bury the heart and say, "So that your heart will beat once more."

Bury the object beside it and say, "Something of yours to help you find your way."

Then leave the portal and wait. Sometimes they will come to you right then and there. But sometimes, as I have said, it can take days.

There are two other things I must warn you of: Once a sleeper returns, it cannot be killed. It will walk for seven days, regardless of what is done to it. The last thing I must tell you is something I have heard, but have not seen with my own eyes. It is said that if a sleeper were to murder a living person and spill his blood within those seven days, then the sleeper will stay awake for all eternity.

Please use these instructions wisely, and only when the time is right.

I love you with all of my heart, Sara Harrison.

Yours eternally,
Auntie

JANUARY 4

ⅇ

Present Day

Katherine

The snow was knee-deep, but they'd stopped at the barn and strapped snowshoes on—the old-fashioned sort made of bentwood with rawhide laces. The procession moved forward, across the yard and field and toward the wooded hillside. Candace was leading them with her headlamp, Ruthie and Fawn in the middle (Fawn shuffling along stoically, holding tight to a dirty rag doll swaddled in covers that she kept whispering to), and Katherine was the caboose.

"Katherine! Don't fall behind." Candace turned toward Katherine, her headlamp shining right in Katherine's face. "You don't want to get separated from us out in these woods."

No. No, she did not.

Katherine looked up from the tiny screen of Gary's camera. He had photographed all of Sara's missing diary pages, and Katherine had been studying Auntie's instructions for bringing back the dead. It was difficult to make out all the words exactly, even when she zoomed in, but she got the gist.

"What are you so busy looking at?" Candace asked. She looked like a Cyclops with one horribly bright eye: a third eye, a mystic all-seeing eye.

"Just trying to get a clearer sense of where this opening we're looking for is," she said, shutting the camera off and putting it back in Gary's pack. Everyone but Fawn had on packs that had been quickly loaded with supplies: flashlights and batteries, candles, matches, rope, bottled water, granola bars, a few apples. Candace had put on the headlamp they'd found by the front door, which Ruthie and her mother used for bringing in firewood after dark. Katherine had the camera, some water, a flashlight, candles and matches, and Gary's old Swiss Army knife in her pack.

"Good," Candace said. "I'm glad you brought the camera."

So am I, she thought.

She concentrated on walking in the snowshoes, a strange kind of duck-footed shuffle through the deep powder. The snow was still falling hard and fast around them. All Katherine could hear was the sound of their breathing, their grunts as they moved up the hill. There were no car sounds, no distant sirens or train whistles. The world was eerily silent, all the sound muffled, as if everything had been swaddled in cotton wool.

The trail ahead of her seemed impossibly steep all of a sudden. They'd left the field behind and were now climbing up into the woods. The trees were bent and twisted, the branches weighted down with snow. She felt the trees were watching her, a terrible army that stood in rows and reached for her with gnarled fingers.

You're almost there, Gary whispered in her ear.

He felt so close. She could almost smell him, taste him. He'd walked this same path at the end of October, on his last day alive. He'd walked along, shouldering this very backpack.

Is it really possible, Gary? Can we bring back the dead?

He responded with soft laughter. *Isn't that why you've come?* he asked.

And then, then she understood. She knew why she'd come, why she'd been led here. She felt his hand take hers. He was beside her now.

Shh, he whispered. *Do you hear it?*

She closed her eyes, heard the music play in some far-off part of her mind, an old jazz song they'd once danced to. She felt Gary's lips brush her cheek. She and Gary moved together, doing a few awkward, shuffling dance steps in the snow.

We can be together again, he told her. *We can bring Austin back.*

The idea of it hit her like a cannonball in the chest, so heavy and unexpected that she lost her balance and fell over in the snow. She looked desperately around for Gary, but he was gone.

She lay on her back, looked up at the dark sky, the swirling snow that fell down on her like a million falling stars. She let herself imagine it: having Gary and Austin back with her, even if it was only for seven days. The three of them snuggled together under the covers. "Did you dream while you were gone?" she'd ask Austin. "Oh yes, I dreamed," he would say. "It was all one big dream."

"All right back there?" Candace called.

"Fine!" she said, struggling to get up again, but it was absurdly difficult with the huge snowshoes hitting her legs and refusing to let her right herself. Ruthie turned around, came back, and offered her mittened hand to help pull Katherine up.

"Thanks," Katherine said, slapping the snow off her jeans. It was no good—they were soaked through.

"The snowshoes take a little getting used to," Ruthie said.

"I don't think I'll be running a marathon in them anytime soon," Katherine said. Ruthie gave her a tense smile, then moved back beside her sister. She leaned in and whispered something to Fawn. Fawn shook her head and pulled her doll tighter against her chest.

They moved through the grove of bent and twisted trees, and the climb got steeper, the trees larger, more looming. She had the directions. They were going to the portal. She had a candle, Gary's camera. All she needed was . . .

"Jesus!" Candace yelped up ahead. There, just off the path, her headlamp illuminated a gruesome sight. A fox had just captured a snowshoe hare, and had the hare by its throat. The animal struggled for a few short seconds before going still and limp in the fox's mouth.

Candace pulled out her gun, pointed it at the fox.

"Don't!" Katherine shouted. The animal was beautiful—the way its rusty fur shimmered and glistened, its eyes seeming to look right at her, to say, *We know each other, you and I. We understand hunger, desperation.*

The gun went off, and Katherine jumped. Startled, the fox dropped the rabbit and hurried off into the trees—Candace had missed. The fox ran with such grace, such quick sureness, that it took Katherine's breath away. And she was sure that, just for one brief second, it turned its sleek head back and looked at her.

See what I left you.

It all felt so impossibly meant to be.

"Can we save the bunny?" Fawn asked, going over to the small white animal, which lay unmoving in the snow.

"No," Ruthie told her. "It's past saving. Don't touch it, okay?"

"Come on, I think we're about halfway there," Candace said, tucking the gun away, turning her headlamp back to the path before them. If they looked carefully, they could make out the barely discernible impressions of tracks from Candace's trip down the hill, hours ago. The hillside was much steeper now, and the walk was more of a climb. Katherine thought of photos she'd seen of climbers on Mount Everest, all strung together with rope so that they would not lose one another, so that no one would fall and be left behind. They began to trudge on, Candace picking up the pace, the girls struggling to keep up. But Katherine slowed down, stopping at the place where the fox had been. Fortunately, there was no rope binding her to the others, and they did not seem to notice she was no longer right behind them. She bent down, took off her glove, and touched the white snowshoe hare. It was still warm, its fur soft.

Quickly she scooped the rabbit up, surprised by how very light it was. Then she slid Gary's backpack off her shoulders, carefully laid the animal inside, and zipped it up tight.

She ran to catch up with the others, heart pounding, ears buzzing.

The rabbit was small. It couldn't be too hard, she imagined, to feel for its ribs, open it up, and remove its heart.

Ruthie

"It's got to be here somewhere," Candace said as she scrabbled around at the base of the Devil's Hand.

"I can't believe how big the rocks are," Katherine said, looking up at them. "The tallest one's got to be twenty feet at least. They don't look that big in the pictures."

"The Devil must be a giant," Fawn said, clinging tight to Mimi. Mimi was still swaddled in the blanket that held the gun.

It had taken them nearly forty-five minutes to climb the hill. Since they'd arrived at the top, Candace had spent at least ten minutes digging randomly with almost spasmodic movements. "The hole could be beneath any of the five rocks," she said. "They all look the same. What are you all waiting for? Start digging!"

The snow was falling steadily, and the rocks were blanketed in a thick white glove. Candace was pawing through the snow with her mittened hands, pushing and pulling any smaller rocks aside.

"Let me see that," Ruthie said, tucking the flashlight into her coat pocket and reaching to take the camera from Katherine, who was staring down at the back display. Ruthie saw that Katherine had been studying one of those close-up photos of the instructions for creating sleepers.

Ruthie fast-forwarded to the photo of the opening at the base of the rock. The picture was taken back in October, in daylight, and now it was pitch-dark, and everything was covered with snow. Ruthie studied the grain, shape, and shadows of the rock in the photo, then shone her flashlight on the rocks before her.

Candace was wrong. They weren't all the same.

"I think it's the biggest one," Ruthie said. "The middle finger. See here, the way it seems like it's kind of leaning to the left compared to the one beside it in the picture? And look at the angle he took it from. He must have been standing right over there, on the left side. There's the big maple in the background." She pointed at the tree, now shrouded in snow.

She handed the camera back to Katherine and took off her snowshoes. She used one as a shovel to pull snow back from the base of the middle-finger rock. Soon she'd uncovered a rock about two feet in diameter, and many smaller ones that rested against the bottom of the finger. She gave the big rock a hard shove, but it held tight, cemented to the ground by ice and snow.

"Give me a hand," she said to Candace. Together, they pried and pushed the rock. At last, it budged, then rolled away, as if they were pushing the bottom ball of a snowman.

Katherine shone her light down on a small hole leading into the ground at the base of the large finger stone. "This is it! The entrance!"

The opening looked narrow, barely big enough for an adult to squeeze through. If Ruthie had come across it out hiking, she would have thought it was the den of a small animal—a fox or a skunk maybe—and passed it by.

Ruthie clicked on her flashlight and shone it into the narrow hole. The darkness seemed to eat up the beam of her light, and she couldn't see how far back the tunnel went. "Are we sure this goes anywhere?" she asked, doubtful. What she was really thinking was, *There's no way in hell I'm climbing in there.*

She suddenly had the feeling that this was all one big trick being played on her, that at any second everyone would start laughing, patting Ruthie on the back, saying, *We sure fooled you!* Her mother would even come out of hiding, in on the joke. Maybe it had all been her brainchild—a way to teach Ruthie some lesson about responsibility.

"One way to find out," Candace said. "I'll go first, but if you all don't follow right behind, you can bet I'll be back out in a jiffy. And

I'm not going to be happy." She patted the holster under her coat in case anyone missed the point.

"I don't know about this," Ruthie said. *What kind of person actually uses the word "jiffy"? Particularly when threatening people with a gun?*

"She doesn't like small spaces," Fawn explained to the others.

Understatement of the year, thought Ruthie.

"I'm not thrilled about it, either," Candace said. "But, like it or not, that's where we've got to go."

Candace shoved her pack down into the hole, then took off her coat and pushed it in, too. The snowshoes she left leaning against the rock. Headlamp shining, she wiggled herself into the hole headfirst and seemed to get stuck midway.

"Maybe it's not big enough. Maybe we can't get through, or it's just a dead end," Ruthie said, beginning to sweat as she watched Candace struggle. Candace kicked her feet, writhed, and squirmed like a swimmer stuck on land. They heard muffled curse words from inside. Eventually, Candace's feet disappeared. A few moments later, there was an echoing shout: "I'm in! Come on! Hurry! You're not going to believe this!"

Katherine turned to the girls and began talking quickly and quietly. "I'll go next," she said. "I'll take as long as I can getting in. But here's what I want you girls to do." She rummaged in her coat pocket and pulled out a set of keys. "Take the path that leads right down to the road. My car is parked about a quarter-mile past your driveway. It's a black Jeep Cherokee. My cell phone's in the glove compartment. Call for help. If there's no signal, get in the car and go to the nearest house. Just get out of here. This Candace woman is clearly nuts, and I'm afraid she's going to hurt someone with that gun she keeps waving around. I can hold her off for a while, give you a good head start."

"Where the hell are you?" Candace yelled from the hole. "Who's coming next?"

"I am!" Katherine shouted into the hole. "I'm on my way!"

Ruthie let herself imagine it for a minute: escaping down the hill with Fawn, calling 911 on Katherine's phone, orchestrating a rescue. But Candace believed her mother was in the cave. What if she was right? What if her mother was hurt, or what if Candace got to her first, with her insane conspiracy theories—and her gun?

Ruthie shook her head, lowered her voice. "I'm not leaving."

She took the doll from her sister's arms, unwrapped the gun, and showed it to Katherine, holding it in her outstretched palm. "I really think my mother might be in there. And I know that, whatever's going on, she'd never leave me and my sister on purpose. So, if she is down there, chances are she's in trouble. And with Candace heading in, things just got worse."

Katherine looked at the gun, sighed, and nodded.

Ruthie turned to Fawn. "You take the keys and follow the path down to the road. Find the Jeep and call for help. You're a big girl. You can do this."

Fawn shook her head determinedly. "No way. Mimi and I are staying with you. We're going to help you find Mom."

"Okay," Ruthie agreed, wishing she knew if she was doing the right thing. But she could stand out here all night debating plans or visualizing scenarios, and in the meantime, her mother might be down there in trouble.

"Both of you just be careful, okay?" Katherine said. "Don't do anything stupid."

"You, either," Ruthie said, thinking of the way Katherine had been studying the photo of Auntie's instructions, how eager she'd seemed to send the girls away.

"What's taking so long out there, ladies?" Candace shouted.

"Sorry," Katherine called down into the hole, "couldn't get the damn snowshoes off. I'm coming!" She shoved her pack in, then scrambled in herself, disappearing quickly.

"Mimi and me next," Fawn said. Ruthie handed the flashlight to her little sister.

"I'll be right behind you," Ruthie promised, making sure the gun's safety was on, just like Buzz had shown her, before tucking it into her coat pocket.

Fawn's size definitely put her at an advantage. She slipped through the narrow passageway with ease, the flashlight beam illuminating craggy walls of dark, damp stone.

Ruthie took a deep breath and followed. The tunnel smelled

like wet rocks, dirt, and . . . woodsmoke? No mistaking it—there was a fire burning somewhere close by. The opening was tight, and she squeezed through on her belly like a cork in a bottle, head low, eyes on her sister's feet ahead of her. Ruthie's heart raced, and she was breathing so fast she was afraid she might pass out.

"You okay, Ruthie?" Fawn called back.

"Fine," Ruthie said, her voice small and squeaky. Was the tunnel getting even smaller? She imagined the stones pushing down, squeezing her until her ribs began to crack and her eyeballs popped out. If her instinct was right and her mother turned out to be in here somewhere, Ruthie might just have to kill her for putting them through this. She was more frightened than she could ever remember being.

"Don't worry, the tunnel gets wider," Fawn promised.

"Who's worried?" Ruthie mumbled, pretty sure her heart was going to seize up at any second. Her elbows hurt from dragging herself along the rough stone.

Suddenly everything went black.

"What happened to the light?" Ruthie called, panic rising.

"I think it died?" Fawn called back. There was the sound of the flashlight being shaken, batteries rattling dully in the plastic case.

It was pitch-black now, darker than anything Ruthie had ever imagined—a darkness that seemed to go on forever.

This is what it feels like to be buried alive, she thought.

"Never mind, just keep going," Ruthie called out, trying to make herself sound brave.

Fawn was right, the tunnel did widen; but then it narrowed again. She closed her eyes tight, tried to trick herself into believing that it wouldn't be dark when she opened them. Ruthie had to crawl on her belly, arms bent, as she used her elbows and toes to propel herself along. The tunnel itself went on for about ten feet at a steep decline after the flashlight went out. Her jacket and shirt rode up, and her stomach was scraped by the rough rock floor of the tunnel.

"Stop," she said out loud.

"We're almost there," Fawn called back, her voice muffled. "I see light." She sounded much farther away than Ruthie had imagined her.

Ruthie shoved her backpack in front of her, listened to the faint sounds of Fawn scrabbling along. When, at last, she dared to open her eyes, she saw the soft glow of flashlights ahead. A few more feet and Ruthie realized she could move to her hands and knees. A few feet beyond that and she emerged into a large, cozy chamber. Ruthie stood up tentatively, stretching, looking around. She shouldered the backpack and checked to make sure the gun was still in her jacket pocket.

Just don't think about being underground, Ruthie told herself.

Fawn held the flashlight out to her. "It works again. I guess I just didn't have the switch on right. Sorry."

"It's okay," Ruthie said. "You're a very brave kid, you know that?" Fawn smiled up at her.

The glow in the chamber hadn't just come from flashlights; there were oil lamps lit all around the room. And a room it was— there were shelves, a table, a wood-burning cookstove with a pipe leading up into a crevice in the rocky ceiling. A fire was lit in it, crackling and popping and almost making Ruthie forget she was in a cave beneath the Devil's Hand. There was even a bed, piled high with old quilts, in a jagged alcove to the left.

The place felt strangely familiar.

Ruthie walked over to one of the sets of wooden shelves. There were jugs of water, sacks of flour and sugar, boxes of tea and coffee, tins of sardines and tuna, canned vegetables and soups, a bushel basket of apples.

Ruthie picked up one of the apples. It had no rotten spots.

"The lamps were all lit when I got down here," Candace said. She held the gun out in front of her, scanning the room with her headlamp. There were three tunnels in addition to the one they had just come down, each leading off in a different direction, each dark.

"Ruthie, look!" Fawn squealed. She was over at the bed, holding a garish purple-and-yellow crocheted poncho.

"It's Mom's!" Ruthie said.

Fawn nodded excitedly. "She was wearing it the other night! When she disappeared!"

Ruthie stepped forward to get a better look at the poncho, then froze when she saw what was sitting up at the head of the bed, beside the pillow.

Her old green stuffed bear—Piney Boy. Ruthie scooped up the bear and held him to her chest; a memory flashed back to her, cloudy and dreamlike. It felt familiar because she'd been down here before, in this room. She'd followed someone here.

She closed her eyes and let the memory take her further.

There was a little girl who lived here. But she wasn't nice. She'd shown Ruthie something dark and terrible.

Later, her father told her she'd imagined the whole thing.

She looked around the room. It wasn't possible, was it? How could a little girl be living in a cave under the Devil's Hand?

"It's yours, isn't it?" Fawn asked. "From when you were little? It's the bear you're holding in that old picture."

Ruthie nodded, still holding the bear tight, struggling to remember more from that long-ago day. What had the girl shown her?

"There's something else," Fawn said. "Under the bed." She pointed. Clutching the bear in one hand, her flashlight in the other, Ruthie peered under the bed.

A purple-and-white ski jacket lay on the stone floor. It was torn and covered with brown stains—old blood.

"That's like the one that missing girl was wearing, isn't it?" Fawn asked. "Willa Luce?"

Ruthie nodded, turning away.

She thought of what Candace had said earlier, about her parents' claiming there was a monster in the woods. A monster that killed Tom and Bridget O'Rourke—her birth parents. Where had Ruthie been when they were killed? Had she been witness to whatever happened to them? The very idea of this made her feel sick to her stomach. The cave walls seemed to be moving in closer; the air felt thinner.

"Alice Washburne!" Candace called, her voice echoing, hurting Ruthie's ears. "I've got your children! Show yourself or I'll hurt them!"

Ruthie set down the green bear, reached into her pocket to find the gun. She flipped the safety lever off and held her breath, waiting.

They listened for a minute. All they heard was the crackling of the fire and a dripping sound from someplace far off.

"I don't like this," Fawn said, stepping closer to Ruthie. "I don't like it down here."

"Me, neither," Ruthie said, hand on the gun in her pocket.

Silence.

"Damn it," Candace barked. She circled the chamber, peering down each passageway with her headlamp. She stuck her head down one and sputtered something Ruthie didn't catch.

"What'll we do now?" Ruthie asked, her eye on the gun in Candace's hand. Surely she was bluffing. She wouldn't hurt them. She'd keep them alive and unharmed to use as leverage when the time came.

"We'll have to explore each tunnel, one at a time."

Please, God, no more narrow tunnels, Ruthie thought.

"We could split up," Ruthie suggested. "Or maybe Fawn and I should stay here. In case my mom shows up."

"No!" Candace spat. "We all go together." She glanced around the cave, eyes beady and glinting. "Wait a minute. Where's Katherine?"

Ruthie scanned the room, shone her light down the dark openings of the three tunnels.

"Damn it!" Candace bellowed.

Katherine was gone.

1 9 o 8

Sara

Auntie.

I blinked once, twice, three times, yet she still stood in my doorway, an actual flesh-and-blood being. Surely this was no spirit: she
had form, substance; snow dripped from her clothes, and her body
cast a long shadow behind her.

Gertie had run off as soon as she heard Auntie's voice outside,
probably gone back to the closet to hide.

Shep was by my side, growling low in his throat. Auntie gave
him a look, and he slinked off, tail between his legs.

"Are you . . ." I stammered. "Are you one of them? Have you
come back from the dead?"

Perhaps I had gone mad after all.

I still held Martin's gun in my hands, gripping the stock so tight
my fingers turned white. Auntie just glanced at it and laughed. It
sounded like wild wind through a dry cornfield.

She was older. Her once raven-colored hair was now steely gray
and in wild tangles, tied in clumps with rags and bits of leather. She
had feathers and beads and pretty little stones woven into her hair.
Her skin was dark brown and wrinkled. She wore a fox pelt draped
over her shoulders.

"Would it be easier for you," Auntie asked, "if I were a sleeper?"

"I . . ."

"Easier to believe you were right all these years, that I lay dead in the ashes of my home?" Her face grew stormy.

"But how? How did you survive?" I remembered the heat of the fire, the soot that rained down and covered us; how, in the end, there was nothing left but a few charred remains and that old pot-belly stove. "I heard the gunshot. I watched your cabin burn to the ground."

Auntie chuckled bitterly. "Did you think it would be so easy to kill me, Sara?"

I remembered Buckshot, his fur singed, taking off into the woods. Was he following Auntie?

"Kill me and leave my remains to rot in the ashes?"

I took a step back, suddenly frightened. "I tried to stop him," I said, voice shaking. "I even tried going in after you once the house was in flames, but Father stopped me."

Auntie moved forward, gave a disappointed shake of the head. "You didn't try hard enough, Sara."

"And you've been alive all this time?" I asked, disbelieving. "Where have you been?"

"I went home. Back to my people. I tried to leave my past behind, to forget all of you. But, you see, I couldn't forget. Whenever I got close, all I had to do was look down at my hands." Auntie removed her gloves, showing hands and fingers thick with white, gnarled scars. "I've got another on my belly, too, from your father's shotgun. The wound got infected. It was a terrible mess."

Auntie rubbed her stomach with her scarred right hand.

She raised her eyes to meet mine; hers were as black as two bottomless pits. "But sometimes the scars that hurt the worst are the ones buried deep down inside, isn't that right, my Sara?"

I said nothing, my eyes fixed on her gruesome pale hands.

"I knew that one day I would return. I would return and keep to my word: you would pay. You would pay for what you and your family did to me. Turning your back on me, after all I did for you. I nursed you, brought you up as if you were my own child, and this was how you repaid me, by trying to burn me alive?"

"But it wasn't me! It was Father. He was mad with grief."

She smiled a sinister smile. "Madness is always a wonderful excuse, don't you think? For doing terrible things to other people." There was a little glint in her dark eyes. "To other people's children."

My heart went icy as a terrible realization bore down on me. "How long have you been back in town?" I tried to keep my voice calm.

"Oh, a little while now. Long enough to see your poor family struggle along. Your limping husband, who fights with the land rather than working with it. Your daughter. Your beautiful little daughter. So tiny. So delicate. So like you at her age."

"Gertie," I said, voice faltering. "Her name is Gertie."

Auntie's mouth twisted into a painful-looking smile. "Oh, I know. We knew each other well, she and I."

I looked into her eyes, and at that moment, I finally knew the truth.

I took a step back, raised the gun, and aimed it at her chest.

"It wasn't Martin. *You* killed Gertie."

She cackled, throwing back her head. "The evidence pointed to Martin, though, did it not? His ring in Gertie's pocket. The ring of mine he unearthed in the field. I don't blame you for shooting him. I would have done the same."

"I didn't shoot him. It was an accident."

Auntie laughed, showing pointed teeth stained brown.

"You put the ring there," I said. "You took it from Martin somehow. It was you who left the notes that were supposed to be from Gertie."

She smiled a wide and crooked smile. "My bright little Sara. My star."

I stepped forward, pushing the barrel of the gun right against her chest.

She laughed, shook her head at me as if I were a foolish child once more. A little girl who simply didn't know any better.

"Would it do any good to kill me now, Sara? Would it help to bring back all that I have taken from you? Your child? Your husband? Your brother and father?"

"You didn't kill my father," I said.

"No. He killed himself with drinking. Because he could not live with what he had done to me."

I gazed into her eyes, so deep and black. Her eyes drew me in and held me, brought me back through time to when I was a little girl and would go down to the creek with her, hand in hand.

You are different from others, Sara. You are like me.

Maybe, I thought. Maybe I *am* like Auntie. Maybe I, too, am capable of murder, of revenge. Killing Auntie wouldn't bring back all that she had taken from me, but it would be justice. I would kill Auntie. I would do it for Gertie. For Martin. For my father and brother.

But I was too late.

In one impossibly quick move, Auntie wrenched the gun from my hands, turned it around, and pointed it at my chest. I had forgotten her quickness and strength.

"Let's go see if we can find your Gertie, shall we?" she said, as if I had a choice. "There are only hours left before she has to go back into the ground. I want to watch it happen. I want to see your face when the sad little phantom you brought back disappears forever."

JANUARY 4

⁊

Present Day

Katherine

Katherine moved forward blindly at first, afraid that if she turned on her flashlight they'd see the glow and follow. It wouldn't take them long to find her. She had to work quickly.

The passage went on for twenty feet or so, taking her steadily down, the walls cool and dripping, causing her feet to slip on the wet stone. She had to walk bent over, stepping carefully over and around rocks, feeling her way like a blind cave-creature.

She didn't know where she was going. Was the portal in an exact place inside the cave? Or could she just pull over anywhere to do the ritual?

She paused to catch her breath, listening. She heard voices, but they were far off, mere echoes. She saw no glimmer of light from the direction of the chamber; she should be far enough away now to turn on her flashlight. She blinked at the sudden brightness and saw that she'd reached a fork. She hesitated, then bore left. The ceiling of the passageway dropped, so that she had to crawl on her hands and knees. About six feet in, it dead-ended. She slithered her way back out and went to the right this time, followed the twists and turns, moved down, squeezed through the passage sideways when it got too narrow. The going was slow, and Katherine guessed she'd only made it about ten feet in.

Keep going, Gary whispered. *That's it. Almost there, babe.*

She couldn't hear the others behind her anymore. She'd moved too far from the main chamber now. And a new, haunting thought filled her: *Will I be able to find my way back out?* She thought of all the images she'd seen in movies—people entering a cave and finding it full of the bones of those who hadn't made it back out.

She should have left marks on the wall, a trail of breadcrumbs—something, anything. How many turns had she made? One right turn, then the fork. Or was it two right turns?

Don't worry, I'll show you the way back out, Gary promised, a hissing murmur in her left ear.

The floor dropped out from under her, and she tumbled down, smashing her knee and left elbow. The flashlight fell from her hand and went out.

"Shit," she yelped.

She fumbled for the flashlight and turned it on to check out the damage. It still worked, thank God. Her jeans were torn, her skin scraped and bleeding, but, all in all, it didn't look that bad. She shone the light around to see where she'd ended up.

She was in a small chamber with rounded walls. There was a circular fire pit in the middle, full of half-burnt sticks. The floor was covered with rocky soil and gravel. On the walls around her were drawings and writing done in charcoal and red-brown paint (or was it blood?). Crude pictures of bodies buried in the ground rising up, coming back to the land of the living.

SLEEPER AWAKEN was written over and over, at least a hundred times.

"This is it," she said out loud. She'd been led right where she needed to be.

She went to work quickly, pulling out a candle, matches, the rabbit's body, and Gary's camera.

She laid the snowshoe hare on its back and used her fingers to palpate its chest. The fur was soft, the rib cage tiny and flexible. Hesitating only slightly, she used the small blade on her Swiss Army knife to slice open the animal's chest down the sternum, gently, delicately. It didn't take much pressure. All her college biology came back to her as she located the lungs and heart with ease and carefully removed the tiny heart. It was still warm.

The old Katherine might have been squeamish about this act—but the new Katherine moved through it effortlessly, as if she did this sort of thing every day.

Fingers sticky with the rabbit's blood, she lit the candle and picked up Gary's camera.

"Gary, I call you back to me. Sleeper, awaken!" She said this seven times, each repetition more urgent, more demanding, until, by the last refrain, she was nearly shouting.

She plunged the large blade of the knife into the rocky soil and found it loose and sandy. Digging with the knife, she easily made a small hole; into this she dropped the heart and covered it up. "So that your heart will beat once more," she said in a voice loud and sure.

She began work on another hole, loosening the soil with the knife, then clawing at the dirt and scooping it away with her hands until the hole was large enough to put the camera inside. "Something of yours to help you find your way."

Katherine sat back and waited. "Come on, Gary," she willed. "I did my part. Now you do yours."

She held her breath, waiting.

She thought of Gary's and her first kiss, in the painting studio at college all those years ago, the smell of oil paint and turpentine all around them. How she'd wished the kiss would never end, that they could stay there forever in the painting building, twenty years old and so in love it hurt. How that one moment had become the centerpiece of the rest of their lives; everything that came after it swirled around it, as if the kiss itself were the eye of a hurricane.

She let herself imagine what it might be like to see him again, to hold him in her arms, smell him, taste him, breathe him in. All the words they hadn't had the chance to speak to each other could be said.

Seven whole days. What a gift! They could live a lifetime in seven days. They could get something of Austin's from the apartment, bring it back to the cave, and call him back as well. Then they'd be a family again.

Still, the longer she waited, the more doubt set in.

What if it didn't work?

Or—what if it did work, and the Gary who came back wasn't the Gary she remembered?

Her mind filled with images from horrible zombie movies: the undead pale and rotting, losing limbs, moaning as they shambled their way through the land of the living.

She packed up her things, deciding not to wait any longer. To leave, get out fast.

As she crawled out of the chamber, she heard footsteps coming from the passageway to the left, the way she'd come. They were slow and steady, coming toward her. Worse still, there was a little scrape with each step, a horrible shuffle.

She turned and ran in the other direction, not daring to turn on her light, hands raised protectively in front of her as she groped helplessly through the darkness.

1 9 0 8

Martin

Martin stumbled as he made his way back down the hill. Home. Yes, home. He was going home.

He'd been out in the woods for at least two hours, running at first, then walking, then, finally, collapsing in the snow; there he lay, trying to convince himself that he'd only imagined the figure in the shadows behind Sara earlier, that he'd been a terrible coward to run.

He didn't need his brother the doctor to tell him that he did not have long. He didn't want to die up in those godforsaken woods. He wanted to see Sara once more, to tell her how much he loved her, in spite of everything. Above all else, he needed her to know that he had not hurt Gertie. He could not die knowing that Sara believed him guilty of such a thing. So he'd pulled himself up out of the snow and begun the slow descent down the hill.

As he took each breath, the wound in his left side seared with pain. The bullet had struck him just below his rib cage. Blood soaked through his shirt and heavy woolen coat. He could not stop shivering.

He was staggering now, his breath ragged as he shuffled his way across the field. The cursed field, where nothing would ever grow. Year after year, he'd plowed, manured, and carefully planted crops that never flourished, despite all his efforts. All the ground produced was stones, broken dinner plates, old tin cups, and, once, that beautiful ring carved from bone.

He looked at the house coming into view, remembered carrying Sara through the doorway when they were newly married. How in love with her he'd been. Sara, with her wild red hair and sparkling eyes. Sara, who could see the future. He remembered her as a little girl in the schoolyard, telling him, "Martin Shea, you are the one I shall marry." How he'd handed her that silly glass marble. She still had it in a little box with Gertie's baby teeth and a silver thimble that had belonged to her mother.

Flashes of their life together filled his head and heart: the Christmases they'd had; the time they went dancing at the hall over in Barre and the wagon wheel broke on the way home so they had to spend the night in the wagon, huddled together under their coats, happy. There were painful memories, too. The loss of the babies Sara carried inside her. The death of little Charles; how Sara held him in her arms, refusing to let go, refusing to accept that he was gone. And, of course, the loss of their darling Gertie.

"Sara," Martin moaned as he passed the barn, feet crunching through the snow. "My Sara." He fell, and struggled back up to his feet, leaving the white ground smeared with red, like a wounded snow angel. Maybe she'd be there in the doorway, waiting for him with the gun. Maybe that's what he deserved.

Almost there, Martin, he told himself.

Yes, he was almost home. He wanted, more than anything, to go inside, climb the stairs one last time, and get into bed. He wanted Sara to cover him with quilts, to lie beside him, stroke his hair.

Impossible wishes.

Tell me a story, he would say. *An adventure story—the story of our lives together.*

As he came across the yard, he saw a figure out back, near the little graveyard. The person saw him and slipped behind the old maple tree.

He moved closer.

"Hello?" he called weakly. "Sara?"

But no one was there.

He must have imagined it.

Such an imaginative boy he'd been once. A boy with the heart of a hero. A boy who'd been sure great adventures awaited him.

He heard the front door bang open behind him, and turned to see Sara stumbling down the steps. Sara, his Sara. Ever radiant.

But something was different. Something was wrong. She moved awkwardly, and her face was stricken with terror.

Behind her, an old woman came through the doorway. She was holding Martin's rifle, pushing the barrel into Sara's back.

"Sara?" Martin called, turning toward them. "What's happening? Who is this?"

Sara lifted her head. "The woman who killed our little girl," she said. She looked at him with such agony on her face. "Oh, Martin, I'm so sorry," she said. "For ever thinking it could be you."

And I for being sure it was you, he thought.

He saw the way the wicked old woman's face twisted into a hideous grin and knew he had to do something. Even if it was his last act here on earth, he had to save his wife. His beautiful Sara. How could he have thought she would hurt Gertie? He'd been wrong. So wrong.

Using the last of his strength, Martin ran and leapt forward, hands reaching for the gun. But somehow he missed.

How could he have missed?

He'd failed Sara again. Probably for the last time.

The old woman laughed, turned the gun around, and swung it like a club so the butt end hit him right in the chest, right in the place where he was bleeding.

He dropped to the ground with a howl and tried to catch his breath, tried to move his thoughts beyond the pain that echoed through every inch of his body. Though he tried to get up on his knees, he just melted back down. The old woman lifted the gun and brought it down on his chest again. He felt himself going under, sinking down to someplace dark and warm.

To bed. Into their bed, deep under the covers, with Sara in his arms.

"Please," Sara sobbed. "Stop."

"Not until I am done," the old woman snarled. "Not until everything you have is gone."

Sara . . . He tried to speak her name. To tell her it was all right, really. He deserved this. And she, she had deserved better than him.

He wanted to say all this to her. To tell her how sorry he was. He managed to lift his head, open his eyes, and saw, coming across the yard, someone else. Someone small, moving forward in a slow, determined shuffle.

A child. A child with blond hair and a long dress.

And she was holding an ax. Martin's own ax. The one he used to split wood and kill chickens. He kept the blade so sharp it could cut paper. He was good at taking care of things, at making them last.

But you weren't able to take care of your wife and daughter, were you?

The child moved forward steadily, coming up just behind the old woman, who had turned the gun back around and aimed it at Sara.

The child raised the ax high up, her arms outstretched. As she turned, he could see her face clearly in the moonlight.

It couldn't be.

"Gertie?"

She brought the ax down with all her might, burying it in the back of the old woman's skull. Blood splattered on the little girl's face. The gun fell; the old woman went down, and the child was on her, ripping at her clothes and skin.

Martin closed his eyes, willing it all to end.

Martin? Martin?" Someone was shaking him, slapping his face. He opened his eyes. He was on his side in the yard, half frozen into the snow, though he no longer felt cold.

Lucius was looking down at him, his face a mask of horror and disgust. Lucius, always calm and stoic, was actually trembling. His shirt was rumpled and stained with blood. "My God, Martin, what have you done?"

I've hurt myself, Martin tried to say. He knew he was dying. He could see it on Lucius's face. His chest felt heavy, and his breathing had turned to wet, labored rasps. He coughed, and a light spray of blood shot from his mouth.

"Sara," Martin gasped. He reached for his brother's hand, gripped it tightly. "Promise you'll take care of my Sara."

"It's a little late for that, brother," Lucius said, pulling his hand away from Martin's, his eyes moving over Martin to something behind him.

Martin heaved himself up and turned to look. The moon was higher now, illuminating the yard with crisp blue clarity.

He saw a pile of torn, bloody clothes not ten feet from him—Sara's dress and coat.

"No," he whimpered.

Beside the clothes lay a woman's body on a bed of bloody snow. It had been stripped of skin—the flesh wet and sparkling, skull gleaming in the moonlight.

Martin turned away and vomited, the spasms ripping through his open chest.

Then he saw the gun.

"How could you do this?" Lucius asked, his voice sputtering. He was crying now. Martin hadn't seen his brother cry since they were small boys.

"It wasn't me," Martin said. But he picked up the gun and turned it around so that it pointed at the middle of his own chest, his thumb resting awkwardly on the trigger. "It was Gertie."

Martin closed his eyes and pulled the trigger. He felt himself falling into bed at last, warm and safe beside his darling Sara. Gertie was down the hall, singing, her voice as high and light as a sparrow's. Sara pressed her body against his, and whispered in his ear:

"Isn't it good to be home?"

JANUARY 4

ʔ

Present Day

Ruthie

"Faster," Candace barked at them. "Keep up, now. I'm not losing anyone else."

They were moving down a narrow passage, Candace in the lead, her headlamp glowing, the gun clenched in her right hand. There was no way to know which direction Katherine had gone, so they had just picked the passageway closest to where she'd been standing when Candace had last seen her.

"Katherine?" Candace shouted. "Alice?"

The tunnel seemed to be moving down, deeper into the earth. The air felt thicker, damper. The walls were jagged rock; the ground was uneven. At least they could walk upright. Ruthie concentrated on keeping her breathing as calm and level as she could, counting, "One, two, three," to herself with each inhalation and exhalation. Step by step, she moved forward, trying not to think about where she was, only what she had to do: keep Fawn safe and try to find Mom.

"Um, Candace, maybe we shouldn't be calling out to them like that," Ruthie suggested. "You know, just in case there's someone else down here. Someone whose attention we might not want to attract?"

Candace turned back and looked at Ruthie. "Who's in charge here?" she snapped.

Ruthie reached into her jacket pocket, wrapped her fingers around the grip of the gun.

"You doing okay?" she asked Fawn.

Her little sister nodded up at her, but her face looked flushed in the dim light. Ruthie put a hand to her forehead—Fawn was burning up again. Shit. Ruthie hadn't brought any Tylenol. What happened to a kid if a fever got too high? Convulsions—brain damage, maybe.

She had to get Fawn out of here; she never should have brought her in the first place. She needed to get her home, give her some medicine, put her to bed, get a friend to come watch her; then she'd make Buzz come back into the cave with her to search for her mother.

"Mimi says this is a bad place," Fawn said, her eyes glassy and dazed-looking. "She says not all of us will make it out of here."

Ruthie leaned down and looked in her sister's eyes. "We're going to get out of here, Fawn. I promise. Soon."

"Shh!" Candace hissed; she stopped suddenly, her left hand raised in the air in a hold-on-now gesture. They stopped behind her, listening.

"Did you hear that? Footsteps! Up ahead. Come on!" Candace moved quickly. Ruthie took Fawn's hand and began to follow Candace, clicking on her own flashlight so she could see the way. She and Fawn came upon a narrow opening in the rock wall that led off to the right. Candace had followed the main tunnel and was far ahead of them now, her light bouncing off the walls. Gripping Fawn's hot hand tightly, Ruthie pulled her sister into the side tunnel. She had to bend over to fit.

"Hurry," she whispered as she ducked into the passageway, towing Fawn along behind her.

"Where are we going?" Fawn asked. "I thought we were all going to stay together."

"I'm not sure that's such a good idea," Ruthie said. "That lady's got a few loose screws."

"Huh?"

"Never mind, just stick close, 'kay? I'm going to get us out of this place. Caves can have more than one entrance, right?"

"I guess," Fawn said; then she whispered something Ruthie couldn't quite make out to Mimi.

The tunnel was tall enough for Ruthie to stay upright, but the opening narrowed until she could barely squeeze through. She struggled out of her coat, abandoning it on the cave floor. Now she was wriggling along sideways, her belly and butt scraping painfully against the rock walls, the gun in her right hand, behind her, carefully pointed downward; she clutched the flashlight in her left hand, extended ahead of her, to illuminate the way. Her back was slick with sweat. She forced herself to keep moving, keep breathing.

"How are you doing back there, Little Deer?" Ruthie asked, unable to turn to look at her sister.

"Fine," Fawn said.

"You just stay right behind me," Ruthie said.

"Uh-huh."

As they slowly edged forward, something seemed to change: the tunnel was widening, and the darkness—was it changing? Ruthie flipped off her flashlight. There was definitely light coming from up ahead. Had they somehow circled back to the main room they'd entered with all the lamps lit? Ruthie's heart leapt—were they that close to freedom?

"Shh," Ruthie said, reaching around to slide the flashlight into her back pocket. They crept forward slowly, on tiptoes, the walls getting brighter, the tunnel widening further as they moved. The tunnel ended up ahead, opening into a cavern that was most definitely not the room they'd been in before. Ruthie pressed her back against the wall of the tunnel and pulled Fawn beside her, putting a finger to her lips. Fawn nodded. Ruthie put up her hand to indicate, *You stay here.* Fawn nodded again, eyes huge and lemurlike. With the gun clasped firmly in her right hand, Ruthie edged forward to peek into the room.

The chamber was triangle-shaped, smaller than the one they'd first entered, with a lower ceiling. There was a table, with an oil lamp burning. At the table, a single chair. In the chair, a woman sat with her back to them. Ruthie recognized her shape, her hair, the well-worn gray sweater. She wanted to call out, but she sensed danger close by. Something about the scene in front of her didn't feel right—it felt like a trap. "Stay here," she whispered to Fawn, pressing her sister against the wall. "If anything goes wrong, you run like hell."

Fawn gave a panicked nod.

Ruthie crept into the room, eyes darting around, looking for anything hiding in the shadows. There was nothing. No other furniture, no signs of life. One other passageway led out of the chamber, like a dark mouth on the other side. It was possible that there could be someone, *something,* hiding in the shadows there, watching.

"Mom?" Ruthie called, moving forward, gun raised as she kept one eye on the dark passageway.

Her mother didn't turn around. Didn't speak. Ruthie held her breath as she approached. Her mother appeared to be twitching, wriggling, having some sort of seizure there in the chair. She reminded Ruthie of a woman being tugged at by invisible strings.

Ruthie froze, suddenly afraid that maybe this wasn't her mother at all—that she would turn her head at any moment and have the gray face of an alien or some hideous, pale underground monster.

"Mom?" she said again, her voice shaky and hesitant now. She forced herself to keep walking, on rubbery legs, first one step, then another.

It was only when she got close that Ruthie understood: her mother was tied to the chair and had a scarf gagging her mouth. Her hair was disheveled, her clothes were rumpled and filthy, but her eyes were alert, and she looked uninjured.

"Mom!" Ruthie exclaimed. "Hang on, I'll get you out of this." She set the gun down on the table and went to work untying the scarf.

"Who did this to you?" she asked once the scarf was off. "How'd you get here?" Ruthie began to work on the rough hemp rope that bound her mother to the chair.

"Shh," her mother hissed in a warning voice. "We've got to be quiet. And we've got to get out of here. Now."

"Mommy," Fawn cried, leaping out of the shadows and throwing her small arms around her mother, burying her face in her chest.

Mom's face was tight with worry. She looked at Ruthie and said, "You shouldn't have brought her here."

"I know—it's complicated," Ruthie said.

"Never mind," Mom said. "Just untie me. We've got to get out of here."

Ruthie was getting nowhere trying to untie the complicated knots in the thick rope. She grabbed the small Boy Scout knife she'd shoved into her pack and began sawing at the rope with the dull blade.

"Hurry," her mother whispered urgently. "I think she's coming back."

"Who?" Ruthie asked.

Ruthie listened. Yes, there were footsteps coming down the tunnel they'd just passed through. Someone was moving in their direction.

"Ruthie," Mom said, her face twisted in panic, "never mind me. You've got to take your sister and go. Follow the other passage, and run. Now!"

"No," Ruthie said flatly, "we're not leaving you. I wriggled into this pit of hell to find you; I'm not leaving you behind now."

Through the fear, she saw something else in her mother's face—something softer. *Pride,* Ruthie realized.

Ruthie stopped working on the rope and grabbed the gun, holding it in both hands like she'd seen in movies, pointing it at the passageway behind her mother's back, even though her arms shook. The footsteps were now louder, closer, and they could hear someone breathing hard and heavy.

"The gun won't help," her mom said quietly, sounding almost resigned to whatever fate they faced. Fawn was at her feet now; she'd picked up the little knife and was cutting desperately at the rope.

Ruthie didn't have time to ask why the gun wouldn't help.

A figure burst into the room—a blur of movement with a clatter of footsteps and heavy breathing. Ruthie took a deep breath and was about to squeeze the trigger when she recognized the runner.

"Katherine!" Ruthie said, lowering the gun. Katherine's hands were bloody; her face was sweaty and panicked. "What happened?"

"Something's coming," Katherine panted, terrified.

Something, Ruthie thought. She said, *Something.*

Fawn sawed through the last fibers of the rope.

"Come on," Ruthie's mother said, as she shook off the ropes and stood up. "I know a way out."

From somewhere close by—it was impossible to tell from which direction—they heard a scream.

Candace, Ruthie thought. Something's got Candace.

1 9 1 0

Sara

September 23, 1910

The winter people, Gertie calls us, though I myself am still living. But we exist outside the known world, on the fringe. And, truth be told, I feel I am little more than a phantom.

Gertie is still not able to speak, but will, on occasion, spell out words in my hand. If I close my eyes, she'll come out of the shadows, sit by my side, and take my hand. Her fingers are as cold as icicles, and I cannot help cringing a little each time she touches me.

"H–U–N–G–R–Y," she spells, and I tell her she needs to wait. "When it gets dark, I'll go see what I can find."

Sometimes her touch is so light I'm not sure she's there at all.

We have made ourselves a home in the cave, the same network of caverns and tunnels I went to over two years ago now, when I first decided to bring Gertie back.

At first, we kept to the cave, only venturing out into the woods to hunt and gather water from the stream. Gertie does not ever show herself in the day. Only at night, when she moves in the shadows, a flash of pale skin, here and then gone. It's as though I have an imaginary friend who is with me all the time but seldom glimpsed.

As supplies dwindled, I began taking midnight trips into town, where everyone believes me dead.

It is quite something, to travel through town in the night hours, a living ghost. The people who see me say a prayer and close the curtains. They lock their doors, paint hex signs over the front entry to keep me away. And they've started leaving me offerings so that they will not suffer my wrath: jars of honey, coins, sacks of flour, even a small bottle of brandy once.

Oh, what power we dead have over the living!

I paid a visit to Lucius—I couldn't help myself. I let myself into his house just before dawn, stood by the side of his bed, and gently called his name until he awoke. And when I saw how frightened he was, I told him I'd come back from the dead. "You think I was mad when I was living? You know nothing of the madness of the dead. There is no bed to bind me to now, Doctor," I whispered harshly in his ear.

Sometimes I walk clear out to Cranberry Meadow and sit atop Martin's grave. I talk to him for hours, until the rising sun begins to color the sky in the east, telling him all that has happened, all I have become. Mostly, I tell him how very sorry I am.

Sometimes it is my own grave I visit, right beside Martin's. How odd it is to see my name carved into stone: SARA HARRISON SHEA, BELOVED WIFE AND MOTHER. Even stranger to know that it is Auntie's bones buried beneath.

Skinning Auntie's body was my own clever idea. After Gertie was done with her, I knew we had to do something to hide what had happened—her body ravaged, her skin torn by nails and teeth, both like and unlike an animal attack. I also hoped that when the body was found people would assume it was my own. Auntie and I, though different in age, had the same slight build. Stripped of skin and hair, of all the superficial differences, she and I were in many ways the same.

It was, truly, no more difficult than skinning a large animal, something I am practiced at—something Auntie herself taught me well. It was strange how easy it was, to see a human being as just meat, a job that needed to be done.

The rumor Auntie had heard was true: Gertie has gone on walking since spilling blood. I believe she will go on for all eternity.

The truth of it is, however, that she is but a mere shadow of the little girl she used to be. Sometimes I catch glimpses of my darling child trapped there, beneath the dull eyes of this creature whose body she inhabits.

If I could set her free, I would.

But the best I can do is to keep her safe, and keep the world safe from her. Indeed, from others like her.

As far as I know, she is the only one. But occasionally, someone will climb the hill, someone who has lost a husband or a child, someone who has somehow learned the secrets of sleepers, of the presence of a portal right here in West Hall. It is almost always a woman, although there have been one or two men. Sometimes my very presence is enough to scare her off, to make her change her mind. Sometimes there is nothing I can do or say to dissuade her from entering the cave to try to bring her loved one back. In these instances, I leave it to Gertie to take care of her.

It might seem cruel, to send someone in to her death. But all it takes is one look at the hollow, hungry eyes of the thing that once was my little girl to know there are worse things than death.

Far worse.

JANUARY 4

❦

Present Day

Ruthie

Ruthie's head pounded. Her body felt as if it were made of cold, gray, unyielding marble. She hurried along on heavy legs, following their mother through narrow rocky passageways, navigating twists and turns.

Fawn kept chirping out questions: "What are we running from? Who tied you up? Where are you taking us?"

"Shh, love," Mom kept saying. "Not now."

And Katherine had questions, too: "You met my husband, Gary. Why was his camera bag in your house?"

Mom brushed off the questions with a scowl. "Quiet," she warned, "we all need to be very quiet."

Ruthie had her own questions burning in her brain: Where the hell was Candace, and what had made her scream?

Something's coming.

The terrain grew more difficult—tiny passageways, huge boulders to crawl over and around. Fawn had shoved Mimi inside her shirt for safekeeping, and now Fawn had the absurd appearance of a pregnant six-year-old.

Their mother led the way, holding a flashlight in one hand and the gun from her bedroom in the other. But she kept hesitating, taking just a moment too long to study each turn.

Ruthie was beginning to have the sense that her mother was taking them in one gigantic circle.

"Didn't we already pass through here, Mom?" Ruthie asked.

"No, I don't think so," Mom said, looking around with the flashlight.

"I thought you knew the way," Katherine said.

"I've only been out this way a couple of times," she confessed.

"Mom, I—" Ruthie began, about to suggest that they double back, try to find their way back to the first room, go out the way they'd come in.

"Shh! Let me think," her mother snapped.

Ruthie's clothes were sweat-soaked, and she was chilled to the bone. Her teeth chattered, her body ached. Her brain felt scrubbed and fuzzy, and there was only one thing she knew for sure: she had to get the hell out of this cave.

"I think I feel a breeze," Katherine said, suddenly looking to the left and walking a few paces in that direction.

"We've already been that way," Ruthie said.

"No, I don't think so," Katherine called back. She was moving more quickly, almost running, jumping over rocks, bumping against the jagged rock walls like a pinball. Soon she turned a corner and was out of sight; Ruthie and Fawn followed, their mother a few steps behind.

"Katherine!" Ruthie called. "Wait!"

"Oh my God!" Katherine screamed from up ahead, voice high-pitched and frightened. "No!"

As they rounded the corner, Ruthie caught a glimpse of what Katherine's flashlight was illuminating. She stopped running; her body stiffened. She leaned down and scooped up her sister, to hold her tight.

"Close your eyes, Fawn," Ruthie said, and her little sister pressed her forehead against Ruthie's shoulder. "Keep them closed until I say to open them, okay?"

"Okay," Fawn murmured.

"Promise?"

"Swear," Fawn said, gripping Ruthie's shoulders tightly.

Ruthie moved forward slowly.

Katherine was standing over Candace, who was on the floor of the passage. She lay on her back, eyes open. The gun was on the ground beside her, as was the flashlight, still turned on, its beam illuminating the floor. Her throat had been opened up. In her right hand were a jumble of yellowed pages covered with neat cursive: Sara's missing diary pages.

"She got what she came for," Ruthie said, without meaning to say it out loud.

"Jesus," Katherine said, pale and shaky. She took a step back.

"What is it?" Fawn whispered, her little fingers kneading Ruthie's shoulders, pinching and twisting the skin through layers of clothing.

"Don't worry, Little Deer," Ruthie said. "Just keep your eyes closed."

Ruthie's mother caught up with them.

"It looks like an animal chewed on her neck," Katherine whispered, leaning in closer and aiming the beam of her flashlight at Candace's ravaged throat.

"Not an animal," Ruthie's mom said quietly. She knelt down and grabbed the diary pages, which were splattered with blood. "We have to keep moving."

"Do you feel that?" Katherine asked. "There's *definitely* a breeze coming from down there." She stepped around Candace's body and hurried down the passageway, without looking back.

Ruthie followed, Fawn clinging to her front like a baby monkey. Yes, there *was* a breeze, a change in the air. She didn't look back, either, but was sure she felt eyes watching them from the shadows.

Ruthie

Ruthie sat with her mother, Fawn, and Katherine at the kitchen table. Mom had made coffee and warmed up banana bread from the freezer; the smell should have comforted Ruthie, but her stomach turned. To go from the dark, airless silence of the cave to this world full of light and color, smells and sound—it was all too much. The cups of coffee and plates of banana bread sat untouched.

Mom had given Fawn Tylenol and a cup of herbal tea and tried to put her to bed, but Fawn protested, not wanting to miss anything. She sat slumped on Mom's lap, Mimi in her arms, doing her best to stay awake.

Katherine had been pestering Ruthie's mother with nonstop questions about Gary, and Fawn had asked over and over how she had gotten to the caves and why they had found her tied up. "I'll tell you the whole story from the beginning," Mom promised. And now, at last, she had begun.

"Your father and I came here sixteen years ago. Our friends Tom and Bridget called us and said they'd come into possession of something that was going to change the world, going to make them rich beyond their wildest dreams. If we helped them, they'd share the wealth with us. It seemed so exciting—a great call to adventure."

The lights in the kitchen felt too bright and seemed to pulsate, to throb along with the pain in Ruthie's head. She wanted to go up to her room, get into bed, put her head under the covers, and try to forget everything that had happened over these last three days.

Mom, sensing Ruthie's misery in that special mom way she had, reached out to take Ruthie's hand. Ruthie gave her mother's hand a weak squeeze, but then she pulled her own hand away and set it on her lap, where it looked waxy and useless. A mannequin hand.

Katherine stirred her coffee restlessly, the spoon clanking against the mug like an alarm bell. "Please," she said, interrupting the story. "Just tell me how Gary found you. How you ended up with his camera bag. What really happened that day?"

Ruthie's mom peered at Katherine over the top of her glasses and gave her a patient nod. "I will get to all that. I promise. But in order to truly understand, you need to hear the whole thing from the beginning."

Ruthie closed her eyes as she listened to her mother's story, like when she was little and her mom used to tell her "Hansel and Gretel" and "Little Red Riding Hood." This, too, was like a fairy tale: Once upon a time, there was a little girl named Hannah who loved to go to a bakery called Fitzgerald's with her mother. Her mother and father loved her very much. They wanted only the best for her. And they felt that the key to their fortune, to their happiness, could be found in these pages that told a dreadful secret: how to bring back the dead.

And, as in all fairy tales, there was bloodshed, there was loss.

"It was a chilly spring afternoon," Ruthie's mother said. "And we'd all gone out into the woods to look for this portal that was mentioned in diary pages Tom and Bridget had." She looked at Ruthie, smiling. "You were wearing a pretty little dress and coat, and carrying a teddy bear."

"Like in that picture?" Ruthie said, remembering the photo, the happy smile on her face. "The one we have in the shoebox?"

Mom nodded. "I took that photo just before we left on our walk up the hill." She looked down into her coffee cup, then continued her story.

"It was lovely in the woods—the trees were just leafing out, and the birds were singing. Tom and James were talking about books; you were chattering and humming little songs. When you got too tired to walk on your own, your mother carried you. When we were near the top of the hill, we saw a little girl hiding behind a tree. We called out to her, but she ran. She didn't have a coat or shoes.

Her hair was in tangles. We chased after her all the way up to the Devil's Hand, but she disappeared in the rocks. Then we searched, and Tom found the cave opening, insisted we go in—we had to help this poor little girl. She was obviously lost and alone."

"We all went into the cave?" Ruthie asked.

Her mother nodded. "We never should have. But we didn't know. How could we? It never occurred to us that the portal might be in there, or that this young girl had anything to do with it. We just saw a child in trouble and wanted to help. I think we forgot everything else."

Mom fell silent for a long moment. No one made a sound. At last she took a deep breath and went on.

"It was dark; Tom and Bridget were up ahead of us. When we got to the first chamber, we saw right away that someone had been living there. There were a couple of lanterns burning. Tom thought he heard footsteps down one of the tunnels. He and Bridget went down, and . . ."

"She killed them?" Ruthie asked.

Mom nodded. "It all happened so fast. There was nothing we could do. James scooped you up in his arms, and we ran."

The sleeper killed her parents. But there were kind James and Alice Washburne to take her in, to raise her as their own.

"I believe we were meant to be here for that very reason," her mother said. "To save you, to take care of you. I knew without a doubt as I held you to my chest that day that we would be your parents. That it was our destiny."

"Destiny," Fawn repeated to Mimi.

Ruthie shook her head. Destiny, fate, meant to be, God's plan—all this kind of talk had always gotten on Ruthie's nerves. To suggest that her true parents' slaughter was somehow guided by the stars just added insult to injury.

"But why didn't we leave?" Ruthie wanted to know. "This . . . *thing* kills my parents—and we just hang around? You actually decide we should *live* here? You knew what was out there!"

For she now understood what the monster in the woods was supposed to be—little sleeper Gertie, awakened for all eternity, just as Auntie had warned.

Something had killed Candace, ripped at her throat like an animal. And the existence of Gertie would explain what had happened to Willa Luce, to the young boy in 1952, to the missing hunter, would even explain some of the stories Buzz and his friends told. She remembered her parents' warnings when she was little: *Stay out of the woods. Bad things happen to little girls who get lost out there.*

Her mother nodded. "Oh yes, I knew what was out there, living in the cave. By the time we got back to the house that day, your father and I understood who she was, though we could scarcely believe it."

"Who was it, Mama? Who was in the cave?" Fawn asked.

"A little girl named Gertie. Only she wasn't an ordinary little girl. She was a sleeper."

"Ruthie said sleepers aren't real." Fawn looked suspiciously up at Ruthie.

"Oh, they're real, all right," their mother said. She was quiet again for a moment, then continued.

"Anyway, we made it back to the house. Your father—he thought we should go, he thought we should get as far away as we could, as quick as we could. But I felt we needed to try to do something—to find a way to protect people from her, to keep what had happened to Tom and Bridget from ever happening again. I convinced him. For better or for worse." She paused again, broke apart her banana bread, pushed the pieces around on her plate.

"She came back that evening."

"Who?" Ruthie asked.

"Gertie. I heard a scrabbling in the closet upstairs and opened the door, and there she was. I thought I would die of fright, but Gertie looked so . . . so sorry almost, so sad and alone. She couldn't help what she was. So I talked to her. I made a deal with her. If we stayed, your father and I would visit her in the cave. We would keep her company, bring her gifts, help her find a way to get food, but she needed to promise that she would never hurt us. She can't speak—I don't think any of them can. But she nodded, even smiled at me."

Ruthie nodded numbly, still not quite able to believe the fantastical story her mother was telling. "So you're basically saying you adopted two little girls that day?"

"Yes," her mother said. "Only one was a much bigger bur-
den and responsibility. I believed that it was up to us to help her,
and to keep the world safe from her. I also believed that it was our
responsibility—your father's and mine—to make sure no one else
could make another sleeper. We had to keep the knowledge safely
guarded."

"So the journal pages weren't destroyed?" Katherine asked.
"You had them the whole time?"

Candace had been right about this part. She'd gotten her proof
in the end, but had died for it.

Ruthie's mother shook her head. "The pages weren't ours to
destroy. It didn't seem right. So we hid them in the caves, with
Gertie to guard them, and told Candace they were gone—she only
wanted to sell them, to make money. We knew there were more
pages out there, the final instructions and map, and that one day
they would surface."

"Gary found them," Katherine said. She looked very tired and
horribly pale—her whole face, even her lips, washed of color. "And
he showed up here with them. He had Auntie's original letter to
Sara, and the map she'd drawn showing the location of the portal
in the cave."

Ruthie's mother nodded. "He came to the house after he'd found
the cave—the map had led him right to it. He'd seen Gertie out
there. Taken her picture. He knew everything. And he was absolutely determined that he was going to go home and pick up something of your son's, then return and do the spell to bring him back.
He wouldn't take no for an answer. I tried to explain to him what
would happen—what a nightmare it would be. But he was determined. I begged him to talk it over with me some more. We went
to lunch in town. I tried everything I could think of to dissuade
him. I told him everything about Gertie. Hell, I even offered him
money—not that I had any to give. But he'd made up his mind."

Katherine turned the ring on her finger, the one she wore above
her gold wedding band. Auntie's ring.

Ruthie's mother rubbed her eyes. "I followed him out of town
that afternoon. I didn't know what else to do. I thought maybe I
could get him to pull over, that I'd find some way to get him to

change his mind. I couldn't let him go back to Boston with those photographs. If he told anyone, if word got out . . ."

Mom hung her head, her whole body slumping forward, broken. Fawn looked from her mother to Ruthie, then over to Katherine, perplexed.

"He was driving so fast. Maybe if I hadn't been following so close . . ."

"You . . . you saw him crash?" Katherine said, swaying a little in her chair as the weight of the words hit her. She put a hand on the table to steady herself.

Ruthie's mother nodded and looked down at her hands, lying flat on the table. "He was just ahead of me, going around a bend. He took the corner too fast and just lost control. It all happened so quickly; there was no stopping it.

"I pulled over and ran to his car, but as soon as I got there, I knew there was nothing I could do. He was gone."

Katherine made a quiet sobbing sound and put her face in her hands.

"His backpack was there, on the passenger seat, beside him. Before I could think about it too much, I reached in and took it."

Her mother lifted her head, looked right at Ruthie. Her blue eyes were full of tears, but behind them was a look of resolute determination. "I just couldn't let anyone find the papers he had with him or see the pictures on his camera. I knew I had to hide the papers with the other things up in the cave, where no one would ever find them. You don't understand what a sleeper is capable of. If word got out, if more were made . . ." Her mother shook her head. "Can you imagine what would happen?"

Everyone turned and looked to Katherine, waiting. She sat stone-faced, staring straight ahead, into nothing, with dark, hollow eyes.

"I guess," Katherine said then, standing up, swaying a little, still terribly pale, "we all do what we think is best. Sometimes we make terrible mistakes, sometimes we do the right thing. Sometimes we never know. We just have to hope." With this, she turned to leave the kitchen, but stopped instantly. "Can you tell me one more thing?" she asked.

"Anything," Ruthie's mom said.

"What did he order?"

"I'm sorry?"

"At Lou Lou's, when you had lunch. What did Gary have?"

Ruthie's mother looked puzzled, then answered. "A turkey club sandwich and a cup of coffee."

Katherine smiled. "Good," she said. "That was always his favorite."

JANUARY 5

ʔ

Present Day

Ruthie

Ruthie woke up to the familiar and comforting sounds of her mother making breakfast downstairs. There was the smell of coffee, bacon, and cinnamon rolls. She dragged herself out of bed and went down to the kitchen.

"Good morning," Mom said, voice chipper. Ruthie looked at her mother and around at the kitchen, and just then, for that one moment, she let herself imagine that everything that had happened these last few days had been a bad dream.

Then her mother broke the spell.

"Ruthie," she said, "I know you've had a lot to take in, and I just want you to know that if you have any questions, if there's anything you'd like me to explain further, I'm here."

"Thanks," Ruthie said, helping herself to coffee.

"You know, your father and I saw you as our greatest gift. We couldn't have loved you more, and it never mattered that you weren't our biological child."

Ruthie nodded, felt her face grow pink.

"I'm sorry for keeping the truth from you. And even sorrier that you had to find out everything the way you did."

Ruthie wasn't sure what to say.

"And now that you know the whole story, there's something I need you to think about. I know how much going away to college means to you, and if your mind is set, we'll find a way to make it happen. But I'm not getting any younger. And someone needs to look after Gertie when I'm not able to anymore. Honestly, I could even use some help with it now—it's a big responsibility for just one person, and with your father gone, I'm afraid I haven't been able to give her the attention she needs. She really likes to have someone with her. She gets . . . lonely."

Her mother turned back to the stove, flipped the bacon, opened the oven door to check the cinnamon rolls, then wiped her hands on her apron and went on.

"Gertie has always had some kind of . . . affinity for that closet in my bedroom. When I didn't come to the cave often enough for her liking, I would find her in the closet. I was so afraid that one of these days she was bound to encounter one of you girls. I finally sealed it shut. Just to discourage her. But that only made her angry.

"When she came for me the other night, there was a rage, a desperation in her eyes that I had not seen before; she thought I had turned my back on her. I had to go with her—I had no choice. I was afraid of what she might do if I refused, afraid she might hurt you or your sister."

Alice took the coffeepot and moved to top up Ruthie's coffee, but Ruthie hadn't yet taken a sip. She refilled her own mug instead, stirred in plenty of milk and sugar.

"But this time Gertie didn't want to let me go. She kept me tied up to the chair, wanted me to tell her stories. She's very . . . strong. And when she heard all of you enter the cave, she reinforced my bonds, and even gagged me so I couldn't call out to warn you." Her mother took a long, slow sip of coffee and looked out the window toward the hill.

"So you do understand, don't you? We've got to work hard, do our best to keep things like what happened with Willa Luce from happening again. What happened to Willa—it was because I failed to do my job. But if I had your help, things could be different."

Ruthie looked up at her mother, who gave her face a gentle, loving stroke.

"Someone needs to keep the secrets of our hill safe; to keep everyone in town safe. I just want you to think about it, that's all."

Fawn stumbled into the kitchen, wearing pink footed pajamas and carrying Mimi.

"Now, who's ready for cinnamon buns?" Mom asked cheerfully, opening the oven.

After breakfast, the girls sneaked into their mom's bedroom while she was downstairs doing the dishes.

"Is it true?" Fawn asked once they were alone, crouching over the secret hole in the floor. "That we're not really even sisters?" She looked down into the hiding place.

Ruthie reached for Fawn, turned her face up so that their eyes were locked. "You *are* my sister, Fawn. You'll always be my sister. Nothing can change that."

Fawn smiled, and Ruthie leaned over and kissed her forehead.

They gathered all of the diary pages, Tom's and Bridget's wallets, and the gun. All of it went into Fawn's backpack, to be carried out to the well.

"Are you sure this is a good idea?" Fawn asked again. "Mom is going to be really mad when she finds out we took all this."

Ruthie nodded. "It'll be okay. It's what we need to do. Mom wasn't ever able to get rid of any of this—she felt too guilty or whatever, and I do understand that, but look at all the trouble it caused. As long as these papers are still around, then people will be willing to do crazy things to get them. And as long as the instructions exist, sleepers can still be made."

Fawn gave Ruthie a puzzled look. "So the monsters are real."

Ruthie took in a breath. "Yeah," she said. "But they can't help what they are. The truth is, I feel bad for Gertie. She didn't ask for any of this."

The woods were still as the girls walked up the hill to search for the old well. They made their way through the orchard, past the place where Ruthie had found their father clutching his ax. Up they climbed, the trail growing steeper as they approached the Devil's Hand. Rocks poked out from under the fresh carpet of snow—some tall and jagged, some as smooth and round as giant eggs. Once they got to the top, they stopped beneath the five giant finger rocks. Ruthie looked for the opening to the cave, but the stone had been pulled back into place and was buried in a fresh drift of snow. There was no birdsong, no sign of life. Only the occasional sound of clumps of snow sliding off branches and hitting the ground.

When they finally discovered the old well, to the north of the Devil's Hand, they were both out of breath, but pleased to have found it at last.

"This is where Gertie died?" Fawn asked, her breath coming out in cloudy puffs. Mimi the doll was clutched tight in her arms.

Ruthie nodded and looked down into the well—a circle of field-stone surrounding a big dark hole that seemed to go down forever.

She tried to imagine falling down it, looking up at the bright circle of daylight, seeing it get farther and farther away, until it was like some distant moon.

The girls stood, bundled in winter coats, snowshoes strapped to their feet. The sun had just come up over the hill, and they could see its hazy glow through the trees. The forest around them was blanketed in white, absolutely still. Not even the wind stirred. It felt as if the whole world were sleeping and they were the only two awake.

"Then this seems right," Fawn said. She slipped off the small backpack she'd been carrying, opened it up, pulled out the journal pages, and handed them over. "I think you should be the one to do it," she said, seeming suddenly like a much older girl, a wise old lady trapped in a child's body. "You're related to her."

Ruthie took the pages in her hands; the ink was faded, the paper stained and wrinkled, splattered with Candace's blood. There, in slanted cursive, were her distant aunt's words. The instructions for creating sleepers she'd copied from Auntie's letter.

She traced the sentences with her finger, thinking that her own birth parents, Tom and Bridget, once held these in their hands, believing they were going to change the world, get rich, make a better life for their daughter.

Then there were the pages Gary found: Auntie's letter to Sara, the map she had drawn, more notes from Sara.

It was all there—Sara's story, Auntie's story. Ruthie's own story, even.

The story of a little girl named Gertie who died.

Whose mother loved her too much to let her go.

So she brought her back.

Only the world she came back to wasn't the same.

She wasn't the same.

Ruthie dropped the papers into the well one at a time, watching them flutter like pale, broken butterflies, like snowflakes, down, down, down, until she couldn't see them anymore.

"This means no more can be made, right?" Fawn asked.

"Yeah," Ruthie said, watching the last page fall. She knew, in that moment, what she would do. She would stay in West Hall and help her mother as guardian of the hill, keeper of its secrets. She smiled as she thought of it, how it seemed so simple really, like something that was meant to be; like destiny, after all.

Then, sensing movement, Ruthie turned just in time to catch a glimpse of a little girl in ragged clothes with a pale face peeking out from behind a tree.

She smiled at them, then slipped back into the shadows.

Katherine

Once awakened, a sleeper will walk for seven days. After that,
they are gone from this world forever.

Katherine stared at the words on her computer screen. She had
the memory card from Gary's Nikon plugged in and was studying
Gary's photos of the missing diary pages, Auntie's letter, and the map.

How bizarre it would all seem to someone looking at it for the
first time, someone who hadn't been to the caves, who hadn't seen
what Katherine had seen.

Losing these pages forever seemed criminal, a terrible waste. At
the very least, they were of historical significance. She had a friend,
a sociology professor at BU, who might enjoy having a look at them.
And wouldn't the man she'd met at the bookstore in town love to
get his hands on a copy?

With a few keystrokes, she shrank the map showing the way
to the cave entrance at the Devil's Hand to postage-stamp size and
pushed PRINT. While the laser jet did its work, she glanced down at
her own hand, at the bone ring on her third finger: Auntie's ring.
Auntie the sorceress. Auntie, who could bring back the dead.

The ring had been Gary's last gift to her.

To new beginnings.

She stood up, stretched. The day had flown by, as time often did
when she was lost in her work. It was nearly ten o'clock at night, and
she hadn't eaten either lunch or supper.

The page printed, she carried it over to the art table and cut out the tiny copy of the map. She'd been finishing up the newest assemblage box since she got back to the apartment in the wee hours of the morning. The outside was painted to look like bricks; there was a door in the middle, and a neat sign above that said LOU LOU'S CAFÉ. To the left of the door, a large window made of thin Plexiglas. Katherine pulled open the door and could almost imagine the smells inside: coffee, freshly baked rolls, apple pie. There, sitting at a table in the center of the café, was the tiny Alice doll. Across from her sat Gary in miniature, wearing the good black pants and white shirt he'd left home in that morning.

I've got a wedding to shoot in Cambridge. I should be home in time for dinner.

And in front of him, his last meal. A turkey club sandwich and cup of coffee. Not an exciting meal, but she knew it was Gary's favorite—his standard order at diners and truck stops—and it pleased her to be reminded that the Gary who sat in Lou Lou's that day was the same Gary she'd known all along.

Using a superfine paintbrush, she applied a dab of glue to the back side of the tiny map, and reached in with a pair of long tweezers to stick it onto the table, beside Gary. The map he'd followed to get to West Hall, to the hill, and to the Devil's Hand, where he'd photographed a little girl who'd been dead over one hundred years.

As she smoothed the Gary doll's white shirt, she imagined that last conversation: Alice begged him to forget everything he'd discovered, to let it go. And Gary, who had been walking around for the past two years dazed and furious and full of pain over the seemingly impossible loss of his son, thought only of Austin—that if there was the slightest chance to have him back, even if only for seven days, he'd give anything for that.

How bright and full of wonder and magic the world must have seemed to Gary on that last day as he sat in Lou Lou's Café. That he lived in a world where it was possible for the dead to awaken and walk again—what a miraculous discovery! What hope he must have felt, glowing all warm inside him.

And had he thought of Katherine, of what her face might look like if he brought their son home to her once more? How pleased she'd be. How amazed.

"I understand," Katherine said out loud, stroking the little doll's head. "I understand why you did what you did. I'm just sorry you didn't tell me any of it." And then, because she needed to say them, needed to say the words out loud and feel their weight leave her once and for all, she added, "I forgive you."

She closed the door of the café, leaving them to circle through that conversation again and again: Alice trying to convince Gary to forget the whole thing, Gary telling her he just couldn't.

Behind Katherine, a small sound.

A scratching at the front door to the apartment, as if a dog or cat wanted to be let in.

She rose from the stool, floated across the room, and paused for a moment, her hand on the doorknob.

Her heart sang.

Gary.

1939

Sara

The midnight trips to town have grown more difficult. My eye-sight is failing. My bones and joints ache all the time. The other day, I caught sight of my own reflection in the stream and did not recog-nize the thin old woman who looked back at me. When did my hair become so gray? My face so heavily lined with wrinkles?

It pains me to think of what will happen to my beloved Gertie when I am gone. She will go on living forever. My time in this world is limited.

And, as old as she may get in years, she is still only a child and makes a child's plans and choices.

Who will be here to keep her company, to help her control her impulses, once I am gone?

"Are there others?" she wrote into my hand one night not long ago. "Others like me?"

I was not sure how to answer. I had reflected on the question before, and decided that surely, in all the years people had been making sleepers, she could not have been the only one to spill blood. "There might be," I told her. "But if there are, they are well hidden."

Secretly, I pray she is the only one.

It seems that she needs to feed every few months. She grows angry and withdrawn, then weak, and we must venture out in search of food. I have brought her squirrels, fish, even a deer on occasion. (How ironic that the hunting and trapping skills taught to me so long ago by Auntie are the very skills that have enabled us to survive.) I leave the offerings outside the cave and go take a long walk while she feeds. She does not wish me to watch (nor am I able to stomach it). The truth of it is, the animals I bring do not satiate her. What she longs for most (how I shudder to write it!) is human blood.

I have brought her this, too.

I shall not share the details of my crimes here—they are too horrific to mention. Suffice it to say that if there is a Hell, the Hell Reverend Ayers always warned us of in his sermons, that is where I belong, where they will find me in the end.

It shames me to say it, to confess all that I have done, but Gertie is, after all, my creation.

My child by birth, and my sleeper awakened.

ACKNOWLEDGMENTS

Thanks to Dan Lazar, who pushed me to go bigger, to paint on a wider canvas; to Anne Messitte, for sharing my vision and finding ways to improve upon it; to Andrea Robinson, for her sharp eyes and keen insight; and to the whole team at Doubleday—I'm thrilled to be working with such an amazing bunch; and finally, to Drea and Zella, for, well, for everything—I couldn't do any of this without you.

About the Author

Jennifer McMahon is the *New York Times* bestselling author of six suspense novels, including *The One I Left Behind, Island of Lost Girls,* and *Promise Not to Tell.* She lives in Vermont with her partner and their daughter.